EXPIRED END

LAST CHANCE COUNTY - BOOK 10

LISA PHILLIPS

TWO DOGS PUBLISHING, LLC

eBook ISBN: 979-8-88552-070-6

Paperback ISBN: 979-8-88552-071-3

Published by Two Dogs Publishing, LLC. Idaho, USA

Cover design by Ryan Schwarz

Edited by Christy Callahan, Professional Publishing Services

1

———————

Kamryn Marshall gripped the wheel as her car crested the hill. Her foot slipped off the gas, and she gaped at the sight in the valley below.

A police officer sat in a white SUV as if nothing was wrong. The vehicle was parked beside a beige truck at the entrance to what had once been a bustling local airport—years ago now, before her world had exploded in fire and blood.

It was real. That scene from her nightmares. It was all real.

Beyond the vehicles was nothing but a wasteland. Buildings that had once been the museum and offices, and smaller structures had been destroyed by fire. Or explosion. Something had wrecked them, and it had happened recently.

Scattered across the secondary runway lay the remnants of a white plane, a Learjet if she wasn't mistaken. Not something she'd flown before considering the nonprofit she piloted for transported missionaries and supplies around the world.

She'd been nearly everywhere. And now she was back where it all started. In the place her world had been destroyed when a plane crashed in the middle of an airshow.

Mama is gone, Katherine. She's dead.

When Kamryn closed her eyes, she could still hear people screaming, even after all this time.

She could still see the whisp of her mother's hair as she ran. And ran.

Escape. It was in her blood. But she'd had to come back here if she was going to finally find out what really happened.

Kamryn eased her car down the incline. She was halfway tempted to turn around and drive anywhere else. Fitz had told her this was a bad idea, and she was going to have to admit to her boss that he was right. Nothing good ever came of returning home. But she needed to see it. One last time.

The occupants of the vehicles spoke to each other through open windows. In the truck, the guy turned her way and then got out. She noticed right away he only had one arm—and she recognized him from years ago. He'd gone into the military. Army, she thought. Jeff Filks. Older brother to her best friend in the world.

Kamryn shut that thought off and watched him instead. No point dwelling on how her life had turned out. It was what she made it now—or, it had been up until they'd told her she was free to come back. This one-armed man, Jeff Filks, seemed to be doing the same, considering his gait was sure even with the missing arm. He looked fit and healthy. Determined to live, despite what life had taken from him.

She felt that resonate to the deepest part of her core. So much that she almost didn't notice the other man. Then he was right on top of her, knocking on her window. She choked back a short squeal and pulled on the door handle, then remembered she hadn't turned off the car.

She twisted the key, but left it in as she climbed out. Some cars beeped an alarm when you did that. Hers was so old it didn't have that function. Then she slammed the door, making the hinge creak.

The suited man frowned at the car. "I'm surprised that thing made it up the mountain to get here."

She spotted the police shield on his belt. "Conroy Barnes?" The man had aged well. All that dark hair gelled back off his forehead, gray above his ears. He was still faint-worthy.

"That's right." He stuck his hand out. "I'm the chief of police in Last Chance County. And I apologize for my comment about your car. My wife is eight months pregnant, and neither of us are sleeping at this point. It was uncalled for."

"Don't worry about it." *He doesn't recognize me.* That realization got her stuck until she managed to shake his hand. "Kamryn Marshall," she said, using the name she'd been going by since she left town. "Nice to meet you." She offered her hand to the other man.

"Jeff." He used *that* voice. The one she remembered. His brother's voice had sounded the same once it broke. And why could she still hear it in her memories when it had been *years*?

Because she was a disaster, that was why.

Kamryn needed to get back up in the air where she didn't have to worry about any of this.

"Not sure what there is to do right now," Conroy began. "As you can see, the place is a catastrophe." He took a few steps, and she went with him, Jeff kind of standing guard as they moved. "Recently there was a situation here. None of that has been cleaned up, and as you can see from the secondary runway the original disaster is largely still there. Though, the wind and trespassers have shifted some of it." He shrugged. "It has been twenty years."

"I'd like to look around." She stepped forward.

Conroy held out a hand to stop her. "I'm afraid that's going to prove difficult."

"It's what I'm here for." He wasn't going to stop her, was he? Kamryn had a shot at finally finding out the truth of what'd happened to her mother. They couldn't think she would let that slip by just because of a little danger.

He had to have read the tone in her voice. "I'll explain so you can understand the full picture."

"I understand that legally I'm at liberty to peruse property that I'm in control of as administrator of the corporation that now owns this land and everything that sits on it." She even folded her arms, so they'd know she wasn't going to be railroaded.

It had taken a lot of legal red tape to hide her identity behind that corporation. Not to mention orchestrate the sale from her birth name to the company so no one would know she still owned it. Kamryn thought they might recognize her, but God had chosen to do something for her. She wasn't sure what she'd done that warranted it. Given the situation, she wasn't going to object.

She said, "I'll be going through *everything.*"

Except for the white building. If it was still intact.

Conroy glanced at Jeff. She spotted when it happened, that shared moment they collectively decided she wasn't going to get what she wanted. They would railroad her for whatever reason they had.

She nodded to the men. "Thank you for meeting me. I'll take it from here." She hadn't even wanted them to be here. She'd preferred to do this privately.

"Ms. Marshall, the previous occupant set booby traps." Jeff waved his one arm toward the main building, now really just rubble. "There are no doubt some that are still active here. It would be unwise to go through what remains of the airport without some kind of safety inspection."

There was more, but she'd gotten stuck on something he said. *Previous occupant.*

Jeff swallowed.

Conroy was the one who said, "A man named Lenny Marks. He was—"

"A psychopath." She managed to hold herself together long enough to say, "I've seen the news reports. He's dead, isn't he?"

Hold it together. They didn't need to know exactly how closely she was connected to this airport.

"Yes," Jeff said. "I was there. Which is how I came to know he placed traps everywhere. Who knows how much time he had here, setting up all kinds of things."

"I'll be careful." She squared off with the chief. "As I said, I will be looking around. And I appreciate you coming out here."

"You don't understand—"

She glanced over her shoulder. "I understand perfectly fine, Mr. Filks."

"I never told you my last name."

Her mouth dropped open. "Uh…" What did she say?

Instead of putting her foot farther in her mouth, Kamryn strode between them. Past the wreckage of the Learjet, between buildings, to what had once been the main runway. Until one day, the year she'd turned four, a plane had crashed into spectators at the Last Chance annual air show.

No one had ever come up here after that. The accident was written off as a tragedy, any evidence to the contrary was buried. Everyone left.

Packed up.

Drove away.

Leaving her completely alone.

Jeff frowned. "Please be careful, Ms. Marshall. It could genuinely be dangerous."

"It looks like a ghost town." She turned, pushing away the cold specter of her memories. "Or a nightmare."

"I feel the same way." Jeff ran his hand through his hair. "My girlfriend and I were tortured here." He winced. "I'm actually the one who blew up that white plane. So they wouldn't take her with them."

"You—"

"Speaking of Toni, I should head out." He didn't move, though. "How did you know my last name?"

"Someone must have told me. Or it was written down somewhere."

The skin around his eyes flexed.

She wouldn't believe her, either. That was why she had to turn away again, this time in shame. It was for the best, though. Kamryn didn't want anyone to know exactly how tied she was to this place.

"What are you going to do with the airport?"

She shrugged in answer to Conroy's question. "I'm not sure yet. Though I'm leaning closely toward flying overhead, dropping some kind of explosive ordinance and just vaporizing everything."

That was what most people would want to do with a place where so many had died, right? It was what they needed to believe so they could put this place to rest as a town. Move on. But Kamryn had her own truth, and it had never mattered what anyone else said. Not when it counted.

"I'm not sure you can buy a bomb at the military surplus store."

She glanced over her shoulder at Jeff. "Shame."

His lips twitched. "It is."

Kamryn spotted something by one of the buildings, coming around the corner. She frowned as a man came closer, stumbling. Covered in something. "What is—"

Jeff spun. "Hey!"

She raced past Conroy. "He looks hurt!"

The two men didn't waste time following. Both kept pace with her as she sprinted to the man who'd lurched around the building carrying something. An older guy, maybe fifty. He had white hair that shone in the afternoon light, but marred by something.

"Careful." Conroy touched her elbow. She saw he had his gun out.

Kamryn looked at the man again. His clothes were covered in blood, along with his shirt and pants. It was even smeared on his face. "Is that a dog?" Lying in the man's arms was a black animal. "It looks like a dog."

The man saw them. Relief had him collapse against the

outside of a building. He slid down the wall, leaving a smear of blood from him or the dog. She couldn't tell. They were covered.

Jeff steadied the man with one hand. Conroy helped him to sit down.

Kamryn crouched. "What happened to you?"

Man and dog didn't look good. Both panted, and the man said, "He was mauled by a bear. I barely escaped." He panted again. "Our hunting guide tried to shoot the bear, and it ran through our camp. It crashed into everything. It killed…" He didn't finish.

"How far from here?" Conroy pulled out his phone.

The man's eyes glazed over. "I walked miles."

The chief of police gritted his teeth. "Forgot there's no cell signal here. We'll have to take you with us to the hospital."

"What about the dog?" They weren't just going to leave him in favor of saving the man, were they?

Conroy lifted the dog and gave him to Jeff, placing the animal over one shoulder so he could hold the dog around its waist. "Take him to the vet."

"You know he won't see me."

"Tell him there's a rogue bear in the woods. I'll need your help finding those people."

Jeff watched as Conroy lifted the injured man to his feet and started walking. Kamryn got under the man's other arm and helped hold him up all the way to Conroy's car. Until her legs were shaking and she wished she was one of those athletic type people who could probably do this for more than a mile.

Conroy got him into the passenger seat of his car. She nearly sagged like the man had, but spotted Jeff. And he wasn't heading to his car. He walked to hers and tugged open the back seat. Legs bent. Body angled back so the dog didn't slide off.

"Hey, what—"

Jeff settled the animal on her back seat.

"—are you doing!"

He slammed her back door shut. "Take him to the vet in town. His name is Brett, and he'll make sure this dog is taken care of."

Brett. She couldn't think about that now.

"I'm not… I can't…" She needed to solve the mystery of this airport, not get involved. But a man was hurt, and a dog needed help. She bit back the frustration building. This was not going according to plan.

"I have to help find whoever's still up there." He touched her shoulder. "Drop the cleaning bill for your car at the police station. They'll get it to me." He rushed to his truck.

Conroy was already pulling out, lights and sirens going even though no one was around to get out of the way.

Jeff sprayed gravel and accelerated to catch up.

Kamryn blinked. Then she hauled her door open.

The dog lay unmoving on the back seat. His chest rose and fell only a tiny amount. Shallow breathing wasn't good, was it? She climbed in and turned the car around before she followed in the same direction. Toward everything she'd said she never wanted.

Kamryn was going to make sure the dog was taken care of, but that was it. No way did she want to see Brett.

She had a mystery to solve.

2

____

Last Chance County veterinarian Brett Filks strode out the front door of his office building eating a PB&J. After three bites, he realized he was hungrier than he'd thought, but since he'd been in surgery with a poodle for the last six hours, it was probably not surprising to anyone else.

He figured he looked like a hot mess too. He hadn't shaved in almost a week, and the air-conditioning in the office was intermittent at best. He needed a shower and a Netflix nap. But considering he'd just sent his day nurse assistant, Pepper, home for the afternoon, that wasn't going to happen anytime soon.

He was just deciding whether or not to eat the crust when a green-blue compact shuddered right out of his memories and into the parking lot. What was it—ten years? She was still driving the same car.

The driver's door flung open, and the occupant jumped out, moving to the back door and swinging that open. "I need help," she called out to him.

It was probably the scrubs he wore.

She muttered to herself as he approached.

"What is it?" he asked.

"You're not going to believe this, but I think he was mauled by a"—she looked at him—"bear." Her face fell, registering disappointment for a second. "It really is you."

He put her out of her misery, moving around her and shifting her out of the way. "Let me see." He crouched in the open door and looked at the dog on her back seat. "Is this your animal?" He glanced at her, but it didn't seem as though she had suffered a bear attack. And why would she have brought her pet here?

"It's a long story."

"It would have to be, considering you're back when you told me you wanted nothing to do with this town. Or me." He tried not to let the old wound seep into his tone. He really tried.

He didn't look at her. The dog was in a bad way and needed to get inside. Brett always found it better to do his job and not worry about his own feelings. There were enough emotions tied up between people and their pets that he didn't need to get caught up in it. Or project.

He tugged the dog out and lifted it into his arms. The fact it didn't whine wasn't a good thing.

"I should go." She shook her head. "I don't need to stay here."

She was going to leave again? Brett said the first thing that came to mind. "Open the door for me, will you? And I'll need some help. I sent my nurse home for the afternoon."

He heard the awful creak of her door shutting and winced. Why was she still driving the same car? She had to have come home because of her father's and brother's deaths a few weeks ago. Taking care of the paperwork and the estate, stuff like that. He could only imagine how she felt about all of it. His own family might not be perfect, but at least his brother wasn't a crazed psychopath.

Not that he was willing to talk to Jeff.

He waited by the door. "Katherine?"

She reached for the handle. "I go by Kamryn now." She shrugged. "Kam is fine."

"Suits you." She was still beautiful enough it distracted him from the fact he had a dying dog in his arms. All that golden hair, and the spark of mischief in her eyes that nothing could extinguish. "Come on, we have to take a look at this guy."

He heard her follow down the hallway. "We? There's no 'we.' I don't know what to do with a hurt dog. Your brother put him on my back seat and told me to come here so he and Conroy could take the man who owns the dog to the hospital. Then they have to search for the people the bear attacked."

Jeff to the rescue.

"It's good they're doing that if people are hurt."

His job was different than that of a cop and…whatever Jeff was. And that was the way he liked it. Brett wasn't simply some muscled guy with a gun. He had a brain, too, and he intended to use it for more than just figuring out the "mission." Whatever that even meant anyway. He was a small-town guy and always would be.

"I suppose that's true." She sighed. "I don't know what it has to do with me. And don't go thinking that because my family were all psychos that I'm some heartless person. If people are hurt, I would do something to help them."

He set the dog down on the examination table that Pepper had cleaned off before she left. "I know you're nothing like they were." Although, he had personal experience with her being heartless. At least to him.

"Is he going to be okay?"

Brett looked down at the dog as he pulled on a pair of gloves. "I don't know yet."

"I have things to do here. I don't like being dragged into stuff I didn't plan on being part of."

He figured that described almost her entire life. He didn't know about the last ten years, though. Maybe she had a family now. A job she loved. Friends who adored her.

"Well?"

Before he could answer, her phone rang.

She said, "Sorry, sorry," and pulled it out, swiped her thumb across the screen, and tapped another button. "You're on speaker because I probably have to explain to the vet here what just happened, and I should just tell you at the same time."

An older man's voice came through the phone. "A vet? Like a veteran?"

Brett said, "Like an animal doctor." He felt around the edges of a particularly nasty gash on the dog's hip that was going to require stitches. So far, she didn't seem to be squeamish, but he was about to test her ability to handle gruesome.

"Oh. Well then, tell me what happened," the voice said.

Brett listened to the dog's heart. When he was done, he realized Kam hadn't said anything.

Before he could, the voice said, "Kamryn?"

Not, 'Kam' as she'd told him he could call her. And she didn't have a ring on her left hand. Not that he had any business even asking about that.

"I'm here, Fitz."

What kind of a name was that? Brett eyed her, then went back to the dog. Pain medicine. IV. Stitches. Antibiotics. He noted the procedure, in order, in his head. As though he was writing it on a chart, or even a napkin. If he pictured himself writing it, he always remembered everything perfectly. Not exactly a photographic memory, but it'd helped him get through school and college with good grades. Now he was Doctor Brett Filks. Though, the qualifications he had didn't mean he could forego writing stuff down.

"I was at the airport."

He glanced at her.

"The police chief met you there?"

"Yes." She sighed. "They didn't even recognize me." Her gaze drifted to his and that connection they'd always shared flared to life. Then she blinked, and it was gone. "They told me not to go snooping around. Something about booby traps, as if I wouldn't know exactly what Lenny probably did with all those buildings."

Brett moved to the white board on the wall, got a marker, and started his chart with the dog's vitals. He added a couple more things, then grabbed the suture kit.

There was an hour until the night nurse assistant came in. He should be done by then, and she could take over the dog's care while he got some sleep. Or took Kamryn to dinner.

He liked the name. It suited her, and he could see how she wouldn't want anything to do with her past. Her family. This town.

Him.

On second thoughts, dinner was probably a bad idea.

"So you agreed with them on it being dangerous," Fitz said, "and you're not going to look around."

"You know why I have to do this." She pressed her lips together, reacting to this Fitz guy whoever he was without him knowing. "Before I could get into that with them, this guy comes around a building covered in blood carrying this dog. He said there was a bear attack in a camp. They gave me the dog and took the man to the hospital."

"'Gave you the dog'?"

"I'm at the vet's now."

And Brett was watching her stress levels rise. "I need your help."

She told Fitz, "I'll call tomorrow, or something. Okay? I have to go."

"For goodness sake, be careful. Please. We already know that place is a deathtrap."

She hung up without a goodbye. "What do you need?"

It took him a second. "Hold this."

Brett dragged over a light and flipped it on so he could see better. He used a magnifying glass to get the stitches right where they needed to be and did probably the best work he'd ever done. Because she was standing close, watching him do the thing he was most proud of in his life.

"You're very good at that."

"Thank you."

His phone rang on the counter across the room.

"Do you need me to get that?"

"Thanks." He put in a couple more stitches, almost to the end.

"It's Conroy." She held it out, and the call connected.

"Filks."

"Are you coming? We're almost to you. We'll pick you up."

"I'll be done in a minute." Still, exhaustion rolled over him. "Did the guy say anything?"

They needed a location. Otherwise, they'd be searching blind through all the campsites people used in the hills around town.

"Jeff got him to describe the location."

Brett pressed his lips together. Kamryn's eyes crinkled, a question in her gaze. He shook his head. "Great."

"Look, there are seven people up there. This guy has been gone from camp for we don't know how long. They might not have the luxury of us dealing with family stuff. They could be bleeding and who knows what."

"My job is the bear, not people. If it killed, it needs to be put down before it hurts anyone else."

"So you *are* coming?"

"Of course, I'm coming." He just didn't want to talk to his brother.

"It's far. We'll need ATVs because none of the pilots are available, so the helicopter is out."

"I can fly it."

Brett lifted his attention from the dog and looked at Kamryn.

"I can fly anything."

He mouthed, *Do you really want to do this?*

She mouthed back, *No.*

"Is that Ms. Marshall?"

She said, "Yes, Chief. I'm right here, and if you have a chopper, I can get you in the air."

"Really?"

"I wouldn't lie about that. My license is in my wallet. I'll bring it with me if you're sure whoever's chopper it is doesn't mind me borrowing it."

"Belongs to the county. You've just been hired." Conroy paused. "I'm getting another call. Gotta go." The phone call ended.

"Give me a minute, I'm almost done."

She nodded.

"Having second thoughts?"

"People are hurt." She took a breath, as though psyching herself up for it. "They could be in serious trouble."

"It's the right thing to do."

She nodded. "What was that about, with your brother?"

"Stick around. I'll tell you."

She bit her lip. "They'll realize who I am. Someone will recognize me, and it'll all come out before I can figure out…"

"Maybe so," he said, "but it's still the right thing to do… together." If he had to face Jeff, she could face the risk of being outed for who she was.

She nodded, a small smile pulling on her lips. "Okay. Together."

The door flew open and Conroy rushed in. "Let's go. Mia said her dad was on that trip with a buddy of his."

Kamryn frowned. "Mia Tathers?"

"She's my wife," Conroy said. "And her father is missing."

Brett noted the confusion on her face. "It's a long story." Mia had been her friend in high school. He didn't know if they'd stayed in town after Katherine—Kamryn—left town.

Her eyebrow rose. "Stick around, and you'll tell me?"

Conroy said, "Am I missing something?"

Brett pulled off his gloves. "Give me a minute to get my stuff, and I'll be ready." Then he realized who stood behind Conroy. "Jeff." He barely managed a nod.

His brother motioned to Kamryn. "Who is she really?"

"None of your business." He tossed the gloves in the trash. "Let's go."

3

———

The second Kamryn felt the helicopter lift off the ground, she relaxed. This was a model she'd flown before, so all the better because she didn't have to worry about unique dials.

Brett sat beside her in the front, a huge rifle bag between his knees that he'd told her was loaded with tranquilizer darts. She figured he was near her to be as far as he could be from his brother in the back with the chief and two other guys. Dean Cartwright apparently ran a therapy center, and Tate Hudson—the oldest—was the local private investigator.

That was good. Kamryn could use a PI to help her, so it was for the best she did this. Maybe he would help her for free.

"You kept up on the flying thing?" Brett glanced over.

It's in my blood.

Before she could answer him, Conroy spoke. "Can everyone hear me?"

They all answered in the affirmative.

Conroy said, "According to Mia, her dad was camping with Craig and Victor Hillier."

Someone groaned.

"Is that bad?" She looked over at Brett and saw his expression. "I guess that's bad."

She figured given her father had likely caused a plane crash that killed a dozen people, and her brother had been a psycho stalker who'd murdered at least one woman—evil was relative.

They could be bad. But were this Craig and Victor *bad*?

"Supposedly it was going to be a group. He was going with a friend." Conroy sounded worried. "Mia is lying down at home, but she'll be on my laptop running searches for her dad's GPS and trying to get ahold of him. We need to find him fast so there's not too much stress put on her and the baby."

"I can't imagine Rich choosing a group to camp with." She thought that was Tate speaking. "Especially these guys."

"Regardless," Kamryn said, "I need to know which direction to head." She was already going toward the airport where they'd found the man. But how could they figure out where the rest of the campers were?

Tate said, "Go north from your airport."

Someone muttered.

"What? It is hers," he said. "I saw the paperwork just like everyone else. The old man died and the airport you'd all forgotten about until recently transferred to the daughter you'd also all forgotten about, and then to a corporation owned by this person with our lives now in her hands."

"Dude." She had no idea who said that, but it didn't matter.

Her plan had held up to scrutiny. Now she just needed to find out what really happened the day of the catastrophe. After that it didn't matter if they figured out she was the daughter.

She would be gone.

Brett bristled in his chair. Just at the sound of his brother's voice? One word spoken, and he shifted. She wanted to ask what their deal was, but now wasn't the time. Jeff had joined the military before she and Brett started high school. Their sister was between them in age.

Her curiosity would simply have to accept being unsatisfied. She wasn't going to be here long enough for an answer to Brett's family issues, and she certainly had no intention of getting involved in these people's lives. She would go as far as asking for Brett's email address. Maybe. They could message each other every once in a while. That was all she was prepared to allow herself.

"You guys get that I'm a private investigator, right?" Tate didn't wait a beat before he continued, "So there's this entire airport with a disaster that happened there and I don't remember that because—*hello*—I was undercover with the FBI at the time. And y'all don't think I might want to look into that in my down time?"

The fourth guy, Dean, said, "I'm sure having four kids means you have a whole lot of that."

"And a wife who's a police detective." That was Conroy.

Kamryn was getting dizzy just listening to their back and forth. It was clear they were friends, and had been for a long time. The kind of friends who shared healthy competition between them—something she'd never found, except maybe with Brett. Now all she had were acquaintances, and her boss.

How sad.

Kamryn banked to the northeast, circling a mountain peak. She scanned the terrain below. They were far from anywhere. "Did someone say if they planned on hiking to the campsite, or going in on horseback?"

Conroy replied, "Mia's dad doesn't do horses, so they had to have hiked in. She said he mentioned it being a couple of miles. Though, she thought it might've been more."

"Couple of miles from where, though?" Brett echoed the question in her mind.

Kamryn said, "If they parked at the trailhead over here and walked north that would put them close to Shaffer's Crest. Maybe the lookout by the creek…what's it called? Where the waterfall is."

"Trinity Falls," Brett said. "Good thinking."

"Yes." Tate's tone was a whole lot more suspicious. "You

know the area, but I've never seen you before. Do you live in town?"

"She knew my name," Jeff said.

Conroy huffed. "She indicated she knew Mia."

"So who are you?" Tate asked her. "And how come you know so much about search and rescue?"

"I don't." She watched the terrain below, feeling Brett's stare. Maybe all of their stares. She didn't want them to see the guilt on her face.

Brett could easily sell her out. Tell them all who she was. He had no reason to keep her secret. Not even nostalgia came into play when people's lives were at risk.

She wanted to find the campsite right away. That would distract them all from interrogating her with questions. Afterward, she could get Tate to help her with the airport. It seemed like he wanted to know what happened—just not for the same reasons as her.

I fly professionally, and I used to live here. Was that going to be enough to satisfy them? It was all she was prepared to say. She was helping them save whoever was still up here. That should prove to them she was a good person. Maybe if she did enough, then when they found out they'd believe she was nothing like her family. Or, she could leave before any of that happened.

She was about to give her statement a try when Brett said, "Back off, guys. She's helping us."

"So you know who she is?" Jeff said. "But you refuse to speak to me, so I guess you'll go back to ignoring me now. As though anything you've been through is my fault."

"I guess it wasn't, since you weren't even here. Then you were dead. It's probably hard to be blamed for stuff if you're dead."

She tried to gauge Brett from just his body language. It gave nothing away. He'd always had to hide how smart he was. Bullies. His father. Her family. Their friends. She was the only one he'd opened up to…and only because she'd had such a hard time figuring out what on earth to write on her history paper. He'd sat down and explained all the societal implications of whatever that war had been, she couldn't remember now. But he'd finally shown her the real him, and she'd had to fight her crush all that much harder.

It had been the beginning of the end of their friendship.

The start of something unexpected.

Being in the same place as him again was beyond weird. She'd been unsure how seeing him would go. He was impressive as a man. They seemed to have fallen pretty easily back into that comfortable connection they'd always had.

But she couldn't stay.

Kamryn might not have ever found another place in the world where she felt like she fit. Or people she fit with. But the answer wasn't here. Not when everyone would know there was evil in her blood, despite all her attempts to fight the truth.

She tried not to shift in her seat. "You must have gone to school for a long time to be a vet."

Brett glanced over.

"You've accomplished a lot since..." She didn't finish. Which made it worse. "It's impressive." Mostly, it was impressive how much she put her foot in her mouth. Why did she always do that?

"So you do know each other," Tate said.

They ignored his comment, and Brett offered her a small smile.

"There," Dean said. "On the right side. There's a clearing, and I see people waving."

She made a circle and came around. Sure enough, two people waved. Not just saying hi to the helicopter overhead, but trying to get their attention. "I see them."

She needed a place to set down.

"You do seem to know what you're doing with search and rescue," Brett said. "Have you done this before?"

Was he going to tell her that she was impressive? Why did

she want that like a parched river bed thirsted for the first spring rain?

Kamryn had to brush it off. "Going after a rogue bear? No." She even chuckled, so they'd all believe it was no big deal.

Jeff said, "You're not military."

"No, I'm not." Maybe she was supposed to say she'd "never had the pleasure of serving." But given the way he'd fired off that accusation she hadn't thought to do so before she spoke.

"So you're unqualified for this."

Brett bristled. She didn't want to leave Jeff's newest statement that sounded a whole lot like an accusation lying.

"I've flown water tankers during wildfires the last four years in a row. I've dropped supplies to the Red Cross when they were cut off because of rebels, and I rescued two missionaries from northern Alaska during a blizzard." Before any of them could respond, she said, "So yes, I am qualified to land a helicopter in pleasant weather in a clearing. Thanks for asking before you all got in this helicopter and put your lives in my hands."

She started to lower the bird, both hands on the stick, very aware Brett's attention was on her again. She felt heat on her cheeks and almost let the chopper drop a couple of feet just to make a point that she was perfectly in control. She smiled over the idea. A little healthy fear might be good for these guys.

Or it seemed that way until she realized that's what her father had raised her to do.

Vindictiveness didn't need to be part of a rescue operation.

She set the chopper down and they all piled out.

Conroy set his hand on her shoulder and mouthed, *Thank you.*

She nodded.

"Mia thanks you, too."

Kamryn didn't know what to say to that. She left the chopper running while the others ran to the campers.

"You're leaving right away?" Brett asked. A wealth of

expression played on his face, much more than could be stated with two words.

"If any of them are injured, I'll need to transport them quickly to the hospital." They both knew that hadn't been his question. "Will you be out hunting this bear?"

He nodded. "If it's hurt someone it needs to be taken down."

"Does that mean you're going to…kill it?"

"If I have to. It could be aggressive, and that's a danger to anyone in its path."

"And that's part of being a vet?"

"Not normally. I contract with the local park rangers as a conservation vet in addition to my other duties. On occasion they need help with wildlife."

"Wow."

"You fly helicopters and rescue people."

"Still."

As he grinned, stress bled away from his face, ridding him of years and making him look like the boy she'd known once.

Kamryn wanted again to ask what the deal was between him and Jeff. But she didn't.

"Dean's bringing in an injured man."

She turned to the back door and nodded at Tate, who continued, "Brett, you'll need to talk to Conroy. This is more complicated than we thought."

"What is it?" Brett didn't get out.

Tate glanced at her. "The man who was taken to the hospital just died. The doc says he was shot."

She felt her eyes widen. "The man we found?"

Tate nodded. "You didn't notice that?"

"There was a lot of blood. But he said *bear*." Was she supposed to have noticed a gunshot wound?

"Doesn't matter anyway. But now there's a killer up here. And a rogue bear."

That didn't sound good at all.

Dean carried a woman over, double-timing it to reach the chopper. He climbed in with her and then donned headphones. "Let's get her to the hospital. We need to be quick."

She nodded. "Copy that."

Brett shoved his door open. Before he took off his headphones, he said, "Later?"

All she could think to say was, "Be careful."

4

———

Brett pulled a beat-up ball cap from his rifle bag and tugged it on. Wind whistled in his ears and ruffled the material of his T-shirt as he watched the helicopter take off and fly away.

Not the first time he'd stood there watching her leave.

After the bird was out of sight, he turned to the campsite and nearly bumped into his brother and Tate.

Jeff brought a hand up to protect himself. That was all it was. But it also meant that Brett walked into his hand.

The collision triggered something in Brett he preferred to have stay deep down inside him, where he could pretend it no longer existed.

He took a step back.

"Who is she?" Tate asked. He was older than both Brett and his brother. He was also bigger, dragging out yet more of those buried feelings.

Brett didn't like facing down two guys bigger than him, even if they weren't bad. He had to remind himself that this wasn't like in high school when he was shoved into a bathroom stall and punched until he peed blood. "She asked me not to say, and she's entitled to her privacy."

"So you have some kind of pact with her?" Jeff frowned.

"You think she showed up here perfectly in time to fly our chopper right when we needed it? That can't be a coincidence."

Brett shrugged. "Why was she here?"

After a second Jeff said, "To look at the airport. Check it out, before she figured a way to drop a bomb on it."

"She…" Brett kept himself from looking where his brother's arm should be. Jeff had lost it in an explosion, serving his country in a war zone like the one Kamryn apparently wanted to create at the old airport. Now Jeff was all happy and no longer had to pretend he was dead.

Brett had mourned his brother for years. He'd remained stateside while the hero saved the world. He'd mourned his sister, even before she got herself killed. He'd watched his mother grieve both of them for different reasons, and try to keep her joy while she took care of women and children who needed a safe place to stay.

All Jeff seemed to care about now was getting his life back. He didn't realize how much had changed since he'd been gone.

"This isn't about her." Brett shook his head. "She's not involved."

Jeff shifted toward him. He probably didn't mean it, but the move was aggressive nonetheless.

"Are you going to hit me again, *Dad?* Or do you want me to go find that bear before it kills someone?" Brett didn't wait for them, just brushed past his brother and made a beeline for Conroy.

He didn't even know why he clipped his brother's shoulder. Because he was such a sucker for contact after all this time, that he couldn't help himself?

It might be all kinds of messed up, but after seeing Katherine—Kamryn—again, he didn't know how else to be. Other than carrying on. Heading out with this rifle to focus on the job at hand.

Conroy stood talking to two campers, dirty and disheveled. But they appeared unharmed. Neither was his father-in-law, or the two brothers who were the ones to shove Brett in the bathroom stall. Maybe that was the problem here. Way too many elements of the past had shown up today when all he wanted was to do his job and go home to his quiet house.

His phone buzzed in his pocket, and he checked the message. The dog he'd done surgery on was stable still, and the nurse assistant for the night was going to keep an eye on him. He sent a quick reply of a couple of things to watch for, then stowed his phone in his front jeans pocket.

Conroy glanced over. "Everything good?" His gaze drifted over Brett's shoulder to Jeff and Tate.

"Everything's fine." As if he wanted to deal with family issues he'd been avoiding for almost a month now. "Briefing?"

Conroy nodded, and everyone gathered around. "You guys want to sit?"

The man shook his head and tucked the woman to his side. Both were in their thirties. "We're good. Ready to get out of here, though."

"I'll try to make this quick," Conroy said. "Can you tell us what happened?"

"The dog was barking. It belonged to that man, the one who ran after him. Victor said he would shoot the mutt if it didn't stop. The owner guy said he wouldn't bark like that unless there was something there. So we figured it could smell a deer or something. Rich—I know him from Bible study—said he would track the animal and shoo it off. He had a pistol, but not his rifle."

Brett nodded. A lot of guys wouldn't go into the mountains without protection from man or beast, and Rich hadn't been here to hunt.

The man continued, "So the bear comes out of the woods and starts running for Craig. We tried to get away. Victor grabbed my wife and held onto her like he was going to use her as a shield. I fought him. We tried to run, but he jumped me as we were going that way. The bear swiped at Charlene—she's

Craig's girl—and then dragged off Craig. Victor went after him, shooting his gun. We hid. The dog ran off, and his owner chased him. We heard a gunshot a few seconds later." He shook his head. "If he hadn't found you all I don't know what we'd have done. We don't know how to get back to where we parked."

Brett kept his opinion of that quiet. These people didn't need a safety lesson when it would be too late for that because the worst day of their lives had already happened. "So Victor went after Craig and the bear?"

The man nodded.

Brett moved far enough he could set his rifle bag down, unzipped it, and got the weapon out. He didn't use it often, and he didn't hunt typically. Mostly he had no time to, considering his duties as the only town vet that treated both household pets and livestock.

"You're going alone?" Jeff asked.

He didn't look at his brother, just kept readying his rifle. Checking and double-checking everything. "I didn't have time to call the state park ranger I usually work with, so I guess so."

He grabbed out a few things from the pouch at the front of the rifle bag and slid them into his backpack. The pepper spray went in the outside pocket, where he could quickly fetch it out it with his right hand.

"So you've done this before?"

Brett stood. "Not my first rodeo."

"Are you ever going to tell me why you're mad at me, so I can fix it?"

"What if it's not something you can fix?"

His brother didn't like that, but he also didn't have a response for it.

Across the horizon, the helicopter made its way back to them. Brett could hardly believe she was here. Sure, she was using a different name and she wanted nothing to do with this town. But spending time with her? Even just a couple of minutes had made him realize exactly what he could've had through all these years of working, and failed romantic relationships.

The problem was, now that he knew what she looked like and how amazing she was, it would be all the more difficult to watch her walk away again.

"Do you really know who she is, this woman whose company apparently now owns the old airport?" Jeff asked.

"Used to," Brett said. "A long time ago."

And if she wanted to keep her identity a secret, then he would respect her need to do that. After all, if his brother was a crazed psycho and his father had been the kind of man hers was, then he would probably feel the need to do the same thing.

But Brett had never been one to run away. After all, he was still living in his hometown. Sure that was at least in part because his father never came around anymore. His brother and sister had both been dead, and going away meant leaving his mom alone. He hadn't been able to do that to her when he was all she had left.

Now that Jeff was no longer dead, Brett wasn't sure what he was supposed to do. Their whole family dynamic had been flipped upside down. His mom only wanted to talk about her hero son being back from the dead. Not the one who had remained here in town this entire time, making a good life for himself the only way he'd figured out to do that.

He decided then he was going to figure it out the same way he was going to work out how to be content with his life being exactly the way it had been for years now—by using the brain God had given him.

"Whoever she is, you need to tell her to be careful," Jeff said.

Brett twisted to him and frowned. "Why is that?" Maybe his brother's highly trained soldier Spidey sense meant he knew something that Brett didn't.

"Just a feeling I got at the airport. She might want to destroy the whole place and forget it ever existed, but first she's planning on looking through everything. That could get dangerous."

"So this is just about those booby traps you and Toni found?" Brett asked. "You think she's going to get hurt because you barely survived."

"I felt like someone was watching us at the airport, and it wasn't the guy with the dog. It was more than that."

"So it was your Spidey sense."

"What?" Jeff asked, as if he didn't know what to make of any of this. "Look, if you talk to her, do you think she'll listen to you? She needs to be careful."

"I guess I can try." Brett shrugged. "After I'm done tracking this bear."

Unless of course…

No, she would never go for that. Aside from transporting the injured, Kamryn had made it clear she didn't want to be involved with this. But if he could get her to fly him around, he might be able to spot where the bear had gone.

If he wasn't able to find tracks on the ground.

Then again, Brett didn't want to manufacture spending more time with her just for the sake of it. That would only prolong the torture.

"Why don't you protect her?" Brett suggested. "Isn't that what you do?"

"Obviously, it's not my job."

"Well, mine only has to do with animals. Not people."

"So you don't care about her at all?" Jeff paused. "What if you get back from the bear hunt and she's dead? Or injured?"

"You think someone wants to kill her?"

"A blast from your past just showed up. Despite you saying otherwise, you're interested in her. Because you can't keep your eyes off that helicopter. So, yeah, I do think she's in danger. Don't you know yet that's how this works?"

Brett nearly rolled his eyes. "Just because it happened that way for Conroy and Mia, Tate and Savannah, Dean and Ellie,

Kaylee and Stuart, Jess and Ted, Will and Hollis, Bridget and Aiden, Sasha and Alex, and you and Toni, doesn't mean it's going to happen like that for me. That's not even realistic."

"I have no idea who half of those people are, but I know what God does. And you're standing right in the flight path." Jeff clapped him on the shoulder and erupted with laughter.

"I still hate you for leaving," Brett shot back.

Then he walked away, not exactly sure if he'd meant Jeff by that comment. Or maybe Kamryn.

Or both of them.

5

———————

The second time Kamryn touched down at the hospital, she spotted a woman in a red blouse with a police shield on the belt of her gray slacks. Her long blonde hair curled below her shoulders, and the wind whipped the strands as she waited on the helipad.

Given the fuel situation, she powered the engine down. This bird wouldn't be going up again anytime soon. In fact, she doubted it would make it all the way back to where the camp had been.

The two passengers, the couple from the campsite, had been silent almost the whole way.

"Is that Detective Wilcox?" the wife asked.

The man said, "I think so."

"Do you think she's here to interview us?"

Kamryn didn't want to get in the middle of the aftermath of their trauma, but said, "I'm sure she's just wanting to help the others find the rest of the campers." She removed her headset and had them do the same. "There will be hospital staff waiting for you just inside."

As she pointed at the window, a couple of orderlies in scrubs emerged with two wheelchairs.

The man frowned. "Did somebody tell them we can't walk?"

"They probably think you've had enough excitement for one day and you could use a rest." Kamryn smiled at the woman.

"I've had enough excitement for the rest of my life," the woman said.

"I know what you mean." Kamryn realized she'd given something away when they both looked at her, as though waiting for her to explain what she meant by that—specifically, what excitement she'd had in her life. But there was no way she would tell them that her worst day had been at four years old.

Instead of doing that, she pushed the door open and aided them in getting out. The blonde made her way to them with a slight limp in her stride, as though her leg had been injured recently. That didn't take away from her obvious authority as a police officer. And not just from the shield on her belt or the gun on her hip.

"You must be Ms. Marshall." She stuck her hand out. "I'm Detective Savannah Wilcox."

"Four kids?" The question just blurted from Kamryn's mouth, but it was the first thing that came to mind as she put the pieces together of who this woman was besides being married to Tate.

The husband of the couple glanced at her as he passed and she gave the two of them a tiny wave. It wasn't like she was ever going to see them again, so if they thought she was a little loony it wasn't anything she needed to worry about.

Kamryn said, "I believe it was mentioned in the helicopter."

Savannah smiled widely, and yet with all the joy evident in her expression there was still a measure of something beneath it. Perhaps to do with how she'd been injured. "I'm supposed to see what you need and then check in with Conroy and Mia and coordinate with them on whether there's more for you to do. But I'd rather talk about the kids for a second."

Kamryn grinned. Savannah's happiness was infectious, especially after the emotional roller coaster of today.

"We adopted them all a couple of weeks ago. Do you want to see?"

Kamryn blinked. "Uh…"

"Sorry." Savannah raised both hands. "I forget not everyone wants to look at pictures, but I'm seriously in love with them already. It's hard, you know? But so worth it when you get to take something broken and help it heal. In a way, it heals you too."

"What happened to you?" Kamryn looked at the ground for a second. "You don't have to tell me. It just seemed like…" She didn't know what to say. Or how to explain what she'd seen in the police detective.

"It's fine." Savannah glanced around the roof, and out to the skyline of the town around them. "You picked up on something for a reason, and I'm trying to allow God to work in my life that way."

The sun was beginning to set, which meant those searching for the campers and the bear were going to have to quit for the night before long and then start again in the morning. Night would be scary for anyone still out there, in danger or bleeding.

"We were already planning on adopting before I was kidnapped by Lenny Marks. Do you know who that is?" Savannah asked.

Kamryn could only nod. If she opened her mouth, she was probably going to be sick.

Savannah continued, "He cut up my leg pretty badly, but my husband is an ace private investigator so you know he found me before the worst happened. It was scary, but I knew God wasn't going to let me down." She gave Kamryn a small smile. "My husband rescued me, and we went ahead with our plans to adopt. After that I was more sure than ever it was the right thing to do."

"That's wonderful." As someone who likely should have been adopted out as a child, Kamryn still felt she knew what it might be like to get that second chance. Even if she'd never experienced it herself.

"It was hard to be helpless. I haven't been reacting all that well since then, and I think the kids and I are just clinging to each other at this point." Savannah smiled a self-effacing smile. "But I don't even care. I just know I love snuggles."

Kamryn felt the burn of tears behind her eyes. "I need to find out what happened to my mother."

Savannah shook her head. A tiny shift in her stance indicated she had switched to "detective mode" from the personal conversation they had been having before. "Why don't you tell me what you know?"

"I was four years old. She died the day of the airport disaster." Kamryn took a breath. "Only, I saw her. After the crash, I…I saw her. And she was looking for me." No one had ever believed her. The second she tried to go after her mother and tell her where she was, her brother had dragged her into the admin building and shut her in the closet. "I need to know where she is."

"Tate can help you with that." Savannah nodded, certain of her husband's ability to get the job done. "You know he's a private investigator?"

"Yes, you did say that." That was the problem. "I don't want to put him out."

"It's no problem. I know he's been looking into the airport disaster himself."

Saying it out loud had felt cathartic almost, but what she didn't need was a private investigator discovering—probably in about five minutes—exactly who she was.

Yet, now she was backed into a corner. She'd seen a kindred spirit in Savannah and reciprocated a moment of deep emotions. She should have known it wouldn't go well. After all, that kind of thing never did.

No one had ever cared enough about her to ask how she felt. Only, that wasn't true, was it? Brett's face filled her mind.

He'd cared. And she'd destroyed it.

"I'll just look around the airport myself and figure it out." Kamryn tried to brush off the whole idea. "I'll be fine."

Savannah frowned. "You were really there when it happened?"

Kamryn nodded. "It's why I came to look at the airport now. So I could finally figure out what happened and put this to bed." She needed to move on. Her father and her brother were both dead. They no longer had a say in who she was. That meant she could finally discover the truth with no hindrances.

"I've heard about the disaster a bunch of times in the last few weeks, but I've only lived here two years or so and I never even knew the airport was there." Savannah shook her head. "It's just crazy to think there was this big disaster, and it's like everyone just forgot about it."

Kamryn brushed away a tickle on her cheek and realized she was crying a little.

"I'm sorry. I didn't mean to upset you."

"Thank you for listening." Kamryn tried to shake off her emotional reaction. "Hearing my sob story isn't why you're here."

Savannah eyed the helicopter. "I'd love to have you take me out there so I can help with the search. But I would only slow them down." She patted the side of her leg. "And I'm sorry, but I don't want to go back to the airport. Not anytime soon."

"I don't blame you after what happened to you there." Kamryn wanted to wince. It was all her brother's fault, and yet she couldn't help but feel at least partly responsible.

There was far too much guilt mixed up with the shame inside her for anything else. She couldn't allow that to bleed into people here, and the good lives they were living.

Someone like Kamryn didn't belong in a place like this where things might not be perfect, but people worked together to do what was right.

Savannah said, "I can't believe Lenny's sister just sold the airport off the second she inherited it. Of course, she wouldn't show her face here, after everything that happened. She probably wants nothing to do with any of it." She paused. "Do you know what your boss is planning on doing with the airport?" Under the bravado was a deep hurt that Kamryn saw every day when she looked in the mirror.

Kamryn shook her head, not wanting to be caught in a lie. "I'd like to learn more about what happened while I'm here."

"But you won't let Tate help you?"

"I'm sure anything about one particular woman was lost a long time ago."

Kamryn's phone started to ring.

She tugged it from the side pocket of her skinny cargo pants and saw it was her boss calling. She held the phone in her hand while she finished her conversation with Savannah. "Maybe I won't ever find out what happened to her. It could be there's nothing to discover."

"And you came all this way?" Savannah asked. "There's no reason you should give up so quickly. Remember what I said about letting God do what He wants to do? That means not giving up hope. If you want to know what happened to your mom, then I'll be praying that you find out. And if you need anything at all, then call Tate or me and we'll do what we can to help you."

"Thanks. I do want to know if she's dead, or if somehow she survived." If Kamryn believed the truth of what she'd seen, that meant her mom was alive. But if she was, why hadn't she made contact in the last twenty years? Or even in the weeks since Lenny and their father died.

Savannah frowned, her gaze on something up in the sky. She tugged on Kamryn's arm and pulled her to the edge of the helipad.

Kamryn's mind registered the fact she was hearing a relentless high-pitched buzzing it took her second to place. She spun around to find a drone swing wildly toward them.

Flying directly, as though targeting them. "We should go inside."

"Agreed," Savannah said. "Just in case—"

It fired at them. Not a gunshot, but something else. It looked like an arrow.

Whatever it was Kamryn didn't want to be hit by it. She shoved at Savannah, who grabbed her at the same time.

Together they toppled over the edge of the roof.

6

The trail was comprised of boot prints, blood, and bear tracks. Brett followed for at least a mile before the bear tracks split off from the blood and boots.

He stopped. "They went in different directions."

Conroy, Tate, and his brother Jeff were all behind him. Brett might have done this a number of times before with state park rangers and even with the wildlife department. Never with the police chief, the town's private investigator, and his brother who he'd thought dead for years.

Normally he would just track the animal and deal with it in whichever way necessary. This time it was that, plus a whole host of emotions he didn't want to deal with right then. Add Kamryn being back, and everything inside of him was going haywire. He needed to get a serious handle on himself, or he would do or say something he couldn't take back. Not to mention the risk of not finding this bear before it potentially hurt someone else.

Tate took a look at the tracks. "Jeff and I will go after the human. You and Conroy take the bear."

Brett wanted to argue that he should go after the bear alone, and three of them should help the human. The only one who was maybe qualified to go with him was Jeff—though, not in any official capacity. He had just done a lot of hunting. Both man, and beast.

His brother stared him down, clearly wanting to say something. But he kept his mouth shut. Finally, he nodded. "Let's go, Tate."

The two of them headed off in the direction of the human tracks while Brett turned to the bear prints.

After few feet, Conroy said, "Do you want to talk about that?"

"About how he pretended to be dead when he wasn't? Or about how I'm supposed to be the one pretending now."

"What do you mean?"

Brett listened for a second as he watched the trees. "Pretending everything's fine all of a sudden because I agree with what he did."

"You and your mom could've been killed if Jeff revealed to you he wasn't dead."

Brett understood that on an intellectual level. He knew Conroy was right, and his mom would've been in danger. "It isn't like I wanted her to be hurt. But the fact is, she was already. He knew how she felt about Annabelle's death, and he still let her believe that he was dead too. And he thinks he was keeping her safe?" But Jeff hadn't been here to see the devastation that his supposed death wrought in his mom's life. He didn't know. He hadn't seen it.

"I understand," Conroy said. "Jeff is trying to understand as well, and you can probably guess these things take time. But you have to come to the table and be willing to talk about it. Otherwise, the two of you are never going to get to the other side."

Brett wasn't entirely sure he was ready for that. "Maybe someday. I'm not saying it's going to take years, but I can't do it right now."

Jeff had been his hero. Off fighting as a soldier to make the world a better place. Something Brett had been extremely proud of.

And then he'd been declared dead.

Brett had lost his hero.

"Does it have anything to do with that woman?" Conroy asked.

"Kamryn? I felt this way before I saw her today. It was just inevitable she was going to bring up a whole bunch of extra feelings. Considering the way she ended things."

His emotions roiled in him, out of control in a way he was having a hard time keeping a lid on. If Jeff continued to press it today, Brett was liable to erupt. The whole thing was messed up in his head. His brother had to understand he just needed space. That could be why he'd split off with Tate to follow the human tracks.

They crested a hill, and Conroy said, "She's the one that got away?"

Brett wanted to shrug but just couldn't do it. She meant more to him than that. "She's the one who tore me up and left."

Conroy winced. "My advice? Don't let her do it again. Talk to her. Convince her to stick around for a while. Because if there's still something between you after all this time, it's worth it to figure out what that means."

"First, we've got to find a bear."

"Can't say I've ever heard that before." Conroy clapped him on the shoulder and grinned. "I'm going to check in with Mia while you look."

Brett studied the tracks while he listened for man or beast in the trees. He walked around the immediate vicinity a little, just to make sure he was on the right path. Every few steps there was a little blood on the grass. He'd thought it was from the human originally, but it was possible the bear was also hurt. Or it was from the dog.

"Okay, okay," Conroy said into his phone. "I know I don't need to tell you to calm down. But if you go into labor early and

I'm up a mountain miles from town, we're going to have a fun story to tell this kid."

It didn't sound like the police chief was entirely happy about that.

"Yes," Conroy continued. "As boring as humanly possible." He chuckled for a second. "Love you, too."

After he hung up, Conroy let out a long sigh. "We need to find Rich before Mia decides to lace up her hiking shoes and come out looking. There's no sign of him on the app that finds your GPS location. Which means his phone is either out of battery, or it's switched off."

"Maybe Tate and Jeff found him already." Although, once Brett had said that out loud, it sounded dumb. They would've called. "Or he's over at the airport, and there's no signal."

"I have Sergeant Donaldson over there looking around to make sure no one else showed up. So we'll get an answer to that soon enough."

"I thought there's no signal at the airport." That was a normal-enough statement. Brett figured it was enough to portray an air of calm, not the reaction he wanted to have hearing that name.

Aiden Donaldson and his wife had been instrumental in finally finding Brett's sister's body. Toni, Jeff's girlfriend, as well.

That must've been where this all started—with the idea she'd been murdered, instead of simply succumbing to the addictions that ruled her life. Annabelle was laid to rest now. Jeff was alive.

Brett didn't know what he was, but it wasn't okay.

"Donaldson will radio the station and they'll relay the information if he finds Rich, or anyone else there," Conroy said. "Got a lead on that bear?"

"Yes, and we'll want to be careful. It might be angry if it's hurt."

"Copy that."

Brett got moving again, following the bear tracks. There

wasn't much time until nightfall, and they would have to quit for the day, starting again first thing in the morning. At least it wouldn't get too cold tonight. Even up at this elevation it wouldn't be freezing overnight the way it would be on a lot of other mountain peaks around here.

Rich would know that. Of all people, Mia's father could take care of himself.

Conroy was probably praying. Brett figured it was enough but still added his own, despite the fact his faith often felt like estrangement. His mom was deeply spiritual and a believer in Jesus. She'd told him many times about her own faith. Considering it seemed like God had rarely ever done her any favors, Brett wasn't so sure he wanted to put his faith in a Being like that. Shouldn't her life be better if God was on her side?

The questions had long kept him from forming a true connection in church. So he left the prayer to Conroy and fell back on his tracking skills instead.

The bear's path wound around the hillside to a clearing where Brett spotted Tate. Jeff was crouched nearby beside something.

The private investigator waved. "Over here. I was just about to call you."

Conroy ran over. Brett needed to make sure the bear wasn't about to race at them from some hidden spot, so he continued to follow the tracks.

Their conversation drifted to him as someone raised their voice. "All his fault."

"Calm down." That was Jeff. He shot a look at Brett, shrugged his shoulder in a question, then turned back to whoever he'd crouched over. "You got attacked by a bear. How is this Brett's fault?"

Satisfied the bear wasn't close by, Brett made his way to them. On the ground with his back to a tree, was Victor. "Where's Craig?"

Victor's face reddened. "He's dead. Because of you."

"What did *I* do?"

"You let his dog die because you didn't even care to save him. Billy would have fought off the bear so we could get away. But he wasn't here, so that bear attacked Craig and now he's dead."

"Where is your brother?" Conroy asked.

Victor motioned with a hand toward the trees beside him. Brett moved with Jeff in the direction he'd indicated.

As they did so, he heard Conroy say, "We need to get you out of here and to the hospital."

Did that mean Kamryn would be back in the helicopter? He wanted to see her, but not when he was busy and things were stressful because people's lives were in danger. This wasn't close to being over, and he had no idea if she'd be here when it was. Conroy's comment about convincing her to stay might be nothing but false hope. Who said he even wanted to have a conversation with her?

"You okay?" Jeff asked.

Brett glanced at his brother, then back at the ground looking for a man's body. Jeff's comment about her life being in danger was simply bizarre. Nothing she'd said, or that'd happened, indicated as much. Why would his brother say that? Still, if she wanted to look around the airport, then maybe he could go with her. Just for support.

Jeff motioned. "Over here."

Brett followed him to the spot where a man lay facedown in the bed of pine needles between two trees. He knelt in the dirt and pressed two fingers against his neck. "His pulse is pretty faint, but this man isn't dead."

Jeff yelled out, "He isn't dead!" Then he turned back to Brett. "All your medical training mean you might be able to help him?"

"Officially? No." He studied Craig, and the visible injuries he had. "But I might be able to stabilize him before help gets here."

Jeff nodded. "All right." He almost looked impressed by Brett. Which had never happened before, considering he left to join the army years ahead of Brett going to medical and then veterinary school.

Brett set down his rifle and looked over Craig.

"What did he mean you were at fault for his dog's death?"

He didn't glance at his brother. "Everything bad that happens to Victor and Craig is my fault. All the way back to when they got Fs in history because I didn't get their papers written in time." The brothers were so close in age they'd been in the same grade at school.

"Bullies?" Jeff glanced down at the unconscious man covered in blood.

"I try not to let that matter these days. But they're still the same, even now. Everything that goes wrong is my fault. Including when Craig's dog got cancer and there was nothing I could do about it but make him as comfortable as possible." Brett was the one who'd been there when the dog passed away, talking softly to him and telling him everything was going to be all right. The brothers had been out getting a beer.

"Is Craig going to live long enough to get to the hospital?"

"Let's turn him over and find out." Jeff assisted, but with one hand he didn't provide much help. Not that Brett expected him to. Down Craig's front, from his cheekbone to his chest, the bear had taken a nasty swipe to him. Bruising from the claw marks had that raked at the skin.

Jeff sighed. "That doesn't look good."

"I'm more worried about the bump on his head and him being unconscious." Brett believed the rest of it could be patched up and would heal, assuming he fought off any infection with the aid of whatever medicine the doctor gave him. "I'm going to get him back to the clearing. Can you carry my rifle?"

Jeff nodded. "Of course."

Brett ignored his brother's amenability and hauled the unconscious man onto his shoulders before he started to walk.

"You know," his brother said, "if you ever want to work out, a few of us go to the gym a couple times a week. Now that the weather is nicer, we also hit the trails."

Brett gritted his teeth, two hundred pounds of unconscious bully on his back. "Maybe, but it depends. I'm on call basically all the time. It's hard to be too far out of town."

"Mom said you usually mow her lawn over at Hope Mansion on Saturdays. Are you going to do it tomorrow, or do you want me to?"

"Why don't we worry about hurt people first, and then we'll worry about the lawn?" Brett deposited Craig beside his brother, feeling the strain of carrying that much weight, then called out to Tate, "Is the chopper on its way?"

"Savannah isn't answering her phone," Tate replied. "Something is wrong."

7

———

Kamryn groaned and pushed off the gravel roof. "Ouch."

"Yeah. Exactly." Beside her, Savannah drew her gun and did the same thing. "I hear that thing coming."

Kamryn listened. Sure enough, she heard the steady buzz of the drone. "Did a drone really just shoot at us?"

"It can reload. So let's not give it another chance." Savannah tugged on her elbow. "Come on. We need to move."

Kamryn looked around. Thankfully they'd only fallen eight feet or so. Otherwise, they would've been in serious trouble, and a lot worse off than she was right now. Her hips smarted with bruises, and the limp in Savannah's stride was more pronounced. "Are you okay?"

Savannah shook her head and tugged Kamryn along. "Come on. I'll be all right as soon as we get away from this thing and get it disabled. We need a place we can be protected, like a defensible position. Then I'll shoot it down."

Kamryn looked around for a place like that out here. In the center of the flat roof was a couple of air-conditioning units. Not big enough for either of them to hide behind, let alone both. The wing of the hospital where they'd landed was a floor lower than the main tower, with a ladder going back up to the helipad. No windows, so it wasn't likely anyone saw them fall.

They needed a door to go inside, and that was clear across the roof. The second the drone spotted them, they would be exposed running for it.

The buzzing grew louder as the drone headed right for them.

"Hurry." She practically shoved Savannah, but got the woman to use some of Kamryn's momentum.

They made it to the door, and Savannah uttered a prayer as she twisted the handle. The door swung open. Savannah grunted as she hauled it wide and they both rushed through. On the other side it was dark, and the hallway looked empty. "Are we still in the hospital?"

"This whole wing is part of the original facility, before the tower was added on. I don't know that I've ever been over here. I think they're renovating it." Kamryn flipped a light switch, but nothing happened.

Savannah peered out a crack in the door. "It's still there. Seems like whoever is flying it is trying to figure out how to get to us."

Kamryn shivered. "There are two more arrows on it. And something else, but I can't see what it is."

Savannah was silent for a second.

"The thing looks deadly." Kamryn wanted to ask the detective who was trying to kill her, but now might not be the time. She patted her pockets for her phone. It must've fallen from her hand. "I don't have my phone. Can you call for help?"

Savannah pulled it out of her back pocket without looking and used her thumb to unlock the phone.

Kamryn took it from her and looked at the screen. "You have no signal." She tried to make a call anyway, just settling for dialing 911. Sometimes that worked even when a phone was disabled.

All she got in response was an angry tone.

"It didn't work. I can't dial out." She looked around at the hallway and found a desk partway down. On both sides there were rows of rooms, alcoves, and plants. Just like a hospital floor. Except the plants were dead, and it smelled in here. "Maybe there's a phone around somewhere. We can call someone. Like hospital security."

Savannah clicked the door shut. "Good idea."

They checked each room as they moved, the police detective going first with her gun. Finally, they reached the nurse's desk.

It was empty. Cleared off, and abandoned.

Kamryn's heart sank. "How are we going to call for help?"

Savannah looked back at the door. "Maybe I should just go try and shoot it down right now."

The door to the last room Kamryn had checked was still open. Out the window she spotted something dark hovering. "I don't think it's outside the door anymore." She lifted a finger and pointed at the window.

Savannah pushed her away from the open doorway, so the drone wouldn't be able to see them. "Please, Lord, don't let this thing have heat sensing technology on it."

"Isn't that a military thing?"

"A lot of that stuff you can get on the black market. Or from surplus stores. Or hobbyists." It looked like she wanted to say more.

Kamryn said, "What is it?"

"I can't help but wonder if that thing on top of the drone is a signal jammer of some kind, and that's why I have no cell reception."

"Who would use something like that, and why do they want to kill you?"

One of Savannah's eyebrows rose. "Are you assuming this is about me? I was thinking it was about you."

Kamryn frowned. "Who would want to kill me? You're a police detective. There must be lots of people trying to kill you."

"Okay, you have a point there." Savannah's lips twitched.

"But I'm not aware of any active threats, which makes you the wildcard here."

"No one is trying to kill me."

The idea was ridiculous.

Kamryn figured she would've had to anger someone…to the point it induced them to send a drone after her. Aside from Brett, there was no one in her life that she'd wronged. No one she even evoked that much emotion in.

That she knew of.

"Could this have something to do with your mom?" Savannah asked.

"How would I know if it did?" All Kamryn had done was return to her hometown. After that quick visit to the airport, she'd been caught up in the rogue bear attack. "What about the man we found with his dog? Or the woman or couple I brought in?"

"The man was shot, and he died in surgery. But why try to kill us over that?"

Kamryn couldn't even process the dead man from the bear attack. That made no sense. Along with other things. "Why with a crossbow and not just a gun?"

"That, I might actually have an answer for," Savannah said. "Bullets are traceable. Arrows from a crossbow, not so much. Although, if I can get someone to look at the drone, I might be able to figure out who sent it after us. But that assumes we've stopped it from trying to kill us first."

"So we need a way out of here." Kamryn bit her lip. "And for whoever is controlling that thing to not use it to hurt anyone else before we can either stop it or get help."

That was exactly how her brother and father would've thought—targeting another innocent because the original victim had slipped away unhurt. So of course she considered it instinctively, without even wondering why she knew that vindictiveness could be how this person chose to act next.

She didn't want to face the fact that her dad and brother

may have very well been correct in their assertions that she was like them. There was plenty that was different. Instead of thinking about the similarities, she wanted to live in this moment right now. To do the right thing and be a good person. To save anyone that needed saving.

After all, she tried to always use her pilot skills for good. Of course, that meant she was going to do the right thing—even when it was hard.

How else would she prove to herself, and everyone else, that she was good?

She wanted to ask Savannah to stay behind her. So anything that came at them hit Kamryn first, and not a woman with four kids just looking for a good life full of the love of her family. She wasn't quite sure the police detective would agree with her, so she kept her mouth shut and just moved ahead of Savannah to the stairs.

She hauled open the heavy fire door and looked at the concrete stairwell beyond. What she saw made her heart sink. "We can't get out this way. It's completely blocked."

Someone had stacked pallets of medical supplies and what looked like office supplies as well as cleaning supplies in the stairwell. They would have to climb over the stacks to even see the rest of the stairs. If it was anything like this landing it was completely blocked and they'd wind up having to climb down the railing of the stairs.

She shivered at the thought of being in a situation where she could fall that far. Going over the edge of the roof had been bad enough. For a second there, she'd thought she was going to slam the ground and die beside Savannah, her last breath full of the certainty that she was the reason a family was going to lose their wife and mother.

As much as she'd tried to believe otherwise, it would've been her fault.

Kamryn might try to do the right thing, but she was toxic

enough that a woman she'd barely met could be dead in minutes.

No way did she want to experience that for real. Not if there was anything she could do to stop it.

"Let's try and find an elevator."

As they moved down the hallway, Savannah looked again at her phone. "I have one bar of signal." She swiped the screen and put it to her ear. "The call won't go through. But maybe a text." She typed quickly.

Down the hall, back where they had come, Kamryn heard glass break.

Before she could say anything, Savannah grabbed the sleeve over her elbow. "Run."

They raced down the hall, and Kamryn looked in every direction for a way out.

"Over there!" Kamryn headed for an alcove where she found an elevator. She jabbed the button, but it didn't light up. The display above the elevator was dark. "Is this thing even working right now?"

Savannah looked again at her phone. "We might be running out of options on how to get out of this. My phone never sent the text."

"You should hide. Don't let this thing hurt you if it's trying to kill me."

"Whatever we do, it's going to be together."

Kamryn didn't exactly agree with her. "Let's find somewhere to hide."

Savannah shot her a look, as though she knew some of what Kamryn was thinking. Neither of them said anything as they found a side room and moved through it to a closet. She couldn't possibly know what Kamryn's idea was.

"That's all there is in here?" Savannah turned on a sigh. "A dinky closet?"

Kamryn studied her. A strong woman, a police detective. Savannah was a mother now, and a wife. Someone who had fought her way through terror and pain to find the good in her life. Now she was determined to cling to it.

Kamryn knew what it would feel like if Savannah's family lost her. Because she'd lived that loss every day since she last saw her mother. She knew what it was like to lose everything good. To become poison when that loss settled into the soul and began to touch everyone else.

"At least it's a place we can hunker down," Kamryn said. "Maybe they'll give up and go away."

She wanted to believe that was true, but couldn't have faith in her own words. Those that wanted to destroy other people didn't care who was caught in the crossfire, or who else was hurt in the process. They just had to get what they wanted.

What Kamryn wanted was for Savannah to walk away from this. Because if anything happened to Kamryn, no one would grieve her overlong. She would never know what had happened to her mother after the disaster at the airport, but it would be okay knowing she'd done the right thing regardless.

"Let's wait in the closet while we figure out what we're going to do." She held the door while Savannah went in first.

Before the police detective turned, Kamryn shut the door and tugged the hospital bed across the room. She jammed it against the handle and pushed on the brake with her foot so the bed didn't move.

The handle rattled. "Are you serious right now?"

Kamryn ran for the hall before Savannah could say anything that might change her mind. She wasn't going to allow Savannah to suffer. Not any more than Kamryn's family had already caused her to.

The drone was close, but she couldn't see it. Maybe it was down some kind of side hallway, searching for them. She raced toward the exit that would lead to the roof, an idea already forming in her head—a way to disable the drone so it wouldn't hurt anyone else.

Could she lead the danger away from innocents?

No, that wouldn't work.

More ideas and random thoughts fluttered through her head, like air currents rushing past the wings of her plane. She struggled to catch one while she sprinted in silence toward the exit.

The noise of the drone grew louder. Kamryn ran faster and pushed her way outside, almost falling. She headed for the ladder that led to the helipad and scrambled up the rungs with sweat slicked fingers. With feet that didn't seem to move as fast as she needed them to.

Help!

She was supposed to have a relationship with God. Instead, she knew she'd have to succeed here first before she felt as though she could go to Him with her needs.

The drone fired again. She recognized the noise immediately—that ping of the arrow being released.

Air whistled as it sang past her head and slammed into the side of the building. She yelped and her entire body flinched, but she kept going. There was no time to think about how close that had been.

Kamryn ran to the helicopter, hauled the door open, and grabbed the emergency kit from under the back seat. She flipped the latches and loaded the flare gun, turning as she did so.

The drone hovered in front of her.

She brought the gun up and fired too early. The flare sailed through the air below the drone.

Another ping sent the final arrow hurtling toward her.

She'd missed, but whoever controlled the drone wasn't going to.

8

The roar of an engine broke through the relative quiet of the clearing.

Conroy and Jeff held up Victor, while Tate and Brett crouched beside Craig, who was still unconscious where Brett had laid him on the ground. It was probably for the best that Craig hadn't woken up yet, considering all his wounds. He'd be in serious pain.

As a group, they turned toward the source of the sound—a four-wheeled all-terrain vehicle emerging from between the trees, Stuart in the driver's seat.

Brett hadn't really ever spoken to the relative newcomer to town, though he knew a lot of the man's story from his mom. She'd told him all about how Stuart had fallen in love with the police department receptionist, Kaylee. Now they were married and the two were expecting a baby. Although, Kaylee was not nearly as far along as Mia. Brett's mom had relayed the entire story as though it were a true-life TV special. One he could hardly believe.

Stuart stopped the four-wheeler but left the engine running when he hopped out. "I got here soon as I could. And I brought supplies to stay out for the night searching. What's the latest?"

Conroy said, "We have two men to get to the hospital, we still have to look for Rich, and we need to take down the bear."

Tate straightened from his crouch, worry in his expression. "I need to get to the hospital to check on Savannah. She isn't answering my calls."

The chief of police nodded. "Okay, Jeff and Stuart head out and search for Rich. Brett, you need to make sure Craig has the best chance of making it to the hospital. Tate and I will bring Victor and come with you."

Brett nodded. The rest of them agreed also. Even Victor grunted, though it was clear he didn't especially want to be in such close proximity with Brett. Maybe he was just in too much pain to argue, though.

"I came up from the airport. My car is there." Stuart handed a set of keys to Conroy. "Keep me apprised by text. I'll do the same with you if we find anything."

Jeff and Stuart began to haul camping equipment and supplies from the back of the ATV. They made enough room getting what they needed that Craig could lay down in the back cargo area.

Victor trudged over, in serious discomfort from his own bruises and cuts. Still, he made the effort to come close enough to speak in Brett's ear. "You make sure he stays alive until he gets to the hospital. If he dies, it's on you."

Jeff planted his hand on Victor's chest and shoved him back a little, though it was clear he hadn't used much force. "Back off."

Conroy said, "Get in the ATV, Victor. Your brother doesn't have time for this."

As he shifted, Jeff moved in front of Brett. Guarding him. Brett didn't exactly know what to think about that. He just knew he had to help these guys get Craig to the hospital so he could prep what he needed and get out first thing in the morning to look for the bear. There was no way he'd make it tonight. In fact, it was possible his brother would find the animal first.

"Jeff." When his brother turned, Brett said, "Be careful if you run across the bear. Don't hesitate."

There wasn't much that could be done if a bear had turned violent and was willing and unafraid to hurt a person. Unfortunately, it was a fact of life in the wild.

Even with people, certain ones were unwilling to accept limitations for their actions, were fearless to face the consequences of hurting someone. They preyed upon others. Whether evil, or simply ill in some way, there was help to be found and there were safeguards. There was also the harsh reality of imprisonment.

Or those people went unchecked, and innocents were hurt.

For the worst of the worst who were caught, the end wouldn't be much different than that of the bear. Though, those who administered such things considered themselves far more civilized. Brett had decided a long time ago that humans weren't so far from the savages they'd once been. Not much had changed despite history moving on.

It was a heart issue, after all.

Jeff took a step toward him and said in a quiet voice, "And if I don't find it? Are you going to go out by yourself?"

Brett could only shrug. "I've done it before."

"If I find Rich before morning, I want to go with you."

Brett tried to think of a good reason to say no. In reality, everything in him wanted to spend time with the brother he'd adored so thoroughly before he left to save the world. Before he died. He couldn't think of a good reason. "Okay. Sounds good."

Conroy called out, "Time to go."

Brett climbed in the cargo area of the ATV and checked on Craig. There were a couple of places he was losing blood in a slow but continuous trickle. If it continued, that could spell serious problems.

Tate handed back a first aid kit, and Brett began to pull open gauze packets. He used medical tape to secure them, and continually checked Craig's heart rate. Not that there was much he could do if there were any changes.

They moved down the mountain at a serious clip, Conroy driving.

Tate left a message for his wife, and then called the police department. After a few minutes of conversation, he hung up. "Kaylee said she's heard nothing about Rich, and she doesn't know anything about Savannah possibly being in trouble. She was glad to know that Stuart made it up here." He had told her while he was on the phone that Stuart was headed out for the night with Jeff. "She did say she's tried to contact Savannah and couldn't get through either. She even called the hospital, but they didn't know anything."

"Once we get to the airport, we'll have no signal," Conroy said. "We'll have to make it to the highway before you can call out again."

Neither man looked appreciative of the fact this was going to take time.

Brett leaned on Craig's side, putting pressure on the worst of his wounds. "Didn't you say Savannah was going to talk to Kamryn?"

What that meant in the context of all this, Brett wasn't sure. But if Savannah wasn't receiving phone calls, or was simply not answering the phone, then it couldn't be anything good. Police detectives were generally supposed to be on call.

With the airport buildings in view, Tate said, "Stop the ATV. Don't go in the dead zone."

Conroy hit the brakes.

Tate swiped the screen of his phone. "Savannah?"

Conroy made a left turn and began to circle the airport so he was moving closer to the parking lot. Remaining out of the dead zone, but making progress.

Tate listened for a second, then tapped the screen again and held the phone up. "You're on speaker. I have Conroy here, one of the injured, and Brett."

"We got shot at by a drone that fired crossbows at us."

"Are you serious?" Tate blinked.

"I know, right?" Savannah said. "It was tracking us when we tried to escape, and then it targeted Kamryn when she headed back to the helicopter. She tried to shoot it with a flare, but she missed. I fired a couple of shots into the drone. It's down now, but it was a close call, and she got hit."

Brett nearly fell from the back at the ATV. "She's hurt?"

"She's seeing a doctor now," Savannah replied. "The arrow cut along the outside of her shoulder. They said it should be just a few stitches, but that she's going to be just fine."

"What are you thinking?" Conroy asked. "And make it fast, because we've got to get the injured guy with us to the hospital."

"Probably protective custody at the least. I'm not interested in taking any more chances with this one. Not considering someone just came at her with a deadly weapon."

Brett needed to get his heart to calm down, or it was liable to pump its way out of his chest. Despite knowing she was all right, and being taken care of, he just couldn't seem to settle down.

He didn't need this. He didn't need her and whatever was going on with her in his life. And not just because it meant Jeff had been correct about her being targeted, her life in danger.

Brett had a rogue bear to find. Whatever Kamryn brought with her was none of his business. But the squeeze around his chest didn't loosen.

"Do whatever you need to do," Conroy said. "We'll be there soon."

Before anyone could add anything, Conroy tugged the wheel toward the parking lot and hit the gas.

"No signal." Tate let out a grunt of frustration.

Conroy said, "We'll be there soon enough."

They shut down the ATV, but left the keys and drove the car to town. It was barely thirty minutes, but felt like much longer with a bleeding man in the back seat.

"He dead yet?" Victor asked.

Brett shook his head. He might not have happy feelings toward his brother right now, but he certainly wouldn't treat him like this. "He's alive. So if you're expecting to come out of this inheriting his truck, you're out of luck."

Conroy called for an escort of two police vehicles, making the last part of the drive much quicker.

Savannah met them by the emergency doors and Conroy, along with his sergeant and one of the other officers, accompanied Craig and his brother inside.

She slammed into her husband, and he held her close as she groaned. "Ouch. I kind of fell off a building."

Brett started toward them. "You…what?"

Tate lifted his head. "Give us a minute, bro."

Brett headed inside while Tate and Savannah had their moment alone. They caught up with him in the lobby shortly after, but he couldn't stop pacing. Kamryn was getting stitched up. Savannah was hurt. Tate had looked worried. He couldn't remember what she'd said. Something about a drone?

"Brett."

He spun to Savannah. "Where is she?"

He wanted to see Kamryn more than anything right now. And how did that make sense? Maybe it was the lingering adrenaline from the day. Performing surgery on top of being exhausted, then rushing up a mountain. Flying in a helicopter was exciting enough on its own, even if it hadn't been his first time. Add all the rest of it? The blood and injury.

Hearing she was hurt.

Getting stitches.

Savannah eyed him. "I can show you the room. She didn't mention you two know each other, though." Her chin lifted. "How long has this been going on? I thought she was new to town, except for being here during the disaster at the airport way back when."

Brett was about to walk away until she said that. "She mentioned it to you?"

Savannah started to speak but caught herself.

"Why does it matter that she told Savannah?" Tate shifted closer to his wife. "What difference does it make?"

Brett was the first person she'd confided in who actually believed her instead of dismissing her memories as a four-year-old's inherent unreliability. Who remembered that time in their life with any clarity—except when it was a seriously intense situation?

Savannah said, "Kamryn is looking to find out what happened during the disaster. And if it has anything to do with why her mom disappeared."

Brett nodded. "Her mom died that day."

"If you think that, then maybe you don't know as much about her as you thought you did." Savannah stared him down. "Exactly what is the nature of your relationship?"

She was seriously asking him that? Brett had no idea what to say about it. They'd shared something special.

Or he thought they had.

Then one day, before junior year…she was simply gone. No wonder she'd been acting strangely in the days before if she hadn't even known how to tell him she was leaving. Her brother had tried to play it off that she was sick, but when days turned into weeks, it became clear she was gone. Brett had even gone to the police. Only her dad and brother didn't want to open a case.

It'd been humiliating.

"We don't have a relationship." It might be the best answer. But no, it wasn't true. "Maybe we did once, a long time ago. Now it's just complicated, and she's been back like five minutes. She'll probably be gone just as quickly."

Like the way she'd split town last time, when she took off and left him here.

Tate got a choked expression on his face, ducked his head, and coughed.

Brett turned, immediately noticing the anger on her pale face. She held her arm tucked tight to her front. "Kamryn."

9

Kamryn turned and headed for the front door of the hospital, not quite sure where she was going to go now. To a taxi, probably. She needed to get her car, which was parked outside the vet's office. She had her purse and phone, thanks to Savannah.

One foot in front of the other. First things first.

"Kamryn, wait up."

All her linear thinking went out the window as she heard him come up behind her.

Of course, Brett was going to go after her. Did he have a car? Maybe she didn't need to pay for a taxi after all. And maybe the discomfort she felt of having stitches, with the injection they'd given her wearing off now, was making her disgruntled.

He got to the front door first and pushed it open for her.

She stepped outside. "I don't want to talk to anyone right now."

"Shouldn't you be staying here a little longer? I thought you'd still be in a room."

"I didn't need to be admitted." She headed for the sign that said taxis. "And they're busy, so I figured they needed the bed."

"Are you really okay?"

"I *really* don't want to talk about it. And if you're going to keep asking me, then you're just going to have to face the consequences of pestering me." She glanced over and saw a tiny twitch of his lips. "Now you're laughing at me."

And wasn't that nice. *Not.* She started to walk faster.

Brett held out his arm in front of her. She stopped just so he didn't wind up with it wrapped around her stomach, and he came to stand facing her. "Please let me take you wherever you need to go. You did a great thing for this town today, and I don't want to worry whether you got to where you're staying okay."

She nodded. He put his hand on the small of her back and led her to the taxi stand, where he opened the door of the first cab for her. It was the only one out here this time of night.

Wait. He didn't have a car?

"You have no way to get where you're going either?"

He grinned at her and shut the door, then jogged around the back of the cab and got in on that side. He gave the driver the address for his office and then shifted on his seat to better face her. "I left my car at the office when Conroy picked me up."

"Oh." She hadn't remembered that. "I'm just glad I've still got my purse. The whole time running from the drone, I had it with me. Though, I dropped my phone and Savannah had to go back and get it."

She looked at it now, more for something to do than anything else. Regardless, she needed to quit blathering on about stuff he probably didn't care about. According to her phone, the call to her boss had connected earlier. He must've answered the phone while she held it by her side and finished her conversation with Savannah.

Before the drone.

Before she'd run for her life to try and fix things, wound up being hit, and nearly could've died.

Tears filled her eyes, as much as she tried to will them away.

The last thing she needed was to dissolve in the back of a taxi because she'd had a bad day. There was a man still lost in the woods—Mia's dad, Rich. Kamryn remembered him being nice, although he'd also had no clue what to do with teenage girls. But that was years ago now. Back in high school—before she split town.

She didn't need to get into that thought spiral. "Is Rich going to be okay, do you think?"

Brett reached over and covered her fingers with his, not putting any pressure on the back of her hand. "If anyone can find him it's my brother and Stuart. They're both highly trained."

She was glad he didn't lean his hand on hers. Everything pulled at the stitches on the outside of her shoulder. She couldn't even turn her hand over and hold his. And she wasn't sure she wanted to, given how he'd dismissed her presence here. Even after all this time, she didn't concern herself with too many people's opinions. However, his had always been one she cared about. His opinion of her mattered.

She might have hurt him when she left town simply for her own survival, but he'd never have gone with her. Had she stayed, it would've torn him up to watch her destroyed and be unable to do anything about it.

Because her family *would* have destroyed her.

Brett gave her hand a small squeeze and then let go. "They'll find him."

The taxi pulled into the vet's office parking lot. She reached for her wallet inside her purse, but the bandage on her arm made her movement slow, and by the time she had her fingers around it, Brett already had money out.

"I can give you cash to pay for my half," she said.

He shook his head. "Don't worry about it."

Before she could object, he was out of the car and coming around. Kamryn didn't want anyone opening her door for her when she was perfectly capable, so she shoved it open and gritted her teeth when a flash of pain erupted in her arm.

Brett crouched beside the open door. "Easy. I can help you if you'd like."

And wasn't that an invitation she would very much like to accept? He was far too tempting, even after he'd essentially thrown away her visit home. It was entirely possible, if she wasn't in so much pain, Kamryn could have seen the whole thing differently. But right now, all she knew was what she'd heard him say. Namely, that she wasn't here for long and then she would be gone again.

Unable to see his expression at the time, it was possible she might have missed something.

But what was there to miss about what he'd said?

Clearly Brett didn't want her here.

She climbed out, and he closed the door after her. Finding her keys inside her purse proved more difficult than she anticipated, and it wasn't long before he held his hand out.

"Would you like me to help you?"

Yet another invitation.

"You could also tell me why you're looking at me as though I'm trying to entice you into something terrible. I offered to take you where you need to go. I'm tired, and you're tired." He shook his head. "And even if we weren't, there are a whole host of reasons why us doing anything other than getting coffee and catching up is a really bad idea."

He wanted to get a cup of coffee with her?

"You look like you're about to fall asleep on your feet." He glanced at her car. "I don't like the idea of you driving. How far is it to where you're staying?"

"Uh…well, I haven't actually figured out that part yet. I was going to do it after I took a look at the airport earlier." She hadn't exactly planned on there being a bear attack, and having to fly a helicopter.

"Then give me a second to check on the dog from earlier, and I'll drive you somewhere you can stay."

"Thank you." She managed to nod. "Just make sure I remember to get my overnight bag from the car before we leave." Kamryn knew there was a bed and breakfast in town. She figured that was where he'd take her. She was glad for his help, considering her arm was starting to hurt a lot. Probably too much for her to drive.

"Come inside with me for a minute. I'll check on the dog, then we'll get your bag and head out."

"I could just get it right now while you check on the dog."

He shook his head. "I'd rather you weren't out here by yourself."

She looked around, but there wasn't another drone anywhere nearby. "Do you think the drone is going to come back?" She took half a step toward him.

If there really was someone trying to kill her, she didn't know what she'd do.

Brett put his hand on her back again and led her to the door. "I'd just rather you weren't out here alone. Even if it's just for a minute."

They headed inside, and she couldn't help but think he was eager for her to leave town so she could take the danger with her. He probably wanted his peace and quiet back.

Was that it?

In the waiting room she turned to him. "I'm not leaving town until I figure out what happened to my mom."

"I know that. I just want you to be safe while you do it."

Before she could respond, he headed down the hallway, leaving her alone in the darkened reception area. She went to the window and looked out.

Was the person who'd been controlling the drone still out there? How was she going to be able to sleep knowing they might come back and try again? Let alone when she was in a lot of pain. No way could she take the sleeping pill the doctor had prescribed her when she'd explained her normal sleeping habits.

Kamryn didn't want to be caught unaware the next time.

If there was even going to be a next time.

She had no idea why she'd been targeted, let alone what the person wanted. Other than for her to be killed by a crossbow that couldn't be traced back to its owner.

"You okay?"

She spun around, shifting her arm in the process, and almost cried out. She managed to bite back the reaction. The same way she didn't allow her feelings to slip through about anything else. Except when she had newly bandaged stitches, and he wanted her to be gone.

"Hey," he crooned. "It's going to be okay. I know somewhere safe that you can stay where you'll be taken care of. There's nothing to worry about." His thumb brushed a tear from her cheek.

Great. She was crying? "I hate crying. I don't like it when it happens. My nose gets all stuffed up, and I felt like I can't breathe." She sucked in a breath. "My arm really, really hurts."

"Did the doctor give you another pill?"

"I think it wore off. I've got a prescription in my purse."

"Okay, we'll fill that on the way there."

"Where are we going?" she asked.

He didn't answer before she got her overnight bag, or after. Or when he had to help her with the seatbelt because she couldn't do it herself.

"Tell me." What was so secretive about the bed-and-breakfast? "Is this a safe house or something?"

"In a way, yes. We're going to Hope Mansion. Mom has run it for years, and now it's a town institution. There are a few open rooms, and enough people you'll be safe."

There was more, she could tell. But he evidently wasn't going to explain it to her right now.

She'd been trying to visit home without actually seeing

anyone in town. Except for Conroy—and as it turned out, Jeff—she hadn't wanted to catch up with a single person. Probably because she'd been avoiding the obvious.

Brett.

She couldn't help but be reminded of Savannah's comment about letting God choose the direction of her life. Allowing Him to guide her.

If He'd ever done that for Kamryn before, she hadn't exactly noticed. And if He was doing it now? Well, then maybe it was a case of too little too late considering everything that'd happened in her life. She didn't exactly want to give over her trust right now. And maybe not ever again.

After all, God told her to leave town. He'd told her to leave Brett and make a new life somewhere she would be free—far from here—and doing that had wrecked her.

"You should probably just take me to the bed and breakfast. I'm not sure your mom wants to see me."

Kamryn had adored his mother. The work she did at Hope Mansion with women and children who needed a safe place, even back then just as a volunteer, was amazing. Hearing now that she ran the whole place was wonderful. A testament to the God she served, and the relationship they had.

"She definitely wants to see you. And she doesn't even know about the drone."

Being reminded of it caused another shiver to roll through her. "I thought I was going to die, and I have no idea why I didn't."

She hadn't jumped out of the way. Instead, she'd just sort of collapsed and still been hit. But she supposed that was better than being dead—most of the time.

"You're safe now. And you will heal." He paused. "I wouldn't take you to my mom's if I thought you being there would put anyone in danger."

It wasn't a promise that she would heal. He wasn't going to personally ensure her safety when she'd hurt him so badly. She didn't need to reconnect with the people in this town. Because he'd been right that she was going to leave again—as soon as she figured out what happened to her mother that day.

Then Kamryn would be on her own again, just like always.

And Brett would be able to move on with his life.

Without her.

10

Brett pulled up outside Hope Mansion, parking in one of the guest spots. His mom's space was absent of her Corolla. That meant Marta, or someone else on her payroll, was in charge tonight. "Ready?"

Kamryn didn't make a move to get out. She sat in the passenger seat and stared at the house.

Brett used a soft voice to say, "What is it?"

"I wanted to run here. So many times. They always let you stay one night, and I'd only have to convince them to let me stay longer. But I knew Brenda wouldn't allow it."

"Why's that?"

Brenda had been in charge before his mom took over when the older woman retired a few years ago. As far as he knew, there hadn't been any problems.

"I was a minor. She would've had to call the police." Kamryn stared out the front, not looking at him.

"Why did you need to come here?" As soon as he'd said it, he realized he already knew the answer.

There was a period of time where he'd been here at Hope Mansion. After their mom took them and left their dad. When he started hitting their sister as well, and Brett and Jeff had been big enough to fight back. It could've been during those days, and she'd have visited as his friend then sought refuge. Or it could have been something else entirely.

"Katherine, did your dad—"

"That's not my name anymore."

"Please answer the question." He wasn't sure he wanted to know, but he had to have an answer so he could help her. Would she trust him? "Please."

"He was in a wheelchair from the accident. My dad was just mean."

"And Lenny?" Her brother had turned out to be a psycho stalker who'd hurt Savannah and targeted his brother's girl-friend. All of them had been caught up in Lenny's reign of terror just a few weeks ago. Until Lenny had been shot. Now they had no justice, just the lingering pain of what he'd done to them and others.

"It didn't matter that I might've needed help," she spoke quietly, as he had. "I figured the cops didn't want to help the daughter of Andrew Marks."

"Because of what happened at the airport? It kind of seems like the whole town just forgot about it."

Everything about her was etched into him indelibly. How could Last Chance County have simply buried their dead from that tragic accident and moved on? It made no sense that the airport was forgotten about. And yet, there had been this decades-old grudge that remained. The town's ill will toward her dad was like a collective decision to pour all their hard feelings on the Marks family.

Brett had seen what she'd suffered from teachers at school who assumed she was a bad seed like her brother and father. It didn't surprise him that no one had taken the time to make sure she was all right—or to see that she clearly was not. He'd even heard one teacher tell her that she deserved everything she got. When Katherine Marks had never done anything mean to anyone.

Their friendship had started when he'd seen in her a kindred spirit. She knew the pain life could dish out but somehow still managed to be good.

Or maybe he'd seen in her what he wanted to be—strong, and good. Nothing like what his dad had always told him he was.

"There's a memorial for the dead over at the cemetery." She glanced at him for a second. "I only know because I used to sit there and read since no one ever went to it."

He wanted to go back to the comment she'd made about the cops, but didn't exactly know how to ask. He also wanted her to trust him. What would get her to do that? Instead he said, "I can't believe they never even investigated and no one asked any questions. It seems like the whole thing was just swept under the rug." Surely there had been some kind of examination into what happened. Someone had to have been held accountable.

"Dad always said everyone just labeled him the culprit because they wanted a scapegoat. But if he was responsible, why didn't he go to jail? People died."

"Maybe Conroy could tell you. There might be an old file over at the police department, where they opened an investigation into it. Or the NTSB did."

"Do you think he would tell me?"

"It wouldn't hurt to ask." Brett shrugged.

"I always heard everyone thought it'd been sabotage brought down the plane that crashed." She shrugged. "But why would my dad do it? The airport was his life, and before the accident I remember him…well, he was never nice. But he was definitely less mean before my mom died and the airport went bankrupt because they denied his insurance claim. And he had no millions stashed away to clean up."

He reached over then and squeezed her hand. He knew what it was like to have a father who used something other than understanding to communicate. And now she was determined to remain silent about what they had done.

"Why didn't you tell me? If Lenny was doing something to you, you could've said. Even if it was me, or my mom. An adult somewhere. Someone would have helped you."

She flinched, but said nothing.

Maybe she thought he was the one who should've noticed.

Her dad and brother were dead now, but she might still need help. Nothing he'd learned and even all he'd experienced in his life didn't tell him how to fix this. His intelligence might be his greatest strength, but it didn't give him the answers he needed now. How was he supposed to help her if she wouldn't talk to him?

Kamryn sniffed.

Brett pushed his door open and rounded the car. If they didn't go inside now, he wondered if they ever would. And where else would she go? She didn't seem inclined to make a move, so he opened her door and tugged her to her feet as tears rolled down her face. He pulled her into a hug, wondering what to say while his heart squeezed in his chest. Maybe she couldn't tell him for some reason. Then, or now. "I'm sorry."

She squeezed his middle with her arm that didn't have stitches in it and then pulled away. "Someone's watching."

He pulled away and looked. Toni, his brother's girlfriend, stood in the doorway on a pair of crutches. He figured it made sense she was here, considering his mom was gone and Jeff was with Stuart looking for Rich. Pretty much everyone in town seemed to have some kind of military or special forces training, if they weren't a cop or if they were. Everyone except him.

Kamryn slipped her hand into his as they walked to the door. "Please tell me Lenny didn't do that, too," she said quietly.

Brett glanced at her. "He was dead by then."

She nodded. "Good."

Toni stepped back as they approached, leaving the door wide for them to enter. "I thought that was you on the surveillance."

He'd met her a couple of times since his brother came back

from the dead. He thought he was doing pretty good with it, considering how unbelievable the whole situation was.

"Hey." He motioned with his head. "This is Kamryn. She's an old friend of mine."

Toni cocked her head to the side. "A drone at the hospital?" Before they could respond, she said, "Savannah told Kaylee, and Kaylee told me." She motioned back over her shoulder with a jab of her thumb as she shut the door behind them. "Kaylee is here as well, but she had a long day at work, so she's in bed already."

Brett loosened Kamryn's fingers from his so she could shake Toni's hand.

She seemed nervous, but more exhausted than anything else. "Is it really okay to stay here? Maggie won't mind?"

Toni made a *pfft* noise that managed to sound slightly British. "Nah, she has plenty of open beds, and even more space in her heart."

Brett felt the burn of tears gather. He could hardly believe it was happening now considering the last time he cried was when he was three. He cleared his throat. "That's a really nice thing to say."

Toni shrugged. "Your mom's a nice lady. She's letting me stay here until Jeff and I get married."

Kamryn looked at him.

"Toni is Jeff's girlfriend."

Before he could ask her anything, Toni turned to Kamryn. "You look exhausted. Let's show you to your room so you can lie down." To Brett she said, "Make yourself useful and put the kettle on."

He figured that was the British version of an invitation to sit and visit a while. Considering he wanted to know where his mom was tonight, just to make sure she was okay, he did as she asked.

She wandered into the kitchen a few minutes later. "Your friend is all settled."

"Thanks. She had a rough day."

Toni winced. "I heard about the crossbow."

"Anything from Jeff yet about Rich?"

"About an hour ago. They hadn't found anything so far. They're pulling out the night vision stuff to get a few more hours in."

She poured the tea, and he sat on a bar stool. "Where's my mom at tonight?" He'd been hoping she would be here to see Kamryn. Maybe it was for the best, considering Kamryn didn't exactly want to see people who knew who she really was. Except him. Then again, considering it hadn't been her choice to bring the dog to his office, maybe she considered this whole situation a total disaster. Him. Everyone. The whole town. Who knew?

"She's on a date."

Brett choked on the first sip of his tea. "She's—what?"

"On. A. Date." Toni shrugged one shoulder. "I guess it's what normal people do when they like someone?"

He figured that was a fair reaction, considering his brother's relationship with this woman. They'd met the night she'd been shot at by Lenny Marks. Toni had fell, hitting her head. She'd lost her memory, and Jeff had witnessed the entire thing. Once he realized they'd had a connection, Jeff had taken her to his cabin. The two had been practically inseparable since.

And when she found out who Kamryn really was?

Brett wasn't sure what the reaction would be given Toni had seen Lenny murder a woman. He wanted to believe the people in his life could see past Kamryn's biological connection to a terrible person, but the truth was he didn't know them all that well. Except for his mom.

"Who is she on a date with?"

"Are you sure you want to know?" When he said nothing, she said, "Zander's team doctor."

"I don't know who that is." But he had better be someone who would treat his mom with respect.

Toni lifted her hands and showed him her palms. "It's all good. I know him pretty well now, and he's a nice guy."

"He better be."

She tipped her head to the side again. "You're more like Jeff than I think either of you realizes." She took a sip of her tea. "So what are we going to do about this young woman in danger?"

"The police are investigating the incident with the drone."

"Do you have to go out and look for the bear tomorrow?"

He shook his head. "The state park ranger emailed. He's going to take over with a team of his. He'll let me know when they leave, and if I'm not busy with work I'll go out too. He knows how my work schedule is."

"So you'll be in town, where you can keep an eye on Kamryn."

"I don't know what I can do if something happens." Not that he thought it would. One drone didn't mean someone was trying to kill her. He didn't think it'd been an accident, or mistaken identity. But that didn't mean it would happen again.

Toni didn't comment on that. "What is she doing in town?"

"She's trying to find out what happened at the airport years ago so she'll finally know what happened to her mother. Everyone said she died, but Kamryn isn't so sure."

"So you need investigators." Toni tapped her chin with a finger. When she spoke again, her tone held sarcasm. "I don't think we have any of those in town. No one trained to protect someone, or who knows how to work a cold case. Or a historian. Or people with the skills to take down the booby-traps. Or people who can keep her safe while she does what she needs to do."

He stared. "Is this how you help people?" If this was some kind of attempt to reverse psychology him into helping Kamryn, it might be working. "You said a historian?"

Toni shrugged. "School is out for the summer, and I might have heard that Ellie is working on research for her new book.

Something about town founders. Maybe she can tell you where to look."

That actually wasn't an awful idea.

Toni grinned. "And Dean can hang around to help you protect Kamryn in the meantime."

"Who says she needs protection? The police are probably investigating the drone thing. It could've just been a one-off random incident."

"You believe that, do you?"

"I'm guessing you talked to Jeff about this."

"Whether I did or not, this is about Kamryn. Right?" She set her mug down on the counter. "She either needs help, or she doesn't. It's either going to be you sticking with her, or it'll be someone else. And who knows? They might not be the kind who'll drive her to a safe place and stick around to make sure she's all right."

She pinned him with a stare that made Brett's cheeks heat. Yes, he'd done that.

"I'm going to help her." And yes, if necessary he would protect her.

After what this town had done to her? He wasn't going to allow Kamryn to swing out there with no support except her boss on the other end of the phone. After all, Brett was the only one in Last Chance who cared about her enough to do it.

The only one whose heart she'd broken.

The only woman he'd ever loved.

"Of course I will."

11

———————

Kamryn walked down the hallway the next morning with her hair still wet from the shower she'd taken. Normally she'd have blow-dried her hair, but there hadn't been a blow-dryer in the bathroom cupboard. Probably it would frizz up as it dried naturally, but that was the least of her problems.

This morning her arm ached worse than it had yesterday. If she was going to take the pain meds the doctor had prescribed, she'd have to eat something. Which just meant she would be grumpy until she found food. Not good, when she was in a strange place with people she barely knew. If at all.

She stopped at the threshold to the kitchen and saw Brett's mom loading the dishwasher. The older woman wore stylish jeans and a tank top, revealing her toned arms. Probably from all the yard work she did around Hope Mansion. Kamryn had spotted her out the window an hour before pulling weeds. Her long red hair was wavy and fell to the middle of her back, and her feet were bare.

Before Kamryn could say anything, Maggie turned. Her face spread into a smile so wide that Kamryn wondered why she'd ever been worried. "They tell me you go by Kamryn now." She spread her arms.

Kamryn could do nothing but walk into the welcome of Maggie's hug. "Since I left."

Maggie gave her a strong squeeze. "Did you sleep okay?"

"Yes, thank you for allowing me to stay."

Nothing about her family, or how she'd hurt Brett so badly when she left. Just a warm welcome that made a small part of Kamryn grieve the fact she'd ever walked away from this. Maggie had still been healing from her own traumatic relationship when Kamryn left town, but she'd always been open and kind.

Of course, she now ran this shelter for women and children as a ministry. A way to help those in need, the way Maggie had been when she took her children and left her husband.

Brett was probably already out looking for the bear, or he was at work. Mr. "good guy" had plenty to do in this town, and it didn't involve watching her like a babysitter. She'd been asleep before she even thought about saying good night to him last night. It was probably for the best, considering how tired and emotional she'd felt. Everything so close to the edge.

"Of course, you should stay here." Maggie ushered her to a stool at the bar. "Have a seat, and I'll get you some coffee."

Kamryn did so, still thinking about Brett. About her silence and his telling her she should've spoken up. The past wasn't something she could change, no matter how much she might wish to.

He just didn't realize he was the only one she'd ever shared even that much with. And he told her it wasn't good enough? That she should have done more? All that at an age when she could barely take care of herself, let alone deal with everything she had to contend with at home. It was probably for the best that he wasn't here. She'd had all night, and she still didn't know how she felt about him.

Maggie set a cup of coffee down in front of her, then put the bottle of creamer beside it. She stared at Kamryn for a moment as if she couldn't quite believe she was here. "He missed you."

Surprise brought tears to her eyes. Of all the things Maggie could've said right now, that was the last thing she thought would come out of the other woman's mouth.

Kamryn tried to speak, but the words got stuck in her throat.

Maggie smiled softly. "Creamer?"

The knowing look in her eyes said she understood. And instead of forcing out Kamryn's emotions and getting her to open up, Maggie gave her a few seconds to get control of herself and decide which direction she wanted the conversation to go next.

Kamryn held the cup with two hands and sipped the warm coffee.

Maggie took a sip of her own. "I'd like to say that the Good Lord told me you were coming, as He often does. But you always were a lovely surprise."

Kamryn lowered the cup, and tears spilled over onto her cheeks. After the day she'd had yesterday, was it any wonder that she broke down in the face of so much unexpected kindness?

The door opened.

She only heard it, turning in time to see Brett step into the room.

His gaze darted to his mom. "You made her cry? Mom, you're supposed to be taking care of her, not upsetting her. What did you say?" His face reddened as he spoke, and he stormed over to Kamryn. He stood right beside her, his hand between her shoulders. His palm rubbed side to side, as if trying to comfort her but unsure how to do it when he also wanted to throttle his mom. At least, he did if she was reading the thunderous look on his face right.

Kamryn needed to resolve this fast. "Brett, it's fine. I—"

He shook his head. "It's not fine. Mom, you—"

"You think I'd say something to purposely upset her?" Maggie set her hands on her hips. "In fact, we were talking about—"

"It's really fine." Kamryn twisted in the chair to look up at Brett beside her. "Your mom didn't upset me." She wanted to explain, but it wasn't as though anyone would understand. Maggie thought she was lovely. Something no one had ever said to her. He didn't need to know, and she didn't want to fumble over an explanation. After all the things she'd kept silent about in her life, she wanted to tell the truth now when she did speak up.

But she also needed to keep that for herself as the gift it was.

His anger didn't seem to diffuse. "We're supposed to be taking care of her, Mom."

Maggie's lips twitched. "Well, you're here now. So I suppose I should get on with my inside chores." She pointed between them. "I'm guessing…you've got this?"

He frowned. "Yes."

She glanced between Brett, and his weighty word, and his mother. It seemed as though Maggie had been hard at work for hours already, and yet it was barely after seven in the morning.

"Do you always move so quickly?" Kamryn usually wasn't up this time of day, normally waking closer to lunchtime. She didn't usually fall asleep until three or four in the morning. A product of her childhood, she supposed. But also simply how her body had decided to regulate itself. The doctor she'd seen hadn't thought there was anything amiss by it. And thankfully, her boss scheduled most of her flights around her unusual sleep patterns.

Maggie smiled. "I like to keep busy."

Brett said, "There's busy, and then there's breezing in and out like a whirlwind."

Kamryn smiled and drank some more coffee, not quite sure what to say to Brett now that he was here.

His mom rounded the breakfast bar and came over to hug her again. "It was very good to see you, Lovely."

Kamryn hugged her back. "Thank you for letting me stay."

As Maggie left, it surprised Kamryn that she wanted to

catch up with her. And yet, she might not get that chance—which only made her grieve the fact she'd been determined to come back and not see anyone.

And then she was alone with Brett. "Maybe I should tell her why I'm here."

"It's up to you." He studied her. "Did you sleep okay? Did Mom get you breakfast?"

"She asked me the same thing." Kamryn smiled. "I think the pill knocked me out pretty quickly last night, but I need to take another one, so I do need something to eat."

"Oatmeal?"

She shrugged, considering she rarely ate breakfast. "I can get it."

He shook his head. "Sit. Drink your coffee." He boiled the kettle and pulled two cup-sized containers of instant oatmeal and two plastic spoons from the pantry. He had her pick her flavor and poured water in before he replaced the lids and handed over hers. "I figure we can eat on the way."

"Where are we going?" She had assumed he'd be looking for the bear this morning.

"To check out the airport. I'm clear until after lunch, so I'm all yours if you want to look around before you need a rest again."

"Oh." She hopped off the stool just as his mom came back in.

Maggie carried a scarf that she unfolded into a rectangle of silky material, then refolded into a triangle. "Let's tie your arm up in a sling. It'll take the weight off your stitches."

Kamryn let out a sigh of relief. "Thank you. That feels much better."

Brett ushered her to the car while his mom watched from the door with a knowing look on her face. He even closed her door for her. When he got in on his side and set off, Kamryn removed the lid of her oatmeal and stirred it. "Okay?"

"Yep." She sighed. "I've just been thinking about the drone

and what on earth it meant. Especially considering I'm fine, and so is Savannah. Meanwhile, Rich is still missing. And you didn't catch the bear, right?" Everything was so all over the place she barely knew where to start.

"Park rangers are taking care of the bear. Jeff and Stuart will find Rich. We just have to give them time."

"So I just carry on with what I'm doing while all that's going on?" She wasn't part of it, but that didn't mean she felt nothing. And besides, they might need her to fly the helicopter again.

He shrugged. "Looking into the airport and what happened to your mom is a good thing. It's important to you." He set off toward the street, where he turned left onto the blacktop. "So that's what we're going to do."

She ate while he drove there and then waited while he finished his oatmeal, staring out at the disaster that was her family's legacy. Fighting the urge to cry again. "At some point I'm going to have to go to the house and go through my dad's stuff." She swallowed. "All my brother's stuff."

"Isn't it evidence, considering he killed that lady who was the gym owner?"

And Lenny had nearly killed both Savannah and Toni by the sound of things. "He was killed, so charges were never filed. That means it's not evidence."

She didn't really want to know what Lenny had hidden. Whether at the house, or here at the airport. "He was obsessed with this place even years ago. I wouldn't be surprised if he had a whole setup here that no one knew about. If I didn't know better, I'd think he might've caused the crash. But he was only seven when the plane came down at the air show. He couldn't have known anything about sabotage back then."

They walked between some of the buildings, mostly just looking around. There was so much destruction here. It unnerved her to the point she wanted to cling to him.

He said, "If you don't mind, I'd like to get some of the guys from town out to check the place for traps. I don't want to stumble over anything that could hurt either of us."

She figured that was probably a good idea. Just the thought of going inside any of these buildings didn't sit well, but it was a fact of what she had to do. It was the reason she was here. She just didn't want to do it right now. "I'm sorry, I don't think I can do this today." She shook her head and wound up shivering. "I think I just want to leave."

Brett tugged her around to face him. "Is this about the whole place, or a specific part of it? Because you keep looking at that building over there." He pointed at the white structure.

Kamryn stepped back, almost involuntarily. She shook her head. "I don't…"

"Hey, it's okay." He could've set both hands on her shoulders, but he didn't. He left his hands by his sides. "We don't have to do this now."

"I'll just come back later by myself." *He doesn't need to waste his time dealing with me.* It was embarrassing after she'd left town and left him here. Being back brought all of it to the surface, and then some. If she stuck around, she might start thinking about living here again just to be closer to him.

Yes, it was better if she came back alone. He could support her as a friend, but there would be no relationship between them now with so much water under the bridge.

That might even be better, being by herself. Then she didn't have to worry about her feelings for him. She could just ignore them, knowing he didn't feel the same about her. She'd hurt him too badly.

"I don't mind coming with you," he said. "I might have to work later, but it's better if you're here with someone else rather than alone."

That was when she knew he had no feelings for her anymore. It was just about keeping her safe, rather than the possibility she could get hurt and no one would know because there was no way to call for help from here.

Because he was a good guy.

There might never be something between them again, but she wanted him to know one thing. "Your mom is more beautiful than ever." Kamryn smiled. "And you were the only good thing in this town."

12

———

Brett stared at her, unsure what to say. The rising feeling was unusual and unexpected. There wasn't much in his life that'd ever made him feel this way, except maybe Kamryn before she left. In the days when she was Katherine, and he'd been besotted with her. In return, she'd shredded his heart.

At least now he knew why. And maybe that was the worst part of it, knowing she'd felt like she had no choice. She hadn't said anything to him, or anyone. She'd simply gone.

He asked her, "Why did you leave?" But he knew the answer to his question.

Kamryn ducked her head.

It was easy enough to figure out the answer—he hadn't been enough for her to stay.

His dad would always be poison in his blood, destroying every relationship in his life. She might not know that was what it was, but he knew. He would always know.

He wasn't worth it.

"Are you going to let me help you figure this out?" he asked.

"I'm here, aren't I?" She lifted her head. "I could've come by myself in the first place." She'd been intent on doing that, and he figured she only didn't argue over him driving her because her arm still hurt from the day before. If she weren't injured, it was unlikely she'd have let him.

"You've been doing things by yourself for a long time, I'm guessing. It's okay to let somebody help you."

She tipped her head to the side the way Toni had, and he saw that beginning of a smile on her face. "I get the feeling you might need to take your own advice."

Brett folded his arms across his chest and kept his expression neutral. "I don't recall any of this being about me."

Kamryn let out a quick laugh. The smile on her face was worth all the questioning and the wondering that had happened since she got back.

He looked at his watch. There were still a few minutes for them to be alone. "Care to take a walk?" He held out his hand. She wasn't going to do this alone. Not if he could help it.

She stared at his hand a moment.

They both knew she wanted to look around.

Finally, she took his hand. "That would be good."

After a few moments of silent walking he said, "Do you come here often?"

She groaned. "That's the worst line ever. Especially considering you're the one that brought me here."

"True, but I've never been very good at this. You of all people know that."

"I don't think it's a case of being good or bad at this. Maybe it's just right or wrong, and you have to figure out which it is so you know where it's worth putting your time."

And she was choosing to spend hers with him? Sure, she was here for a reason, but she'd allowed him to come with her even though it was only to protect her when she didn't feel she needed protecting necessarily. Given the strength of her grip on his hand he thought she might just be a little bit scared and unwilling to say that out loud.

Brett said, "I think you're right that it's important to figure out what happened here, and why everyone seemed so eager to move on."

She glanced over, but nodded as they made their way toward the runway where the white plane had blown up recently—courtesy of his brother, Jeff.

"And if we can find out what happened to your mom as well, that will be a good thing."

She nodded, biting her lip.

They both knew she might wind up with the worst news a person could hope for. It was unlikely the result would be good, and he figured it was going to wind up somewhere between. The fact was he still cared about her. For someone whose entire existence was characterized by their intelligence, he had to wonder what was going on when his emotions surged once again.

It'd happened when Jeff returned—that uncontrollable urge to throttle his brother. He was in no way confused about the fact his reaction was out of anger. And underneath that anger was a whole lot of hurt.

He'd had to resist the urge to do the same with Kamryn. She didn't need the same over the fact she'd hurt him when she left.

What she needed was support. And if she just happened to realize what he already had in the meantime, well that was just fine with him. Because the truth was that she was everything that'd been missing from his life all these years.

There was something beautiful in her that her brother and father had never been able to destroy.

"This was a very nice plane." She stopped and surveyed the damage. "Did I hear it right that Jeff was the one who blew it up?"

He nodded. "To his credit, he was trying to stop a bunch of crazy guys from taking Toni out of the country."

"Oh. Okay, I guess that makes sense."

Brett had to laugh. "I don't think any part of their story

makes sense. She had amnesia, but they knew each other. Only, they'd never met so neither recognized the other one because they'd only ever talked on the phone."

"He didn't recognize her accent? She's British, right?"

"She tries to acclimate, and more than that. Before she got amnesia she was hiding out in town, so instinctively she used an American accent even though she had no idea who she was." He shook his head. "So there he is, trying to figure out why she has his super-secret, no one-knows-about-it address in her pocket, and meanwhile she's trying to get her memory back. Only, then…"

"Lenny grabbed her."

He'd forgotten for a second that was where the story headed. "Lenny murdered her boss at the gym. Toni witnessed it, and he went after her to silence her too."

"Did Jeff kill my brother?"

Brett shook his head. "One of the men trying to take Toni killed Lenny first."

He could see how that might cause some friction, even knowing how evil her brother had been. It might make Thanksgiving a little awkward.

And yes, his intentions were headed in that direction. He just had to convince her it was the best idea ever.

Because it was.

They walked between two buildings, one of which was nothing but debris. She was doing a little better now, but hadn't relaxed. As they emerged onto the street that ran down the center of the airport like a small-town main street, a car crested the hill.

"Are we expecting someone?" she asked.

"Yes, that should be Tate."

And it was, given the car he was driving. He'd upgraded when they adopted the kids. Going from his old beater to a slightly less old SUV that would fit four kids in the back.

He tugged her hand, and they met Tate as he got out of his car.

Kamryn stood stiffly beside him once again, so different from just a moment ago when they were alone. He wondered if it was simply how she reacted to men she didn't know very well. Or was it some other reason?

Tate held his hand out for Kamryn. "How are you feeling this morning?"

She let go of the hold she had on the outside of her sling with her other hand. "I'm fine, thank you."

Tate shook both their hands, which meant they had to disconnect their handholding. Something Brett let the other man know from his expression how he felt about, which meant Tate shook his hand with a wide grin on his face. "Morning."

Brett wanted to put his arm around her, but it would be more about staking a claim than comforting her so he didn't. He told Kamryn, "Tate is also looking into what happened here, and was even before you came." *Home.*

He nearly said *home.*

Brett had asked Tate to meet them for exactly that reason—and it was also why he'd set up a lunch meeting for right after, before he had to go to work. The more people who could help Kamryn figure out this mystery, the quicker she could find peace.

It occurred to him that might mean she left town as soon as she knew the truth, but he was willing to take the risk. He had time to convince her. Besides, if she left, maybe this time he would go with her.

Tate looked around. "I'd like to know what you can remember, and anything else you found out. What I've discovered isn't much."

"Was there a police investigation?" Brett couldn't see how there was nothing.

Tate shook his head. "There's literally one page of a report on file, and it mentions the NTSB coming out, but nothing else. It was ruled a tragic accident."

"I always heard it was sabotage, not an accident," Kamryn said. "Have you seen anything about that in what you found?"

"Not officially. So I'm hoping if there's something to find that it's still here." Tate waved in the direction of the crash site on the other runway. "Should we go take a look? I know you were very young but I'd love to get your impression. It'll give me a unique perspective as to what happened."

So far they'd steered clear of it, but it was looking like they were going to have to go over there now. Would Kamryn be able to do it?

The truth was, he hardly wanted to when so much death and destruction had occurred here.

Brett hadn't realized he had his own resistance in looking into the airport disaster. He wasn't here when it happened, but he'd heard about it plenty of times. Spending time with Kamryn in middle and high school meant he'd heard plenty about her dad's involvement—from the townsfolk, and her dad. People might not be inclined to remember what happened. But they were more than happy to share their opinion on Andrew Marks.

Which only made him wonder who'd decided Andrew was culpable, and where it had all come from. Sure, he'd owned the airport. But that didn't mean he was responsible. Like an elaborate game of telephone, the story seemed to have evolved as it was told from person to person for the last twenty odd years. Whispers. Buried truth.

He took his cue from her as to whether she was able to do this.

She stared over at it. "Most of the wreckage is still there, as you know. It was never cleared away. Just the human remains."

Brett took Kamryn's hand again as they walked, silently offering support.

"The plane that crashed was from the Vietnam War, a

passenger carrier they would load people in and take them up for a scenic tour of the local area from the sky. I've seen brochures at the house. It was a popular part of the airshow to score a ticket in the raffle and get to go up and see Last Chance County from the air. My dad said a lot of people in town had never flown on a plane, or didn't go very far for vacations. It was a big draw to win."

"That was the plane that crashed?" Brett asked.

She nodded. "There were fifteen people on board, plus the pilot and the tour guide. All of them died when the plane lost power and fell from the sky as it was doing a pass over the air show."

"Do you remember when it happened?"

They stopped to stare at the wreckage of the slate-gray airplane. A piece of debris close to him still had part of the American flag on it, singed and charred from flames. He couldn't even imagine seeing something like that happening.

She stared out at the runway littered with airplane pieces. "It sputtered. I remember people screaming as the plane dropped. But I see it now from the perspective of someone with years of flying experience. Mechanical failure like that doesn't just happen. And sabotage, if it was going to evade all the preflight checks, would mean someone on board had to have done it. That doesn't make sense." She shook her head. "Everyone was running, and the plane flipped. Fire erupted, because I remember it being so hot it felt like my face was burn-ing. Lenny grabbed me, and dragged me"—she turned and pointed—"there." That same tiny white building she'd avoided. The one that was barely bigger than a shed. Everything in her shuddered.

"Kamryn, it's—"

She broke free of his hold on her hand and took a few steps back, almost stumbling. They both reached for her but she shook her head. "Don't touch me right now."

Tate stared at Brett, as though he should've known this

would happen. As though he should know what it was, and how to deal with it.

"It's okay," Brett said. "We knew this was going to be hard. There are plenty of other places to look, and people to help us do it. That's why Tate's here. You could rest, and they can let you know if they find something."

She shook her head and stared at him. "What are you talking about?"

"We have a lunch meeting with Dean and Ellie. She's a historian, and she can—"

"No. I can't believe you." She let out a noise of frustration. "I don't need to be micromanaged, Brett. I've been just fine all this time. Without you."

13

Kamryn couldn't believe what she was hearing. Tate coughed into his hand and then wandered off, moving away quickly. She thought she heard Brett say, "Coward," under his breath.

"I'm just trying to help you," he said.

"By organizing this whole thing for me so I don't have to lift a single finger?" She didn't give him time to answer her. "I don't need you to do that. I'm not completely helpless, and I happen to have some experience with airplanes. Do any of your 'friends' know how to decipher a maintenance report?"

He looked exasperated, but she wasn't going to have any sympathy for him. Not when he thought his ideas were better than hers. Sure, she was too exhausted to have any ideas. But was that the point?

"I didn't think so." She sighed. "You want half the town to help me solve my problem?" There was no way they would accept her when they found out who she was. "How do you know they're not just going to react the same way everyone else did for years?"

"I know they essentially shunned you. But did I ever do that?"

"Okay, so that's one person." She had to shrug, although she could only do it with one shoulder. The other one hurt too much. "And maybe your mom, too. Everyone else? I'm just not sure they'll be as accommodating."

"Isn't it worth a try?"

"Honestly?" He really needed to ask that? "It's been years, but I don't think I could take it, and I don't want to have false hope."

He seemed intent on pushing it, but she just couldn't get past the fact no one had ever seen her beyond who her father was. Who her brother was turning out to be, back then.

Now that Lenny had caused so much havoc in town, murdering a woman and nearly killing two others, there was just no way anyone wouldn't paint her with the same brush.

Anyone except Brett and his mom.

His expression softened. "I want to say it'll be okay and that everyone will be welcoming. But you're right. False hope doesn't do any good."

"I can say from experience that it does harm."

He looked like he wanted to hug her again, but he'd done that so much already it would probably be weird if he gave her another hug. So she stepped away and turned to look at the wreckage.

That was better than facing him. Knowing he just wanted to fix her problem, and not that he still had feelings for her. She had to fight that draw he'd always had. The way he seemed to pull her to him like gravity, and she was left struggling against the inevitable.

"I know this town," Brett said. "It's a lot different than the one you knew, and so many people here have been through what you have. Maybe not the same exactly, but similar." He paused. "You wouldn't believe some of the stories I've heard. People I've met, and relationships that've sprung up. That's where I get this hope from."

People who'd been through what she had? Kamryn didn't

exactly believe that, but Brett seemed convinced he knew what he was talking about. "Do you mean like Conroy and Mia?"

He shrugged. "Sure. She thought he was responsible for her sister's death. The guy who was, they brought down together. When a bad guy came to town with a revenge plan against Mia for something she did when she was an ATF agent, he helped him. Making him culpable."

"Mia became a federal agent?" She tried to picture her skinny friend, taller than anyone else in the eighth grade. She'd really grown up to be a cop?

"After she quit, she became the lieutenant here, and now she's the police liaison for City Hall."

"I never thought she'd come back to town. It seemed like she hated it here as much as I did."

"Now she's back. She found something here that she'd never found anywhere else."

Kamryn wanted to ask her friend that for herself, not just take Brett's word for it. Though it sounded good, Kamryn still needed to hear from Mia what she'd gone through and where it had brought her. After all, she was now married to a man she'd hated for so long. And having a baby with him. That just might be crazy. But it was definitely a story she wanted to listen to.

Kamryn didn't say anything then. Mostly because if she did then she would wind up telling him she hadn't found the same here—something she'd "never found anywhere else." All that would accomplish was hurting his feelings all over again. He was trying to help her, and she was making this about her own emotions. By trying to convince herself—and him—that she didn't need him, she was only causing him yet more pain than she already had.

She let out a long sigh. Out of habit, she pulled her cell phone from her little purse with the strap across her body. "I have no signal. Do you have any?"

He shook his head. "There isn't any here. We think it's the valley this place sits in. The airport was here before cell phones.

They probably figured it was a good place to tuck away an airport where it's not an eyesore."

The sides of the valley would protect the surrounding area from all the noise of takeoffs and landings. Still. "My dad probably figured no one would worry too much about what he was doing if they couldn't see it."

"Was he like Lenny, before the accident?"

She knew what he was asking. "How am I supposed to know? Maybe they were both psychos, and there are bodies buried all over these hills. People who went missing every once in a while, and no one even noticed they were gone."

She supposed she could look through cold cases at the police department. If they would even let her do that. However, it wasn't like she actually wanted to know, or that she'd be able to help them solve the cases when she didn't have any information that would help. She'd either been too young to recognize what was going on, or she'd already left town. Neither her dad nor brother had ever told her what they were up to, but they were forever having private conversations she wasn't privy to.

As much as they had always reminded her she was one of them, there was certainly plenty they'd kept from her.

"Brett. Kamryn. Come look at this."

They both turned in the direction where Tate had called to them. The last thing she wanted was to go inside the white building. She'd spent enough time in there on the worst day of her life. Just looking at it now made every muscle in her body tense and every nerve ending go on edge. Bracing.

Thankfully Tate was outside. With what looked like a big book.

Brett walked with her to him. Not holding her hand, or leading her with his hand on her back. Perhaps they were past that kind of support. Maybe she didn't deserve it now that she'd questioned his method of helping her. Who knew? It was likely for the best though, considering how on edge she felt just walking toward that building.

The shiver came again, erupting through her like a volcano that had built for years. Ready to blow at any moment.

"What is it?" She managed to get out the question without sounding like she was about to lose it. "What did you find?"

Tate handed over the book with a dark expression on his face.

It was a photo album. Dusty, dirty. As though it had lain in debris for years—which it probably had.

She felt Brett shift closer to her as she opened the hard cover to the first page. A woman's handwriting crept across the inside. *Georgette Marks, Family Album.* Kamryn sucked in a breath and the book shivered in her trembling hands.

"Kam—"

She turned the first page.

Then the next.

The next.

Tears tracked down her face as she stared at a blonde woman feeding a bottle to a tiny baby wrapped in a pink blanket. The picture had an off-color tint to it, aged and brittle. Like Kamryn's memories.

"This belongs to you?" Tate asked.

She could only nod in response to his question. Brett hugged her to his side. She wanted to bolt, but he felt strong. Steady. She let him support her while she swiped the moisture from her cheeks and flipped more pages.

Tate came to look over her shoulder, as she turned another page.

Andrew Marks. Lenny Marks. Beside them, Kamryn and her mother. One of those awkward family photos where everyone was far too starched and no one appeared exactly happy, despite the smiles.

"That's… Oh, right." Tate's tone had a knowing edge to it. He'd figured out who she was. "The little sister who left. Who inherited the airport and immediately transferred it to a holding company."

"I didn't want this place associated with my name." She looked at Tate. "I barely want anything to do with it."

This was her legacy, whether she wanted it or not. A place of death the good people of Last Chance had deserted.

"Your mother, Georgette Marks, is the one you're looking for?"

"Yes." She braced for his reaction.

He pulled out his phone. "Let me see the front page, so I know I get the spelling right. I'll broaden my search. Help you find out what happened."

She turned the next page and looked down at it, baffled by Tate's response.

He wanted to help her?

The subject of the next photo caught her attention. "Who is—"

"That's Mia." Brett flipped a page. "Kaylee. Savannah."

Tate flinched. "Show me."

Brett continued flipping. "Hollis…and Jessica." He took the book from her and kept looking. "These are all new. Contemporary. Added to the family album."

Tate said, "Lenny?"

Kamryn fought the way her stomach seemed to want to sink to the ground. Along with the rest of her.

"Hey, Tate." Brett glanced up, angling the album away from her. "Isn't this the woman he killed?"

Tate came over. He nodded. "That's her."

Kamryn took a step back. She wanted to snatch the book from their hands, or slap it to the ground. Lenny had added stalker photos to their family album.

What else had he done here?

She wanted to fly as far as possible away from here, but this place would always be a snare around her neck. Brett was an enticement. Temptation to believe things could be better.

He might be all in to help her figure this out, but that was because he didn't understand just how deep the poison in her life went. He couldn't fix that. Not the way he thought he could help with her other problems.

Kamryn snatched the book from his hands. She flung it like a frisbee toward the wreckage of the plane with every ounce of strength she had. The way she wanted to do with her past—and that white building. But she couldn't toss a building, so she settled for the photo album.

Then she realized she'd thrown away pictures of her mom.

"Kam—"

"No." She didn't want what her brother had poisoned. "Let's go to lunch. I'm hungry." Now she was lying, just like her dad and brother. "Actually, that's not true. I want to meet your friends. To see what they can do to help."

The quicker she figured out what happened to the plane, and her mom, the better.

Then she was *gone.*

14

As they approached the front door of the diner, Brett heard rapid footsteps from behind. Tate hadn't said much after Kamryn stalked back to the car.

He shifted so she was in front of him now and turned to meet the threat as it approached. But it was only Tate.

"Hey—" Brett began.

"A word." The private investigator gave him a two-handed shove.

Before he could say anything else, Brett turned to Kamryn. "I'll meet you inside." Her expression shifted and he saw a flash of the stubbornness he knew she cultivated, and he realized she wasn't going to go in. "Please. I'll be there in a second."

Whatever was going on with Tate, she didn't need to hear. Even though she probably figured, as he did, that this was about who she was.

The entire drive here she hadn't said one word about the photo album she'd thrown on the wreckage of the airplane.

He'd been surprised she threw away pictures of her mom— even with what the album had contained. Brett planned to go back later and retrieve them, gifting her with something of her mom that'd been lost until now. She needed at least a picture of the two of them.

Aside from that, he didn't exactly know what else he could do.

Kamryn glanced between him and Tate, then headed inside. Given the look still on her face, he figured he would be hearing about this later.

He'd just have to convince her he was only trying to protect her—the way he would've done if she'd stuck around in town instead of leaving years ago. Even back in junior year, before she left, he'd been planning on taking her to college with him and getting an apartment. Which probably meant he'd have married her right after high school graduation. It might've seemed unusual, but he hadn't had many options for taking care of her in the way she needed. Which meant protecting her from her family.

And he hadn't even known the extent of the damage they were doing to her.

Not until she left him. And not until now.

The door clicked shut behind her.

He turned to Tate. "What are you—?"

"When were you planning to tell me who she was?"

"You chased me into town, all the way to the diner, just ask me that?" He hadn't said anything at the airport, but they'd left pretty quickly.

"You should've told me when you brought me into this." Tate folded his arms across his chest. "You knew who she was."

"Are you gonna run her out of town now that *you* know who she is?" Brett needed to hear exactly what extent Tate was going to go to before his friend felt like he'd resolved this.

"No, I'm not. You really think I would? But you know what Savannah suffered—and now I find out Kamryn, who Savannah cares about, is Lenny's sister. It's my job to keep her from taking any more hits. I have to make sure she's good so this isn't a surprise that will upset the healing she's been doing for a month already."

Brett looked at the ground. "It wasn't my secret to tell. Kamryn asked me not to say anything to anyone."

He wanted to tell Tate all about exactly how bad she had it growing up in this town. But how would that help? He would only wind up sounding as though he was trying to justify her hiding her true identity. Or defending her because he was so besotted he couldn't see straight.

Brett checked his phone for the second time since he came back into the area where he had a signal. Still nothing from Jeff. "Have you heard from Stuart, or my brother?"

Tate shook his head. "Don't change the subject."

"Look, I'm sorry I didn't tell you, but she asked me not to." Still, the fact remained that Brett should tell Toni for the same reason Savannah should've known. If his mom hadn't done it already—inadvertently or otherwise. He hoped Stuart and Jeff found Rich soon so he could ask his brother first before he sprung the truth on his future sister-in-law.

"Savannah is on her way. I'll wait for her out here, so you can save us two seats at the table. Because we're all going to talk about this."

Great. That sounded just perfect. He shot Tate a look that probably expressed exactly that and headed inside, where he found Kamryn speaking with Dean and Ellie already.

Brett had to admit that Ellie, feminine and intellectual, was nearly perfectly his type. Too bad Dean had snatched her up first.

Or so he'd thought…until Kamryn showed back up in town.

If he could get over his anger at her having left him, and help her find some sense of peace, there just might be a chance for him and the petite pilot he'd always wanted in his life.

Dean spotted him and lifted his chin.

Of course, Ellie noticed. She said to Kamryn, "Why do guys always do that? As if it's sufficient as a greeting."

Brett glanced at Ellie and did the same chin lift. She burst out laughing as he put his arm around Kamryn's shoulders and tucked her to his side. There was just something about having her close to him that made him feel better. He hoped it did the same for her, whether it was about feeling safe and protected, or something that could lead to a relationship. "You guys introduced yourselves?"

Kamryn said, "I already know Dean from the helicopter. It's nice to meet you, Ellie. Everyone says you're a historian?"

"Currently I'm a high school history teacher on summer break." Ellie grinned. "I'm also researching my new book. And finishing our wedding plans."

Brett said, "Let's get a table for six, because Tate and Savannah will be here in a minute. They'll want to hear what you have to say."

Ellie nodded, looking a little surprised.

Maybe that the audience would be bigger than this.

Dean pulled her chair out for her and sat in the seat beside hers, his arm across the back of her chair.

Brett asked him, "How's the center going?"

Dean nodded. "Good." To Kamryn, he said, "I'm setting up a therapy facility. Mostly for veterans, but also those who have suffered a trauma. Or anyone who just needs someone to talk to."

"Oh, wow." She smiled. "That's amazing."

Brett wanted to put his arm over the back of Kamryn's chair, but knew exactly what kind of claim he would be staking. First, he needed her agreement.

"We have one final set of inspections, and then we're ready to open. It's been a long road, but it's so worth it to finally see the finished product. We should be seeing clients in just a few weeks."

Ellie beamed up at her fiancée.

Kamryn shifted in her chair, and Brett reached over to

squeeze her hand under the table. The waitress came over, and he ordered "the Steve."

The waitress, a young woman he didn't know, said, "That's on special today."

Kamryn said, "A chicken Caesar wrap."

Ellie practically bounced in her chair. "Those are so good. I want Hollis to make them for our wedding."

"When are you getting married?"

"Early August. So we can honeymoon before school gets back in."

Brett said, "Finally, someone makes sense. It seems like everyone around here gets married in like five minutes."

Dean and Ellie both got sandwiches and soup, smiling at each other.

"That may be true," Dean said. "But Jess and Ted will probably take the longest. They don't seem in any hurry to be saddled with matrimony."

Brett figured if he was going to do that with anyone, it would be Kamryn. After all, why rush into it unless there was a reason not to wait and make the most of the journey to the altar? She felt like some ethereal thing that could slip through his fingers at any moment. He realized then exactly why everyone seemed to get married so quickly.

He understood when he looked at Kamryn.

She glanced at him. "What?"

He shook his head. "I'll tell you later."

Tate and Savannah approached the table. Savannah looked a little sick, but managed to smile at them all and sit down. The waitress took their orders as well, and then wandered off.

Kamryn said, "What is 'the Steve'?"

"It started a while ago," Brett said. "People making adjustments to the breakfast menu, like leave out the peppers or add more grilled onion. Eventually Hollis just decided to call them by the name of the person who'd figured it out."

Dean grinned. "I prefer the Saturday Tate."

"It's like the regular Tate." The man himself grinned. "But with extra bacon."

Ellie nodded. "It's good."

Kamryn shook her head. "This town is almost nothing like I remember."

"Good thing?" he asked.

She shrugged. "I haven't decided yet."

All their food was delivered. Before the small talk could continue, Savannah said, "Ellie, why don't you tell us all what you found so far."

She didn't even look at Kamryn, something Brett noticed and didn't like. But he knew her injuries from being captured by Lenny Marks had been deep and painful. He thought she might like Kamryn for who she was enough to overlook it, but this whole situation could turn out to be more difficult than that.

Ellie nodded. "I found the pilot's name, and the name of every passenger. I also have every newspaper article, local and national, that was written about the airport disaster."

"Already?" Kamryn asked.

Brett nodded in agreement with her question.

Ellie shrugged. "All that stuff is digital now, and mostly posted on the internet. Although there is a local museum that has some stuff for me to look at, but I have to wait for Dean to go on the field trip."

Brett figured if it was him, he wouldn't want his fiancée put in a potentially dangerous situation. Given what'd happened to so many of the couples on their journeys to each other, it probably wasn't going to surprise anyone when something else happened. He definitely knew what Jeff had been talking about in assuming Kamryn needed protection.

Brett checked his watch. He didn't have long before he had to go to work, which meant he needed a plan to look out for Kamryn while he was on shift.

Dean said, "I made a call to Bill, the old police department dispatcher. He was here back when the crash happened. I didn't get a reply back yet, but I'm hoping to find out what he knew."

Ellie glanced between Dean and the rest of them. "Could this have to do with the founders?"

Tate shrugged. "It's possible, I suppose. Most of them are dead or in jail these days. It stands to reason, if this happened long enough ago, that they had some kind of hand in it. Especially when it seems like the whole thing was swept under the rug."

Dean shook his head. "I thought we were done with those guys."

Brett told Kamryn, "Some of the founders of this town were particularly dangerous, and their actions hurt a lot of people. But I also thought we were done with them."

If the threat was coming from multiple places, it would be harder to defend against, making him want to sweep Kamryn up and disappear to his cabin where he could keep her safe.

Savannah still hadn't spoken past her initial question. Kamryn watched her for a minute while everyone continued the conversation and their lunch. Eventually, Kamryn pushed her chair back. "I have to use the restroom."

She hurried from the dining room and Savannah let out a sigh, as though she'd been holding herself together in front of Kamryn.

Brett didn't exactly know what to make of that, or even what to say to her to settle things. When he glanced at Tate, his friend shook his head. So Brett didn't say anything.

He finished his lunch, and Kamryn still hadn't returned.

She was gone long enough he started to get worried.

"I'm going to go check on Kamryn." He pushed his chair back and stood.

Praying she hadn't left him.

Again.

15

"She said to get this to you."

Before Kamryn could respond, a woman shoved a white envelope into her hands. Then she turned away before Kamryn could even see who she was.

She'd barely come out of the bathroom before the woman appeared in front of her. All too consumed with how Savannah had looked at her to be aware of her surroundings. She was sure now that Tate had told Savannah exactly who she was—and that was why the detective was so upset. A nice woman, who by all accounts was a good cop, was upset because of her.

And on the heels of discovering her brother had added sick stalker photos to a family album?

Her nerves were fried, leaving her seriously on edge.

Kamryn had never wanted things to be like this. She'd rather have avoided contact with people in this town altogether than cause someone pain who didn't need more of it.

Maybe she never should've even come here.

As wonderful as it had been to see Brett and his mom, and spend time with him, it wouldn't last. She'd dreamed her mom could be alive when the fact was she just needed to accept reality. She wasn't going to find anything but disappointment if she carried on with this search. Not with him, and not with finding her mom.

Kind of like the way every moment she spent with Brett also seemed to only be headed for disappointment. Perhaps if he'd have listened to her, things might be different. Not once had he done anything but push the situation the way he thought it should go. Asking her to open up to him, or bringing in others to help them. No, to help *her*. Or that was what he thought he was doing, at least.

Instead, the fact was that none of this was any of his business. He hadn't been there when the drone attacked Kamryn and Savannah. It wasn't like he was involved with her life—though, maybe he thought he was. He had enough of his own things going on. He didn't need to be embroiled in hers.

And she didn't need him, anyway.

Kamryn looked down at the envelope with the name Katherine on it. When she looked up, the woman was gone.

She glanced both ways down the empty hall at the back of the diner. At the last second, she heard the door click shut. She followed to the heavy fire door and pushed on the exit bar. When she looked around outside, the woman was already nowhere to be found. How quickly had she rushed away?

Kamryn caught her thumb under the edge of the flap and pulled the envelope open. Inside was a folded piece of paper.

She stepped back inside and the door shut but didn't click, closing out the bright daylight outside. The disparity between the heat of the sun and the air-conditioned hallway caused goosebumps to rise on her arms as a shiver moved through her.

My darling Katherine,

Kamryn gasped as hope rushed through her in a way it never had before. Every part of her ached for what this could be, and she found herself soaking in every flick and curl of the handwriting.

I'm alive. Please meet me out back so that we can be together. It's not safe, so tell no one. I'll explain everything. Only you have to hurry.

The letter was signed, *Love, Mom.*

Too many emotions overwhelmed her. She couldn't process them all, let alone acknowledge what they were. Her mom was alive? And not only that, but she was here?

Now, after all these years? She was going to go with her mom. But it wasn't safe, and the letter had said to hurry.

She looked back once toward the direction of the main dining area. There was nothing there for her. Not when things were so up in the air with Brett. She could call him later and explain what'd happened. When it was safe.

Kamryn tucked the letter in her purse to keep it secure and pushed again on the bar to go outside. Light from the sun almost blinded her as she stepped out. She shaded her eyes with her hand and looked around to see where her mom was waiting.

The woman she remembered from so long ago wasn't beside the building, or around any of the vehicles in the parking lot. She didn't see her mom across the street, hiding behind some tree ready to wave Kamryn over. Where was she?

Kamryn twisted around, about to call out, when a man came up to her. About her age, he was probably a local. A man she wouldn't talk to otherwise, flushed and sweating in the day's sun. Not that she was a snob but he seemed like he wasn't okay. She'd been living alone, traveling alone, for a long time. She knew to be cautious.

"Have you seen a woman around here, waiting for someone?"

He said nothing, just kept moving toward her. Coming way too close. Instinct had her take a step back a second before he grabbed her. Kamryn yelped as his hands clamped onto her arms, and he started to pull her with him.

"What are you doing?" Her thoughts caught up with her mouth. "Let go of me. What are you doing?"

"Shut up, Katherine." There was something familiar about his voice, but she couldn't place it.

"That's not my name." She tried to plant her feet and then pull her arms from his grasp. "Who are you?"

She needed to use some of those self-defense moves she'd learned. Jab his eyes. Get out of his hold. But it was no use. He was much stronger than her, and his grip right now wasn't anything she'd practiced with.

Kamryn wasn't going to give up, though. Not when her mom was waiting.

This must be the danger her mom told her about in the letter. The reason why she should've been faster getting out.

Hurry.

She wiggled as much as she could to make it hard as possible for him to take her.

He grunted and stopped trying to drag her. He grabbed the strap of her purse with one hand and dragged it over her head. She wasn't going to let him get her phone.

She held her elbows down. He pulled. Her arm got tangled and she twisted. At the last second, she realized what a bad idea that'd been. The strap of the purse snagged on her chin. It tightened across her throat.

He pulled on it.

Kamryn nearly fell over, her body's quick reaction to the potential threat of being choked. Like being suffocated, there was no way to get air. The strap squeezed her neck. She swallowed. Tried to breathe.

I can't get air.

Kamryn tried to kick him. He grunted, and she knew she'd made contact with his shin. But her sneaker only glanced off his leg. She tried to grab him with her hands the way he'd done with her, but he held her in front of him, dragging her back while he pulled on the strap of her purse.

She reached up and grabbed the sides of his hair, tugging on the over long strands.

The strap on her neck only tightened.

She managed to make a high-pitched noise, but with little

air left it wasn't loud. And it used up the last of the oxygen in her lungs.

He stumbled and let out a curse, grunting again.

Kamryn renewed her fight as black spots began to flash like fireworks at the edges of her vision, warring with the afternoon sun for supremacy.

Her mom wasn't here. It had only been a ploy to get her out back, alone where this guy could kidnap her.

Who are you? Why are you doing this?

The questions, spoken only in her mind, went unanswered. She had to get free of him.

The alternative was…

Darkness threatened to swallow her into that pit where she would lose her sanity. It had almost happened before. Enough times she recognized now that despair would override everything in her. Until she lost herself. Even her soul.

No one was going to save her. Kamryn needed to do it herself.

She grasped again with her fingers, her arms almost up behind her head where she found his ear. Kamryn pulled using every ounce of strength she had.

The only person who can save you is you.

God gave her the strength to do that. He gave her the wisdom to know how. And He was pleased when she followed through.

Proving to herself that she was fully capable of protecting her own life was one of the most important things to her. And she was going to get to do that right now.

Thank You.

God knew how much she needed to feel strong and independent.

He yelped as she got his head to the side, fully committed to never let go of his ear. She was fighting for her life. He pulled harder on the strap around her neck. Together they struggled, a battle for supremacy she wasn't going to give up.

He jabbed a hand into her back. The strap loosened a fraction, and she dragged in a ragged breath, still fighting against his grip on her. Still pulling on his ear.

"Kamryn!"

The exit door flung open so wide it cracked against the wall of the building.

Her attacker let go. She toppled forward and fell to her hands and knees, trying to breathe.

"Go!"

She didn't know who yelled that. She couldn't catch a breath.

"Hey." A hand touched her shoulder. A body crouched close beside her.

Every muscle tensed. She wanted to cry out at the sensation of being grabbed again, even though that wasn't what happened. She didn't have the strength to push them away, whoever they were. She'd fought that man and he was gone.

Was he gone? Maybe he would try again.

She tried to turn and look where he'd run off, twisted, and felt her hip drop. It slammed the asphalt before she could stop it. She cried out as someone grasped her elbows and helped her stay upright.

Brett.

"Breathe." His concerned face swam into view in front of her. "You need to breathe, Kam." He hadn't used her old name. He'd called her by her new one.

He was here.

Everything went fuzzy. One moment she saw the sky, and then it all flipped upside down.

"Whoa. Careful."

She didn't know what was happening. Not until she landed flat on her back, her head cushioned by a hand.

"Dean!" Brett sounded worried. "She almost passed out."

Kamryn blinked. *Brett.* Her mouth made no sound.

She spotted Ellie. Then Dean, his gaze assessing her. Then Brett again. She couldn't keep her focus still.

"What *on earth* happened?" Brett grasped her shoulder a little too hard.

She sniffed. Her throat felt like that man's hands were wrapped around it. Like her purse strap was still there. She struggled to get it off her neck, but her fingers found nothing.

"Easy." Brett took her hands. "Let Dean look at it."

"I don't think she can breathe right." That was Ellie.

Dean touched her neck. "Ellie, call an ambulance." He pulled back, wearing gloves.

Her entire body flinched. Why didn't she want an ambulance? Everything in her wanted to run. She was panicking.

You're just panicking. The rational thought managed to break through.

"It's okay. He's gone." Brett's face came close enough she could see the stark fear in his eyes. "You need to breathe, babe."

"There's a lot of damage to her throat. She might need to be intubated."

Ellie hung up her phone. "The ambulance will be here in a second."

Footsteps approached. More than one. Panic rose again, and she tried to sit up.

"Relax. It's just Tate and Savannah. You're safe now."

Kamryn didn't know that was true.

"He got away." Savannah sounded mad. Was she angry at Kamryn still?

Tate said, "He jumped in a truck and sped off. I got a partial plate. We're going to find out who it belongs to."

"And then we're going to arrest him." Savannah nodded.

Kamryn didn't understand the look on the detective's face. She only knew one thing.

Whoever had tried to kidnap her was still out there.

16

———

Brett held onto Kamryn's elbows. As soon as the ambulance pulled around to the back of the diner, she began to sit up. "Careful," he said, a little worried about her falling back onto the ground again.

The second her eyes had begun to roll back in her head, everything in him jumped into action and he'd managed to get his hand behind her head before she fell. Kamryn had enough injuries without earning a few more because he wasn't fast enough.

Her upper body righted itself, and she started to tip forward. He let her slump against him and held her tightly as she sagged in his arms.

"Okay. I've got you." He felt her shudder against him and put a hand between her shoulder blades so he could feel her breathing. "Come on. Take a breath for me."

Both Dean and Ellie looked on, clearly concerned for her as he was. Was she going to stop breathing before the EMTs got here?

Kamryn shifted her arm not in the sling to grasp a handful of his T-shirt, but her grip was a lot weaker than he would've liked. He felt her inhale, and soon her breathing was matching his. They breathed together like that while Dean went and spoke with EMTs.

Brett didn't want to know what he was saying to them. He had enough education to know what the words meant, and none of them were going to be good.

He ran his hand up and down her back. "That's it. There you go."

He was seriously worried about her throat collapsing on its own. That much bruising was going to leave her feeling like she'd been in a fire, with everything scratchy and inflamed. Even a few days after this, she could suddenly have a sharp rise in severity and end up not breathing. She should be in hospital when that occurred, if it was going to happen. Otherwise, he wasn't about to let her out of his sight. But he'd have to let her go in a second so the EMTs could look at her. They would take her to the hospital, and he wasn't a family member. He couldn't be privy to anything that occurred there.

Once upon a time he'd thought they would be family eventually. That it would last forever. Now he was next to nothing to her—at least on paper—and didn't know how to help her.

He still couldn't believe what'd just happened. Watching her fight off an attacker who was trying to kidnap her had every nerve ending in his body sparking like he'd touched an exposed electrical outlet. He wanted to curse and rage, but reined that in. She didn't need it from him when she was already freaking out this much. Though her breathing had slowed a little, it was shallow and she was still extremely tense.

He just hoped he was helping by holding onto her.

The EMTs pushed their stretcher up beside her, and Dean helped Brett lift her onto it. The second she was settled he felt her hand on his arm.

"What is it?" Brett asked.

She couldn't speak. The angry red line on her throat was turning purple, a deep bruise from nearly being asphyxiated.

Just the sight of it brought a lump to his throat so that he could barely speak.

Brett leaned down and touched her cheeks. "Keep breathing. I'll come to the hospital as soon as I can, okay?"

She closed her eyes and leaned her cheek into his touch. Then he felt her hand shift. She pulled a paper from her purse and motioned to him.

"What is it?"

The look on her face wasn't fear, it was anger. Exactly what he felt right now after a second attempt on her life. What if he hadn't been quick enough to realize something was wrong? He could've come out too late. And if he had, then he would never know what'd happened to her.

She held the paper out. As soon as he took it, she looked at the EMT and nodded.

She'd wanted him to have this before he left?

As they moved to the ambulance, Tate and Savannah came into view. The detective sat in the front passenger seat of her police vehicle, talking into the radio while Tate stood in the opening, his elbow on the top of the door. Neither looked happy.

As soon as they'd realized what was happening to Kamryn, Tate and Savannah had both taken off after the fleeing man. Hopefully one of them got a look at the man's face because Brett had been entirely focused on Kamryn.

"What is that?"

Brett realized Ellie was beside him, but didn't get the chance to answer her question before Dean huddled up and said, "What did she give you?"

Brett unfolded the paper and read what was written on it. He felt his eyebrows rise along with anger from deep inside of him. It fanned out to touch every part from the top of his head to the soles of his feet.

Tate and Savannah strode over.

When all four were gathered around him Brett said,

"Someone wrote Kamryn a letter from her mother as though she's still alive. It says she shouldn't tell anyone. Which I'm guessing is why she slipped out the back without saying a thing to any of us." Mostly he meant himself, not the rest of them. She could've said something to him, but she hadn't. "And whoever it was tried to grab her."

Tate shook his head. "He was too fast. He got away before we caught up."

Brett remembered him saying something a minute ago about a truck, but hadn't been paying much attention to his friends when Kamryn lay on the ground barely breathing. "Did you get a look at his face?"

Both Tate and Savannah shook their heads this time.

He wanted to tear the letter to shreds, but Savannah held out her hand. "I'll take that, thank you."

He let her have it, then felt desolate with the loss. That was likely about the fact Kamryn was in the ambulance currently speeding away. Lights and sirens going full blast as they whisked her to the hospital.

She was gone.

Despite the fact everything in him wanted to feel about this the way he had when she'd left him before, he had to face the fact it was different. She wasn't leaving town. He could go see her at the hospital. As soon as he got off work he could swing by and make sure she was all right. Until then the police could make sure she was safe.

"Savannah, can you get a uniformed officer to watch over her at the hospital so this guy doesn't try again?"

"There was a day or so between the two attacks, but we can't assume if it happens again that I'll follow the same plan." Savannah frowned. "Attacking someone with the crossbow on a drone is quite different from tricking and trying to kidnap them."

Tate glanced at her. "Do you think it was two different people?"

She met his steady stare. "I think you and I are going to find out."

Tate gave her a knowing look. "Because I work for the police department now?"

"No." She shook her head. "Because you can't stand to let a mystery go." She grinned and slid her hand into his.

"I don't like innocent people being in danger." Tate's expression shifted as he realized what he'd said.

Worried it might not be true?

Brett wasn't about to let that slide. "Just because her brother and her dad were terrible people doesn't mean you can paint Kamryn with the same brush. She's nothing like them."

"We know that," Savannah said. "It was just a shock. It might take time to work through everything, but I know she isn't evil. If she was, then she wouldn't have risked herself to save my life." She took half a step back and tugged on Tate's hand. "We're headed to the police department. I'll let you know what we learn and I'll get a cop on the door."

Brett nodded.

Ellie took her phone from her purse. "I'm going to pay our lunch bill, and I need to call Jessica. She'll want to know what just happened."

Dean held out his hand. "Wait in the diner for me, okay?"

She nodded, leaned up on her tiptoes and kissed him on his cheek.

The comfortable sweetness they had between them was almost palpable. It spoke clearly that they were at peace in knowing they were going to get married in just a few weeks. Brett wanted to know what that would feel like for himself, but there was also a chance it would never happen. As much as he might wish it would.

Still he said, "It must be nice not being in the thick of things anymore."

Ellie and Dean had uncovered a decades old crime involving a founder of Last Chance. The victim had been buried in a cave in the mountains and the murderer—the town doctor—had assumed he'd gotten away with it. Now he was dead, they were safe. The truth had been brought to light.

Dean studied him. "Just because we aren't being personally targeted by somebody intent on harming us doesn't mean things are all smooth sailing. Life still has ups and downs even when things are peaceful."

"I suppose there aren't any assurances that there won't be bad in the future."

"What is it that you're worried about?"

"Aside from the risk of Kamryn dying before she gets to the hospital?"

Dean waited. He said nothing, allowing the silence to give Brett the space to figure out what he wanted to say.

"I want to know the past isn't going to repeat itself. But life doesn't work that way." Even God didn't provide certainty in life —just in Him, according to Brett's mom. "I don't have the strength to lose her again."

God had helped him last time. Brett had survived it, but only barely. He'd left for college and felt every one of those aching lonely days, missing her and trying to drown himself in his education. After that, he'd drowned himself in veterinary school. Then in his job. The truth was he'd been wallowing in the solitude since she left him.

But now she was back, and he knew he wouldn't get through it if it happened again.

"God can help you get rid of that fear, but you have to trust Him to do it."

"It seems like it would be better to just hold onto everything and make sure myself." And yet, that would be foolish if there were circumstances beyond his control. But it was how he felt.

Dean nodded knowingly. "It's the biggest struggle of our lives as believers. Knowing what we're capable of, and yet giving everything over to God so He can do the work. There are things for us to do, and there are things only He can do."

Brett wasn't even sure where he stood on the subject of faith now everything seemed to be shaking with no foundation. He had an intellectual knowledge of what God had done for him. That was what his "relationship" with God had been—an agreement. There was gratefulness in him, a response to what he knew to be true. His faith had survived on intellect for years, but it hadn't ever gone deeper than that.

Now it was on the verge of collapse. He knew that the way he knew intellectually life without Kamryn would be unbearable.

He'd just gotten her back. Would God really ask him to let her go all over again?

Brett scrubbed his hands down his face. "So there's no certainty? I mean, I can believe He's capable of keeping her alive. But is He going to do it?"

Dean spoke carefully. "If the worst happens to her, it isn't because God made it happen. You could say He allowed it. It's a complex subject, but you either believe He's sovereign…or you don't."

"And I either yield to it, or I'm at odds with Him."

"Exactly. It's a path only you can take. Kamryn has her own journey, and you can help each other, but at the end of the day it's only between you and the Lord."

Was this why God had brought her back to town, so Brett could help her through solving the mystery of her mother's disappearance and she could put the past to rest, burying it along with Lenny and her dad?

So an entire town could move on from the pain they'd suffered and find peace in the future.

A fresh start.

"In the meantime," Dean said, "someone is trying to kill your girl, and I'm guessing it has to do with everything she's looking into here."

17

Kamryn spent the night in the hospital, slept beautifully until eleven in the morning and then was discharged. Now it was just after two and Brett led her down the hallway in the vet's office. He'd picked her up from the hospital, and she'd grabbed a couple of things from Hope Mansion and her car so she could spend the afternoon in his office. Mostly just hanging out and resting while he worked.

He opened the door to his office, and she went inside. His desk was almost completely bare except for the computer monitor and keyboard, beside which was a desk phone.

"It's…"

He laughed. "We've gone paperless. There are no files to leave around and no clutter because instead of sticky notes I just get texts with my phone messages." He sighed. "Sometimes I miss the good old days where you could pretend you never saw the message and that's why you didn't call the person back."

She glanced at him, feeling the pull in her bruised neck as she turned her head to the side. "Did you do that often?"

"Only when Craig Hillier brought his dog in."

She thought that sounded familiar. "Weren't those two guys from the wrestling team who used to hassle us Victor and

Craig?" She remembered them being brothers, so close in age they were in the same grade.

"They're the ones who led the camping trip. Craig is in the hospital still, and Victor should be answering a whole lot of questions put to him by the police department."

"Speaking of." She needed to go in today and look at mug shots, try to ID the man who'd nearly kidnapped her. "I'd forgotten all about those two. They still bother you?"

He shrugged. "Every business has dissatisfied customers. It doesn't matter what you do, there's always someone who wants to complain about something." He motioned to the old couch along one wall. "Make yourself comfortable. Or you could sit at the desk if you want to."

"Thank you for picking me up. It's not going to bother anyone if I'm here?"

"You can go ahead and tell me if anyone bothers you. But they shouldn't, because there's plenty of work to do."

She studied the frown on his face and wondered why he thought he needed to shield her from the people he worked with. "Are they not nice?"

"They will be today." He took a step back. "I'm going to go check on the dog you brought in. Do you want to see him later?"

She did want to know how the animal was doing, even though she never would've said she was much of a dog person. Or someone who invited animals into their life much at all. Given how much she was in the air, flying on jobs, and gone from her tiny apartment, her life wasn't exactly conducive to taking care of a living creature.

"I'll be back in a few." He tugged on the door but didn't shut it completely.

As she settled onto the couch and stretched out, some of the tension eased. She let out a sigh and wondered about the fact that, despite her having slept more than twelve hours under observation at the hospital, she was still apparently exhausted.

Why was Brett so determined to protect her from the people he worked with?

She'd been hoping to maybe hang out with some of them, if they were nice. Otherwise, she'd feel like she was bothering him while he worked. And why would he employ people that weren't nice anyways? That wouldn't produce a good working environment.

She realized she'd dozed off for a few minutes when she opened her eyes and saw him at the door again, this time with a softer look on his face.

"I should get you a blanket." He moved to a tall cupboard in the corner and pulled out a fluffy throw from the top shelf. "Sometimes I stay over. If there's an animal that requires observation."

"You always were taking care of animals." She took the blanket from him, but he tugged on the opposite end and spread it over her all the way to her feet. "I remember that bird we found at the park. Didn't you nurse that thing back to health?"

"Yes, the broken wing. I barely knew what I was doing, and I could've done more harm than good very easily. But it was worth it to see that little guy fly again."

She stared at him while tears filled her eyes. He didn't even realize he'd done the same thing with her, in a way. And when she'd flown away, he'd been hurt by her healing. The independence she'd found all because he set her free.

He'd taken what felt like brokenness and put her back together. Enough she found the strength to fly when God told her it was the only way to survive.

He crouched and brushed hair back from her face. "What is it?"

She wasn't going to tell him. And yet, he'd pushed her before and when she opened up he'd only got mad about that, too. "Isn't there something people say about letting something go, and then if it flies back to you…"

"It was meant to be." He ducked his head for a second. "Is that what you think?"

"It feels like an amazing dream. My life has never lived up to the things I dreamed of."

"What do you dream?"

Kamryn desperately wanted to answer that question but couldn't help thinking it was far too soon. He might brush it off. Or worse, laugh at her like it was a wonderful joke. Her feelings were too new and too fragile, buried underneath all the exhaustion and pain of the last few days. She wasn't going to be able to handle much from him. Instead, she said, "Aside from being chased by a drone? I've also dreamed about falling off of buildings, falling out of the sky in that helicopter, being chased by a bear…and my favorite was being kidnapped."

"You know that's not what I meant."

"You might need to give me some time on that one." She bit her lip.

He spoke softly. "You reminding me of that bird makes me think of the time you and I packed sleeping bags and went to the hills above Makewitch campground and stayed up all night just watch the sunrise. You brought your camera, and my mom gave me cookies for us…along with a lengthy lecture about respect."

"Those cookies were good."

He laughed. "I didn't even realize then how I felt about you. I thought you were just my best friend, and when she said that I started to wrestle with it. By the time you left I realized I was in love with you."

Kamryn felt a tear escape the corner of her eye. He brushed it away with his thumb. She had to know. "Did we miss what we should've had? Maybe it's too late."

"I don't think it's too late. But this right here might be our last chance for something good and real. Maybe something we always should've had but weren't ready for."

His phone buzzed in his pocket. He let out a groan of frustration and pulled it out. "I've got a patient to see, and a schedule of back-to-back appointments for the next few hours. Maybe we could talk more over dinner."

She nodded. "I'd like that."

"Text me if you need anything? Or you can go to the front desk and tell Cheryl."

"Thanks."

Brett leaned down and pressed a light kiss on her cheek. "You're welcome."

He was gone so long she wondered if she didn't dream that entire exchange when she woke up again, alone on the couch in his office.

Kamryn stood and stretched. She found a bathroom in the hallway and took care of pressing business without looking at herself in the mirror. The doctor had left the bruising exposed, though he'd slathered something on it. Apparently, it was supposed to heal better if it wasn't all taped and bandaged. He'd also mentioned the possibility she could have breathing trouble in a day or two.

As if that was the worst of her problems.

When she came out of the bathroom, she saw Conroy in the hall with a tall woman who was very pregnant and still managed to be slender. When Kamryn dreamed of the day she might be pregnant, which was probably never going to happen, she always figured she would wind up as big as a house. Wasn't that part of having kids?

Kamryn made her way to them.

She smiled when she realized the woman was Mia. "Hey, Mia."

They spotted her, and Mia smiled. She came over with her arms out. "Katherine. But I'm supposed to call you Kamryn now?"

"Kam is fine." They hugged. "But if you slip and say Kath, it's fine as well."

"Wow, I can't believe you're really here."

Kamryn laughed. "I could say the same about you considering you said you were leaving and you'd never come back."

Mia laughed.

Conroy said, "Why am I suddenly remembering the two of you getting up to some serious trouble?"

That caused them to erupt into even more laughter. Until Kamryn realized that meant the chief of police knew who she was.

"Exactly." He eyed her.

Kamryn sobered. He didn't seem wary—and he'd brought his pregnant wife to see her. "We should go sit down in Brett's office. I, for one, need to take a load off, and I can imagine you do too."

Mia nodded. "That would be good."

Conroy held the door for them, though there was no need. "Not only is she supposed to rest, she's also supposed to stay as far from any inkling of danger as humanly possible."

Mia shot her glance. "Hopefully nothing happens, because I'm pretty sure Conroy is about to wrap me in bubble wrap and stash me in the only room in our new house that's actually finished."

"You think I'd let you go to a construction site?"

Kamryn grinned at his incredulity. "I'm guessing that's a no."

Mia shifted on the couch. Kamryn handed her the pillow and she put it behind her back. "You remember Ed Summers?"

Kamryn nodded. Brett had told her the story of them taking him down together the year before.

"We bought his house. Actually, Conroy bought it and began renovations as a surprise. But it's been taking longer than he thought and it won't be ready until after the baby comes." She rubbed her hands together. "So now I get to go to the hardware store and look at paint samples."

"You're…domesticated, Mia. This is weird."

Mia laughed at Kamryn's statement. "When the danger is

over, and you realize you have everything you've ever wanted, believe me strange things start to happen. I drink smoothies now."

Conroy shot her a look. Kamryn and Mia erupted into laughter all over again.

"Thank you," Kamryn said. "I didn't realize I needed this. Things the last few days have been crazy, and it's nice to see a familiar face."

Mia patted the back of her hand, and Kamryn saw she wore hearing aids. The sight of them made her want to stay in Last Chance and find out what happened. But if she did that, then she put the people around her at risk.

Conroy said, "Are you still prepared to come to the police station later and look at mug shots?"

Kamryn nodded. "I think Brett has it figured into our schedule."

"Good," Mia said. "Let's get this guy brought in, Chief."

Conroy nodded, a smile on his face that was for Mia alone. "Yes, ma'am."

He'd taken a chance bringing Mia here. Even though it was a controlled location he couldn't guarantee she wasn't in danger. Then again, no one could be completely protected from the things that happened in life purely by chance.

The uncertainty of it bothered her. She wasn't able to control everything, which meant there would be things that happened that she couldn't fix by herself. And the last thing she wanted was to put the people of Last Chance in danger. Especially now she knew they were nice, and at least a handful of them cared about her.

Brett had done the right thing by stashing her here.

But she needed to find a way to tell him she had to leave.

18

———

Brett stood in the hallway listening to the laughter between Mia and Kamryn. It took him a second to realize why he hadn't simply gone in there and joined them after Cheryl at reception told him the police chief and his wife had arrived. Cheryl had sent them straight to the office, and he'd been delayed with a patient. Now he paused where they couldn't see him, standing alone in the hall outside his own office.

Since she'd arrived back in town, Kamryn hadn't once laughed like she did a second ago with Mia. And why did that make him irritated? Other than just being jealous someone else was able to get that reaction from her—and it not being him— he didn't know what to think. He just knew he didn't like the feeling.

Having Kamryn back in town meant he couldn't afford to be territorial. He couldn't do anything that her brother and dad would've done, otherwise he was no better than them. Trying to control everything she did, everywhere she went, and everyone she connected with.

Since that was the last thing he wanted, Brett headed for the door to join them.

Just before entering he got a text. As soon as he read the message, he stepped inside. "Jeff said they found Rich."

Kamryn and Mia sat on the couch, watching Conroy. The chief paced by the window, talking on his phone. As soon as Brett spoke, they glanced at him.

"Is that what it's about?" Mia looked about ready to burst out of her seat and demand answers about her dad.

Brett kept his voice low so he didn't disturb Conroy's call. "Jeff said he's dehydrated and disoriented but otherwise all right. They're bringing him back now."

"Did he say where they were?" Kamryn sat up straighter in her seat. "I could get the helicopter and go pick them up."

"I don't know."

Conroy hung up the phone. "They're about an hour out. Dean is going to meet them with his truck." He turned to Mia and held out his hand, assisting her in standing. "We can go meet them at the trailhead and follow them to the hospital."

"He's okay?" Worry showed on her face, as if the relief was enough she couldn't hide how she felt anymore.

Conroy tugged her to his side and gave her a hug. "Let's go."

Mia squeezed Kamryn's hand. "It was really good to see you. I'm glad you're back."

Kamryn's smile faltered. "It was good to see you, too."

They headed out quickly, and he was left with Kamryn in his office. She hugged her arms to herself, her healthy arm holding the sling where her arm had stitches in it. She looked lost enough he closed the gap between them and pulled her to him in a gentle hug.

She sighed. "I'm glad Rich is okay."

He nodded against her hair. "Me, too." Looking for something to occupy them, he said, "Do you want to go see the dog now? I still have an hour here."

When she nodded, he took her hand. As they walked down the hall Brett said, "He seems to be doing a lot better. His tag says Forest, so I guess that's his name, but I've never treated him."

"So he's not from around here?"

"I mean, there are other vets around town. I'm not the only one." Did she think he was the only one?

She glanced at him. "Huh."

Brett had to smile. It seemed like she didn't think Last Chance having any other vets in town was entirely necessary. "I can't treat every animal in town. I'd be even busier than I am now." He entered the code for their observation room and the second the door opened noise greeted them. A wall of sound that included dogs barking and a couple of screeching cats. "Bingo, sit."

The black lab in the corner pen planted his butt on the floor.

"Good boy."

"Whoa, that was loud."

"I don't even think I notice it anymore." Brett walked her to the one with Forest in it. The dog lay sleeping, his leg and hip bandaged. "I'd probably be creeped out if it was totally silent."

"I love silence. Especially when I'm up in the sky, above the clouds."

Before he could tell her that sounded amazing, Pepper strode in through the other door. She smiled widely. "You must be Kamryn."

Beside him, Kamryn stiffened. "Oh, uh…"

He rescued her. "This is Pepper. And my business would fall apart if it wasn't for her."

"It's nice to meet you." They shook hands. Pepper grinned. She glanced at Brett and raised her eyebrows.

He frowned.

She burst out laughing.

"Uh…nice to meet you, too." Kamryn glanced between them.

"Pepper was just getting ready for the night shift."

His coworker laughed. "Why would I do that when this is *far* more interesting?" She folded her arms, a wide grin across her face. "You've brought a woman in to meet us. And when has that happened? I'll refresh your memory. It's been almost *never.* You've never brought a woman in, or even mentioned more than a single date with one in the four years I've worked here."

Out the corner of his eye Brett saw Kamryn turn to him. "We're just checking on Forest. Then we're leaving."

"Good idea. Take your girl to dinner, since you *finally* have someone in your life now." Pepper gasped. "Better yet, take her to your house. The boys will love her, and you can make your BBQ chicken pizza." She turned to Kamryn. "Doctor Workaholic makes it every time it's someone's birthday. It's the whole reason we had a real kitchen put in here, not just a fridge and sink in the break room."

"Bye, Pepper." He tugged on Kamryn's arm, all the way to the run where Forest was asleep.

"The boys?"

He glanced at her. "My dogs."

"Oh."

"Forest should wake up before tomorrow. After that, it'll be a day or so and he'll be able to go home. Though, with his owner dead I'm not sure what'll happen to him."

Life didn't always work out for the best, with people or pets. He did what he could but simply wasn't always able to save the life under his care. Sometimes there just wasn't anything he could do.

Kamryn stared up at him. Face kinda pale, dark circles under her eyes…and a tiny curl to the edges of her smile.

"What?" he said.

"Nothing." She shook her head, that smile never leaving.

He wanted to lean down and kiss it.

"BBQ chicken pizza sounds good."

"I make the dough from scratch, so it has to be done ahead of time, but I have some pulled pork in the fridge." Not waiting for either woman to laugh at him more than they had already, Brett ushered Kamryn back to the office, where she picked up her stuff.

Then he took her to the police station, and she poured over photos for almost an hour. She never found the man who tried to kidnap her.

Finally home, he pulled under the carport he'd erected beside the house he owned. Brett turned off the engine, which killed the music. He cracked his door so the dome light came on and he'd be able to see her face. "Okay?"

"I am. I was going to ask if you are."

He shrugged. "Just hungry."

"Me, too. Mostly since you mentioned pizza earlier." She smiled. "Was that why you didn't want me to meet your employees? I thought it was because you thought they'd be mean to me. Instead, it was…"

"Because I knew they'd embarrass me? Pepper's just happy for me. Though, she has a funny way of going about saying that. She decides to be hilarious and try to infer things, which doesn't work at all."

Kamryn giggled.

He smiled. "I'm glad you think it's amusing."

"It was pretty funny. Have you really never introduced them to a girlfriend?"

Brett wasn't sure he wanted to admit his dismal relationship history to her. Not that it'd be better if there were a string of successful romances in his past. Or even one. Had she come back to town and he'd been married. Even if the relationship was a happy one, he couldn't help wondering if he'd have been just a little disappointed. The fact she was single, and he was single, had to mean something.

"So the short answer is no, right?"

"Let's go inside. I need to change." Brett unlocked the side door and heard the dogs come in from the yard.

"This is a really nice place."

"Twenty-two acres. Two dogs you're about to meet, four cats that mostly live in the barn, and I board horses for a few people. Though, there aren't any here right now."

"Wow."

He didn't know if she meant his home, or the two dogs currently scrambling over to him at full speed. The Airedale, Pesky, had most of one ear missing and hadn't ever given up his tendency to jump on everything and everyone to show affection.

"Hi, Pesk." His other dog was a Goldendoodle, currently badly in need of a haircut, with only three legs. She hopped over, and he let her lean her weight against his other leg while he petted her from head to shoulders. "Hi, French."

Both dogs noticed Kamryn and went over to meet her.

"That's—Pesky, down." Of course, the dog ignored him. Brett got a treat from the jar in the corner and said, "Place." The dog spied the treat and decided to obey. Brett tossed the piece of chicken jerky to him, and he laid down on his bed long enough to inhale the treat.

French sniffed Kamryn's knees and got a head rub. "This is Frenchie."

"They're adorable."

"Adorably irritating. Which is pretty much par for the course with dogs like these. But they're generally happy going, and smart enough to figure things out. Like how to get the bathroom door open."

Kamryn giggled.

"They also don't eat stuff that's not food, so that's helpful. I don't find random socks in the uh…piles on the lawn."

She made a face similar to one he imagined she had on when she'd been giggling with Mia.

He said, "Dinner?"

"If you tell me where everything is, I'll put it together while you change."

"I'll feed the dogs and show you." He glanced over at where

Pesky had gone when he decided he didn't want to be on his bed anymore. "Pesk, you wanna eat?"

The dog practically slipped on the floor he tried to run so fast toward the pantry.

He heard her laughter as he poured dog food into their bowls. After he'd set the bowls down and told the dogs to eat, he found her tapping out a message on her phone. "Everything okay?"

"Mia said her dad is at the hospital. They're waiting to hear about his condition, but she said he didn't look good."

"That's rough."

She nodded. "I was also filling my boss in on what's been happening. He wants to come to Last Chance so he can 'keep an eye on me.' But I told him there's no need."

Because I'm here?

"Because you're here."

Brett crossed to her. "I'm going to do everything I can to keep you safe if it comes to that."

"I know." She clapped her hands together, dismissing everything except food. "Tell me where the stuff for dinner is and I'll get working on it."

"Thanks." He thought he saw something move across her face Brett wasn't sure he was going to like. Before he could ask what it was, she headed for the kitchen. If she wanted a few moments to ignore the fact her life had been in danger and she was hurt, he'd give her that peace.

She wouldn't be able to ignore it forever.

Brett watched her move. He loved having someone with him at his house. Not just him and the dogs, or occasionally his mom when she took pity on him and came over to make him dinner. Or when he had a few of the guys over to watch a game, which was rare.

Kamryn being here was like having a new lease on life.

So why couldn't he help thinking something was going to go wrong?

19

"Have you heard any more news about Rich?" Kamryn asked. "I don't want to bother Mia again."

Brett shook his head and reached for her empty plate. It'd been a couple of hours, eating and talking, when he stood back from the table and took both dishes to the sink in the kitchen.

Kamryn took a moment to look around.

His living space was a little dated, but clean. Most people would've at least thought about renovating. Maybe upgrade a few things. Though he seemed to have already done that with the refrigerator. Could be it was a guy thing to worry more about the fridge than the cabinets.

"I can call Conroy and ask for an update. If you want me to?"

"Maybe later on." She brought over her empty water glass. "Your pulled pork is really good. That was delicious."

And now things were awkward. He shrugged one shoulder. "It was just leftovers."

Both dogs were on their beds, the tan and black one asleep on his back with his legs in the air.

"This is a nice house."

"Thanks. I don't spend all that much time here with the hours I work, but when I'm off I like to sit on the back deck."

"Can I see?"

He nodded and led the way. Kamryn left her phone in her purse by the door. Fitz had left her a few messages, but she hadn't texted back except to tell him she was fine. She was protected.

Being here with Brett, even only eating leftovers which she survived on most of the time, was better than any fancy date she'd ever been on. To hear he'd never had a serious romantic relationship…

She didn't want to think about the implications—or the promise—of what that meant. Hope never amounted to anything.

After she left Last Chance, she'd taken a job cleaning airplanes at an airport a couple of hours away, going to school at night to finish her diploma. Once she'd graduated high school, Kamryn spent every spare dollar she had on getting her pilot's license. After that, it seemed as though the perfect job fell into her lap when she was asked to fly for a local nonprofit. She'd been working there ever since, making a difference in the world her way. Proving to herself that she was a good person deep down inside.

Brett turned on a light before he stepped onto the back porch. Kamryn heard the jingle of dog tags as the two animals raced to the door, suddenly awake, and rushed into the yard. The deck was at least eight feet deep and as wide as the house. "Of course, if I left the light off we'd be able to see the stars. But then you'd probably trip over my boots."

Kamryn instantly had a mental image of her tripping. He'd catch her and hold her in his strong arms to steady her. Then they would be nose to nose, and things would get interesting.

Too bad her life wasn't some cute romantic tale. The last few days it was more like a tragedy.

She looked at the yard, barely able to make out the two dogs chasing each other. The one with only three legs kept up valiantly. It made her think again of that bird with the broken wing he'd nursed back to health. Brett may not have seen it the same way, but he'd done it with her as well. He'd given her the wings she needed to fly while he stayed behind and did everything right.

"Everything okay? You had a rough past few days."

Kamryn didn't want to talk about that. "Did the state park rangers find that bear?"

"Not yet." He leaned his forearms on the porch railing and watched the dogs while she tried to pretend as though she wasn't watching him. "I'm hoping Jeff and Stuart have something that will help. I passed on the park ranger's info so they can let them know if they saw anything."

She was quiet long enough he glanced at her. "What is it?"

She tried to shrug off his question, but wanted to know. "What happened between you and Jeff? When he left for the Army, it seemed like you looked up to him. Like he was your hero."

"That's because he was." Brett shifted and leaned his hip against the railing this time. He had on the jeans and T-shirt he changed into after work, leaving his feet bare. "He didn't come back to town too much, but he did sometimes. And he called mom every few months. Then two years ago he was on a mission and we got word that he died."

She gasped. How was it possible that he'd died, and now he was here?

Brett folded his arms across his chest. "About a month ago he decided to inform us that he didn't die, and he's been hiding out in the mountains above town almost since the end of that mission. He said it wasn't safe for us to know he was alive. But there had to be some way he could've contacted us anonymously and told us he wasn't dead."

Kamryn bit her lip. It wasn't that she disagreed with his assessment, it was that he was so obviously deeply hurt by it.

Maybe his brother hadn't known exactly how much Brett looked up to him. "What about Annabelle?"

"She was killed a few years ago."

Kamryn's heart sank. "So when Jeff died, you had no siblings left."

"Annabelle had a lot of problems. She was in and out of trouble, showing up here in the middle of the night drunk or high. One time she broke into my office and tried to steal medication."

"How did she die?"

"She was murdered by the fire chief." Before Kamryn could respond he said, "There's a woman in town who married a cop, and they have a daughter together. She's the one who saw it happen, and she and Toni—Jeff's girlfriend—worked with this new canine officer the police department has. They found her body, and we had a memorial service. Bridget, that's the woman who witnessed the murder, is starting a community center that's named after Annabelle."

Kamryn didn't even know what to say. She tugged on his elbow until he released the fold of his arms, and she ran her fingers down to hold his hand. "I'm sorry you lost her."

He nodded but didn't say anything.

"It kind of seemed like you were mad at Jeff." Wasn't he glad to have his brother back? She wasn't the foremost expert on family relationships, but she knew it wasn't worth throwing away good ones. Was it simply stubbornness that kept him from talking it out with Jeff, or did his brother need to apologize for something?

She figured it was unlikely it was Jeff's fault they'd been in danger and he couldn't see them. She wasn't quite sure what the problem was, aside from the fact Brett didn't like that he'd been lied to. But it was a whole lot more preferable to thinking about whoever was trying to kill her.

Which only made her think about whoever was trying to kill her.

"Hey." He tugged her to him and gave her another of his nice hugs.

When he loosened his arms, she said, "Why would somebody be trying to kill me?"

"I've been thinking about that, and it probably has to do with you being here. Looking around the airport. Maybe they don't want you to find out what happened, so they're trying to scare you into backing off."

"Maybe it's working." She shook her head. "I don't care about what happened at the airport. All I want to know is where my mom is."

He nodded. The dogs raced in another circle around the yard. "You think I shouldn't throw away the family I have, because you don't have one at all?"

"I don't know. You'd have to tell me all the tiny details of what happened, and how you feel. And maybe that's none of my business because it's private stuff that's about your family."

"And you're not family?"

"You know what I mean."

"We should call my mom." He lifted his chin, a certain look in his eye that meant he was pleased with himself because he'd figured something out. "We should ask her if you're not family."

"I see you're willing to break out the big guns and bring your mom into this."

"She's always loved you. For a while after you left, I thought maybe she might've been more devastated than I was."

Kamryn looked out over the lawn. "I'm sorry I couldn't stay. They would have destroyed me."

"I would have gone with you, and both of us would have resented it at some point." He sighed. "Maybe it's for the best that it happened this way."

"Like your brother? Finding Toni, and not only making her safe but making it that way for the rest of you as well. Now he can live his life."

"I really didn't need you to be wise as well as beautiful."

She laughed it off. "Please. You're literally the only person in the world who thinks that about me."

"Do you need anyone else to? I'll send them an email and tell them to get their act together."

"You know there was never anyone else." She didn't look at him for fear that it would break the spell, and she would lose her nerve to say it. Now that she knew he'd never had another serious long-term relationship, she felt like she could. "I might have tried, but there was just no getting over you."

"Now I know why I never managed to either."

She looked at him then, and he lifted a hand to brush some hair from her face that didn't need to be moved. Still, it was a sweet gesture. The need for touch was still evident between them, even after all this time. Nothing had changed.

And at the same time, everything seemed to have changed.

"I'm scared," she said.

"Me too."

"Maybe we should hold off until we know for sure that someone isn't trying to kill me anymore. After the police figure out who tried to kidnap me and why, and who sent that drone."

He started to speak, but caught himself and closed his mouth.

"You said Jeff hid without telling you he was here because it wasn't safe."

"What's your point?"

"I'm not going to lie to you, but I would make up some big scenario just so you stay safe. I think I can understand why he did it." Why would she not do everything she could to keep him safe when there was a serious danger?

The thought brought with it a tickle between her shoulder blades. The idea she was being watched. That someone was staring at her with malice, looking for a way to hurt her. Maybe even kill her.

What she needed to do was figure out who it was. But that

was a job for the police, and she only wanted to know what'd happened to her mom.

"So you're going to leave again just so I'm safe?" He shifted, frustration in his body language. "There's a lot more to this than physical well-being."

"I know that. I feel like I'm fighting for my sanity just being back in the town where my dad and my brother were. The town might be a lot different than I remember, but it's still where they lived."

"I want to help you through that if you'll let me."

"And you don't care about being in danger?"

"Why would I?" He shrugged. "Just because I'm not some soldier or cop doesn't mean I can't protect myself and you. I just need you to give me a chance."

"I don't want you to get hurt."

"Newsflash, Kamryn. I feel the same way about you. And I haven't been able to help you so far. You've been hurt, and there was nothing I could do about it."

"I have something you can do." She put her hands on his elbows and shifted closer. "Come with me to my dad's house and help me look through all his things."

Before he could answer, his phone rang. After he'd spoken to the caller for a few seconds, he ended the call. "That was Conroy. Rich is awake, and he wants to speak to you about what happened."

She frowned. "Why would he want to speak to me?"

20

Brett's mom waited in the hallway outside Rich's room. She waited for Kamryn and him to make their way down to her.

In the car on the way over they'd gone around and around as to why Rich might want to talk to her when he'd only just been rescued from an ordeal. Neither of them were able to come up with an answer other than the fact Kamryn was back in town, and she and Mia had been good friends as teens.

"Do you want me to go in with you?" His mom's question wasn't a surprise.

Brett squeezed Kamryn's hand. "You two head in, I'm going to talk to Conroy."

He also assumed Mia was in there. That meant Kamryn would have plenty of support for whatever Rich wanted to tell her. If it was going to turn out to be something not good.

He wanted to find out how the police investigation was going, and what Conroy knew. After that he could help Kamryn if she needed it.

She glanced back at him, as though unsure of herself. He nodded that she should go ahead, and waited until the door shut before he headed for the police chief. "Do you know what he's going to tell her?"

Conroy blew out a long breath. "I'm barely processing it myself. He's more coherent than I'd have thought, but clearly not tracking all the way. Still, enough of his story makes sense. I'm inclined to take him at his word on this one. At least until I find out more."

"What is going on?"

"Hang on a second for Lieutenant Basuto and Tate to get here. I'll tell all of you at the same time."

Brett figured that was fair. "Where's Mia?"

"Getting checked out by the doctor since she's here. Her blood pressure was a little high, but considering her dad was missing for a few days that's understandable. She's going to text me if there's a problem."

"Can you tell me about the dead guy, the one whose dog I have at my office?"

Conroy nodded. "So far we don't know who shot him, because we're still waiting on ballistics. Plus we need more than just two of the guns that were there at the time, even with a match. We'll need everyone's weapon, and Victor still hasn't turned over his and Craig's. I have to rule out the other guns."

Brett figured it was a pretty safe bet that Mia's dad hadn't shot a man, even accidentally. He'd been hunting with Rich a couple of times and thought he had a decent read on how he was with firearms. However, Conroy was right that he needed to dot all his i's and cross all his t's.

"After that, we'll be able to figure out what happened. None of them are talking beyond just their basic statement."

"Isn't Craig still here getting treated?"

"Not as of this morning," Conroy said. "The doctor told me he signed himself out after he got patched up."

"That doesn't sound good."

"I've got Sergeant Donaldson heading up a search for him, and for his brother's whereabouts. There's just way too much of this that makes no sense to have people disappearing when I might need to talk to them. And one dead man is one too many for me."

Tate and Alex, the police lieutenant, showed up soon after. Brett glanced at the door to Rich's room, wondering what they were talking about in there. Was it just a pleasant chat because they hadn't seen each other in years, or was there some other reason Rich wanted to speak to Kamryn now? Something so important he couldn't wait until he was out of the hospital.

Tate clapped him on the shoulder and sat. Brett figured that was an apology and a greeting all rolled into one as far as the private investigator was concerned. Brett shook Alex's hand. He didn't want to ask Conroy to get on with it, so he was glad when Alex did it for him.

Basuto said, "What's going on, Chief?"

Conroy pulled up a chair and sat on the edge of it, elbows on his knees. "All this is more complicated than we thought. And if Rich turns out to be right, it's feasible everything going on with Kamryn relates to the bear attack on the campers."

"How is that even possible?" Brett didn't understand how they were even remotely related. After all, the carnage that went on up in the mountains was a far cry from a drone attack—even with the gunshot. And the near kidnapping.

"It's why he wanted to talk to Kamryn. Rich is pretty sure the bear was drugged or hurt in some way and essentially pointed in their direction. Though, I'm going to have to do some investigation into that once the state park rangers finish their work locating the bear. I also have two officers that have headed up to the site where they were camped. Where the incident happened. They'll tell me if there's any forensic evidence of what went on." He took a breath. "According to Rich, everyone who participated in this camping trip was specifically targeted. They were all brought up there for the exact reason of putting them in danger, and he thinks they were supposed to be killed. It's why I've got people looking for Craig and Victor."

Brett didn't like the way this was going. "You think they're involved?"

"Why would they be specifically targeted?" Tate asked, before Brett even got done talking.

"Rich says they were all employees at the airport, except him. They all had a hand in the crash that happened, each in different ways. I need him to explain more to me, but from what he told me it at least tracks as possible since he knew them all. He didn't give me the exact details because he was saving his energy to talk to Kamryn."

"Does he know what happened to her mother?" Brett figured she was in the room asking the same question. Was Rich able to give her an answer finally?

That would mean her search was over.

Would she leave?

The way his chest tightened felt like panic, but there was no emergency here. Just a boatload of fear that she was going to up and disappear all over again with no word.

Conroy said, "I think he does know what happened to Kamryn's mother, though he didn't tell me. He was pretty closed off about it."

"Doesn't sound good." Tate glanced over at Brett.

Brett nodded. "What about the people who were camping? Not all of them were old enough to have been there. Were they?"

"Apparently the couple who were there both worked at the airport in high school."

"I did some digging," Basuto said. "And the man who died from the gunshot was in charge of maintenance when the accident happened. But he moved away years ago."

"And Rich?" Tate asked.

Conroy said, "I'm guessing he knows more about Kamryn's

mom than he's ever told anyone. That's all I can figure, because he never worked anything to do with the airport."

Brett blew out a breath of his own. This was turning out to be far more complicated than he'd imagined. More complicated even than his messed-up family situation, with all the emotions it was evoking that his brother was suddenly back in town and alive.

"So who is trying to kill Kamryn? Because that's what we need to find out, right?"

"It's bigger than that," Conroy said to him. "If these people were all brought up to a campsite and specifically targeted because of their involvement in the disaster, then someone isn't just trying to prevent Kamryn from figuring out what happened. They want all these people to never be able to tell their stories again."

Basuto said, "Do we have someone sitting on the couple, making sure they're safe?"

Conroy nodded. "And at this point we have to figure Craig and Victor are both involved. Victor could've even been the one who tried to kidnap Kamryn."

Those two had been thorns in his side for years. If they were targeting Kamryn now, Brett was willing to go pretty far to get payback. But he would just be retaliating out of spite. He had to figure a way to keep her safe and not go off burning with the fire of his emotions. Hating them for all those swirlies in middle school.

Conroy continued, "Something Rich did say was that he was certain Kamryn's mother was having an affair. He also mentioned she had a plan to run off with the guy."

Brett figured if she'd done that then she would've taken Kamryn with her. Why leave a child with a father and brother like she had? And if her mom hadn't been able to take Kamryn with her, then what was the reason for that? Why never come back?

He couldn't imagine Kamryn hearing that news. She would

be devastated when she found out her mother might've taken off and left her at home. Running away to live her own life instead of being here for her daughter.

Brett knew plenty of parents chose to be selfish rather than do what was best for their children. His father had been that way, consumed by his anger or powerlessness. It was human nature to choose oneself over someone else. Even a child. Selflessness was something quite different.

Brett didn't know what would push a person to abandon a child they cared about. And he didn't have kids, so he couldn't say what led a parent to make that kind of choice. But he could imagine what it would feel like for Kamryn to learn her mom had chosen to leave her.

She would be devastated.

What did all of that have to do with a plane crash? This whole situation was crazy complicated. He didn't know who was around still to tell them what'd happened—maybe the couple who'd been camping. Did they know who might've been interested in covering it all up?

He wondered if it was possible that this was Kamryn's mother, determined not to allow anyone to find out where she'd gone.

Considering her husband and son were dead, he wasn't sure that tracked. Probably it was someone else. A person with so much to lose if the truth came out that they were willing to kill to keep the secret.

Tate shook his head. "If she was planning on running away with a boyfriend, what does that have to do with the plane crash?"

"I was wondering the same thing." Brett shifted in his seat, eager to get done with this conversation so he could make sure he was available when Kamryn came out. She had to know he was here to support her, because he would rather do that than be anywhere else. Even when things were out of control, he wanted to be in the middle of it with her.

Conroy said, "It's crazy to think the crash might've happened as a means for her to escape. Maybe Andrew Marks caught wind of what she was going to do and he caused it in retaliation. But she wasn't among the dead. So why would he do that, except out of spite?"

"Are we thinking she's dead?" Brett didn't know how police investigations went, but he thought that might be a logical conclusion. As much as he didn't want to broach the subject with Kamryn, maybe it needed to be floated as a theory. Not that he wanted to upset her with something unsubstantiated.

Basuto leaned back in his chair. "Could be she's gone. Maybe we'll never find her body. But we thought that about your sister for a long time, and it seemed like God had a hand in bringing that darkness to light."

Brett nodded, while his insides clenched. "It's probably better if it doesn't take years to find her."

Conroy reached over and squeezed his shoulder. "We'll figure this out. In the meantime, Kamryn will be safe because we're going to make sure of it. I gave the drone to the state police forensic technician, and they're looking to figure out who was behind it. Someone controlled the thing when it was chasing Savannah and Kamryn, and shooting at them."

"And that someone orchestrated a kidnapping attempt."

Brett stood, ready to find out if Kamryn was okay. But she still hadn't come out of the hospital room, and neither had his mom. He couldn't believe they were even thinking that her mom might've up and left her in Last Chance, going somewhere else for a better life. It was more likely that her dad had retaliated and her mom was dead.

But then she wouldn't ever have justice.

And if that was true, then who was trying to kill her?

21

———————

Kamryn jumped from the chair beside Rich's hospital bed and stumbled back.

"I'm sorry, but it's true." Guilt suffused his expression. "I should've told you a long time ago, and I'll regret that for the rest of my life. The way I regret pulling away from your mom when she needed me."

Kamryn ignored Maggie's stare. The woman seemed as confused as she was about everything Rich had told them. She dragged open the door and rushed out to almost collide with Brett. "I need to get out of here."

He didn't ask any questions. He only nodded, and glanced at the room where she'd been.

Instead of him, it was his mom who said, "I'd like to come with you if that's okay."

Kamryn turned to meet Maggie's stare and read something in her expression. As if maybe there was more Maggie wanted to tell her.

Kamryn nodded.

Brett spoke then. "Let's go. But we'll be informing Conroy of our whereabouts, and I wouldn't be surprised if a police car shows up wherever we go."

Conroy nodded. "It would be good if you're not surprised."

Kamryn was too consumed with everything Rich had said to be able to respond. Except to say, "Can you have Mia text me? I want to talk to her."

Conroy frowned a fraction. "I can."

"It's nothing bad. Just about what her dad said."

She could barely get the words out in a coherent manner. Why had he never told her, even before she'd left town? That and so many other questions rolled through her mind like a checklist prior to takeoff.

They headed to the elevator and down to where he left the car. All the while his mom walked quietly behind them. Brett glanced at her, but neither of them said anything. He held the car door for her and closed it after she'd pulled her legs in.

She sat in silence as he did the same for his mom, and then rounded the front of the car.

As he turned the engine on, he glanced over. "Where are we headed?"

She said the first thing that came to mind. "My dad's house." It made sense that she look through everything there. "That's where I want to go. My dad's house."

For a long time, she hadn't thought of it as her childhood home. Or any place she associated with family. Now she knew exactly how warped that situation had been she wanted to destroy the place. Take what she wanted first, and then break everything in the house. Smash it. Get a sledge hammer and start swinging. Probably before she set fire to the whole place.

Her dad and her brother were dead, though. So what would that solve? It probably wouldn't even make her feel better.

That was the worst of it. That they'd left her with nothing good.

She didn't want to think it, but it was likely they'd also left her with no way of finding out what happened when she was four.

"Mom?" Brett said.

Maggie took a minute before she answered. "Yes, honey?"

Just hearing a woman she'd always admired use an endearment for someone she cared about like that made her ache. About as much for the lack of that in her life as the fact she now knew Brett was on the receiving end of it. He got to enjoy it. She'd always been drawn to Maggie as a mother figure, but couldn't ever allow herself to accept it. Maggie probably would've taken Kamryn under her wing. And she had, as much as Kamryn had allowed her to. Which wasn't much.

Had she jumped in with both feet and given that gift to Maggie, at the same time receiving the gift from the sweet woman in the back seat, Kamryn knew her dad would have destroyed it.

"Is one of you going to tell me what Rich said?"

Maggie said, "Didn't Conroy fill you in?"

"I'm guessing he didn't give me the whole story." Brett glanced at her. "What did Rich say?"

Kamryn clenched her hands on the sides of the seat. "My mom confided in him that she was going to run away with her boyfriend."

"She told Rich?"

"She probably wanted him to look after me." Because Rich hadn't said anything about her mom wanting to take her child with her. No, not one thing about that. Just the plan to leave town—and her dad—and live her happy life. Leaving Kamryn here.

"Your mom knew him back then?" Brett tapped the steering wheel. "That could be why he was targeted with the other campers."

She didn't know what he meant by "targeted," but the rest of it she could answer. "Rich is—or was—her brother. He's my uncle." She could hardly wrap her mind around any of it. "Which makes Mia my cousin, and not just the best friend I had growing up aside from you."

Brett's foot slipped off the gas pedal.

She saw him look at her out the corner of her eye, but kept her gaze forward while she tried to figure this out.

All along she'd thought she had no family. Just her dad and her brother, poisoning her life. Now she found out that a person she cared about and the best friend she'd growing up were her blood relatives? Her uncle and cousins weren't a perfect family by any means. Not given everything they'd been through when Mia's older sister had been killed in a car accident. Mia's younger sister had turned out a lot like Brett's with the problems she had. Kamryn still would have wanted them in her life. She'd have liked to know they were part of her family.

Then again, if she had known then she would've likely tried to escape to their house. And her dad would never have allowed that, considering he wanted to know who she was with at all times if she wasn't at home. He'd have made their lives as miserable as he made hers.

And yet she knew their family would've been there for her.

"You really want to go to the house?"

"I have to finish this. There could be something tucked away that'll tell me more about the accident and her disappearance."

Searching would help her feel as though she were doing something. Because the alternative was looking deep in her memories to try and figure out what the mess there meant. Her dad and her brother had told her so many times that what she'd seen wasn't real. Kamryn didn't believe a word they'd said, but she also wasn't entirely sure she could trust the memories of a four-year-old—even if it was her.

"I'm sorry."

"Yeah," she said. "Me too."

As soon as he pulled into the driveway, everything in her sank.

She stared at the house. "Maybe I don't want to go inside."

"I could go in first. Have a look around. Or we could ask the police department if they can spare officers to do it. If it's part of an investigation."

Kamryn shook her head. "I have to do this. They might overlook something that I'd immediately know was important."

She had no key for the house, so she went around to the back door where she used to keep a hidden key. She found it still buried under the rocks, even after all this time. It'd been for those times when she snuck out to Mia's house and spent half the night there.

Inside, the house still smelled the same. No one had turned the thermostat on, so the house sat stuffy and void of any fresh air. She tapped buttons until the fan came on, spooling up the air-conditioning unit to begin bringing the temperature down.

She should probably look through the attic, but if it was this hot in the house, then it was unbearable up there.

Sweat ran down her spine. Probably it wasn't because of the temperature, though.

Maggie started to wander around the living room.

Brett said, "Is there anything in particular you want us to look for?"

Kamryn didn't completely know what she was after. "Just stuff about my mom. Not that I think she left her diary lying around, and it's been here for twenty years. But I guess it's possible he packed up her things and put them away somewhere."

Her dad could have a storage unit. Or he could've destroyed everything when he accepted the fact her mom was never coming home again.

Had he known what happened to her? It was entirely possible he could've killed her, or knew what'd happened and kept the secret all these years. Her dad had been injured when the plane crashed—part of the spectator crowd.

What happened to her mom could've happened before, if he was the reason she'd disappeared.

But what about her memory, the one where her mom searched for her? Was that before the plane crash? She squeezed her eyes shut. It had to be, because the runway had been clear. Her mom had raced through the crowd searching for her.

The plane had crashed later. How much later, she didn't know. Part of her had always thought her dad responsible for the airplane disaster. Even though he'd always denied it and claimed he never knew who sabotaged the flight. How her brother came into it, shoving her in the white building and locking her up in the closet, she didn't know. Just thinking about it still made her shiver.

She'd never liked enclosed spaces.

Or thinking she heard voices.

Kamryn wandered down the hall, trying to shake off the nervous feeling, and found her brother's room. Inside was so much the same as it'd been when he was a teen that she didn't bother stepping inside. It wasn't worth the torment to know what he kept hidden in there.

Her bedroom was next door, with the bathroom across the hall. Her dad's room was at the end. Now that she was here, she didn't exactly want to go in any of it.

She expected her bedroom to be exactly as she left it the day she split town. Preserved like her brother's room. Instead, someone had converted it into a guest room, complete with a floral bedspread on the twin she'd slept in. Conroy had mentioned to her that her dad had a nurse close to the end of his life. She'd also been killed by Kamryn's brother. Another poor innocent life caught up in their destruction.

The walls had been painted, and everything personal she'd left behind cleared out to make room for this new person.

So where had they put it?

The same place they put her mother's things?

She didn't believe they cared enough to preserve anything. It was more likely they'd been too lazy to clear things out and take anything to the dump. Except when her dad had required a nurse. After all, why would Lenny's bedroom still look like it always had when he didn't even live here anymore?

Kamryn got a chair from the dining table and carried it down the hall. She stood on the seat and pushed back the ceiling panel that led to the attic. A hot wall of air rushed out. Musty, and stale.

She pulled down the stairs and kicked the chair away so she could climb up to stick her head inside the attic. There were so many boxes up there. Her heart sank at how long it was going to take to go through them all.

"Find something?" Maggie stood beside the stairs.

Kamryn sighed. "Just a whole lot of stuff that could be full of old newspapers and magazines for all we know. I doubt we're even going to find anything. It was probably wishful thinking to come here." All because she was too scared to go into the white building. The very place where Tate had found that family album.

"Brett and I don't mind helping you. Where else would we be?"

Kamryn ducked her head as she fought off embarrassment. She was unused to having people on her side, let alone standing with her when she'd been in danger recently.

This whole thing with the setup bear attack was crazy. Maybe Rich had hit his head and got confused. It wasn't like it was a conspiracy.

It was nice to have the other woman here. She provided a buffer between Kamryn and Brett when she needed one, entirely too battered and confused to figure out what to say.

Maggie spoke. "I didn't know he was your uncle. If I had, I'd have told you."

Kamryn shifted to sit on the middle step of the ladder. It was awkward, but she needed to conserve her energy. The stitches in her arm stung, so she figured she was past due for another pain pill. Her neck felt swollen and she was mostly trying to ignore it. "I know you would've told me. Thank you for coming here."

"I'd like to know what happened to your mom, too. Especially if she was in danger and no one ever helped her." Maggie paused. "There's no way she would've willingly left you. I saw how she was with you. You were her entire world."

A tear rolled down Kamryn's face. Because if her mom hadn't taken her too, that meant maybe she hadn't left willingly. She swiped away the tear. "What happened to her?"

Glass shattered, and there was a loud explosion. Maggie's body jerked before Kamryn could even react to what was happening.

A second later Maggie fell to the floor.

Kamryn screamed.

22

Brett heard the shot. Seconds later a woman screamed. He thought it might be Kamryn, so he dropped what he was holding and ran for the source.

He'd been looking at a framed picture, the original patent for the airplane. Brett wouldn't have thought Kamryn's dad was the nostalgic type. Or even someone to have something that was actually kind of cool in his house. Maybe it'd been a gift.

The picture hit the floor and broke.

Brett was already in the hallway, where his mom lay on the ground.

Even before he got there, he could see the blood.

Kamryn stumbled down a wooden ladder from the attic. She fell to her knees beside his mom. "She was—I didn't…"

Brett focused on his mom. Unconscious, she'd been shot low through her shoulder below her collarbone. It could have hit her collarbone on the way through. He didn't know. He wasn't a medical doctor, so he couldn't tell.

What am I supposed to—

Brett called 911, then set the phone on the floor with it on speaker.

Another shot fired through the shattered window at the end of the hall. Kamryn yelped.

He reached out to tug her shoulder down and spotted blood on his fingers. "Get down."

She ducked, letting out a whimper—a sound he very much wanted to make.

"911, what is your emergency?" a woman asked. She sounded professional, like a big city dispatcher. Nothing like the previous one Last Chance police department employed. Bill had been older and a lot more informal. The trade-off was that she sounded competent, even though she was new to town. It was good she knew what she was doing. This was someone who could handle herself in an emergency.

"Maggie Filks has been shot in the shoulder, and the shooter is still active." He lifted his mom a fraction and looked at her back. The bullet had gone all the way through her, which was good. Any time a round remained in a person's body, things could be markedly worse. He'd treated enough animals inadvertently hit during hunting season.

"Units and an ambulance are on their way to you. Please confirm the address."

He looked at Kamryn, but she didn't seem to have heard. Or she wasn't processing. "Address?"

She blinked and gave the street name. The house number.

"Understood." The dispatcher asked questions about his mom, and he answered as best he could before he hung up because he needed to focus. An idea was gathering in his mind.

Brett pulled off the buttoned checkered shirt he wore and pressed it against the wound. At least he'd worn an undershirt today. Random thoughts flitted through his head, bringing him back to his idea. He tried to rein it all in and glanced at Kamryn. "You with me?"

Her eyes were slightly glassy, her face pale. Sweat gathered at her hairline.

Another round fired through the window, not far above their

heads. He hunkered down and twisted, covering his mom's body. Kamryn screamed and curled her body tighter into a ball, knees up. The bullet embedded itself in the doorframe behind him.

"Kamryn?"

She blinked and nodded, a jerky movement. "She got shot." Her body was hunched in a crouch, close to the wall.

Yep. Definitely in shock. "Just stick here with her. Okay? Stay low." For the first time in his life, Brett was glad for the ability to be cool under pressure. Plenty of times he'd saved an animal's life in a crazy situation, or when all the odds were stacked against it. Things didn't always work out perfectly, but he knew how to handle himself.

"Are you going somewhere?" She frowned at him, not tracking with what was going on.

"As soon as the ambulance gets here, they'll take her to the hospital. But they can't do that if the shooter is still firing at the house." He couldn't think about it too much. Otherwise, he would want to stay here and hunker down.

A shooter. His mom, injured. Kamryn clearly needed him to help her through the shock and stress. But if he stayed, the shooter would still be out there. Instead, he needed to force whoever was still out there to stop so the police and EMTs could come inside.

Find out who it was.

Tell the police where they were.

"Stay here with her." He took Kamryn's hand and pressed it against the shirt over his mom's shoulder. "Don't let up on pressure. Keep pushing on it."

"Where are you going?" She blinked at him. "Why are you leaving right now?"

"I have to make sure the police and paramedics can come in the house. They can't do that if someone is firing." He touched her cheeks and pressed his lips to hers in a quick kiss, not nearly the one he wanted to have with her. But there was no time.

"Stay with her." He handed her his phone. "And call Jeff if you get a chance."

Brett left his mom laying bleeding on the floor of the hall and crouch-walked to the corner. It hurt to move away from them, knowing they needed him. But he had to.

Once he was out of sight of the window, he stood up and ran for the front door.

Only by disabling the shooter—however he needed to do that—was he going to clear a path for the cops and paramedics to come in the house. Not to mention, Kamryn was still in danger until that happened. She could easily get hit by the next shot if the shooter had line of sight to adjust and aim for her.

He just hoped it wasn't another drone, or he might not be able to take it down. He was a vet and not a police officer or some kind of special forces operator. It was possible he had zero skills at all to do this. Could be a fool's errand. But there was no one else here to disable the threat.

Despite his lack of training for anything other than dealing with animals, he raced along the sidewalk to the end of the street and headed right, trying to figure out where the shooter had set up. He'd been hunting before, and taken plenty of training classes on safety. But firing in a residential area? This person didn't care who got hurt.

All they cared about was keeping their secret.

His chest ached, not just from running so fast. Part of him didn't want to leave his mom in that hallway, but the EMTs couldn't come in until it was safe, and it would take time for the police to make sure the shooter had stood down.

His mom had been his only family for years. Hope Mansion couldn't lose her, and neither could he.

The street that backed onto Kamryn's dad's house had only dirt lots on the north side. No one around to spot a shooter currently standing in the bed of his truck with the stand of his rifle perched on the roof of the truck.

Brett sprinted to a backhoe and crouched behind the tire.

He needed some way to force this guy back from his rifle so he would quit shooting and Brett could possibly subdue him for arrest. He realized then he'd left his phone in the hallway and looked around for a weapon. He was bringing nothing useful to this gunfight, but figured it'd be hard for this guy to lift and turn the rifle quickly enough to fire at him.

That could mean the difference between life and death.

Brett just needed a way to hit him fast. He spied a palm-sized rock on the ground. That was going to have to be good enough without heading back to his car and getting his softball bat from the trunk.

He hefted up the rock and tested the weight in his hand. This would do nicely. And it was probably all he had, considering he was crunched for time if he wanted to do this before emergency services showed up at the house.

Brett came out from behind the backhoe, one thought uppermost in his mind.

Mom could be dead.

No, he couldn't think that way, even if the pain of it fueled his muscles.

He tossed the rock as hard as he could toward the man on the back of the truck. The guy's attention was on the scope of his rifle, no sign he was about to pack up and leave, when Brett's projectile slammed into his shoulder and clipped the side of his head.

He would have taken a second to congratulate himself on his accuracy if he hadn't been racing toward the man, sprinting at full speed. Perhaps God had helped him.

Brett raced toward the back of the truck, where the tailgate was down. But before he could hop up there, the man turned.

Anger seemed to wash over the man's expression, so strong it would be visible even in the dark of the late hour. But with a hood up and a bandanna tied across his mouth, he was unrecognizable as he leaped the couple of steps across the bed and jumped.

Seeing the man coming, Brett shifted, but the guy clipped his shoulder.

Just as he had hit Brett's mom's shoulder with the bullet.

Brett twisted around, spun by the force of the tackle hitting his shoulder. The guy fell to his hands and knees, and Brett kicked him before he could stand.

He'd never been this angry in his life. Faced with the prospect of his mom's life ended, Brett didn't care that he wasn't trained. That there were so many people in town much better suited to doing this than him. All he knew was that he had to disable this guy somehow. Make sure he didn't fire another shot from that weapon. Not only did his mom's life depend on it, but the lives of police and EMTs and Kamryn as well.

Too many people had died over the last sixteen months. The town didn't need to lose anyone else to death or injury. A friend of Brett's who had been a police officer was currently paralyzed from the waist down. Frees didn't seem content to allow that to hold him back, though. He was determined to keep living his life.

More than once, Brett had seen him at his house. The last time he'd helped Frees figure out how he could still ride his horses even with the injury.

The shooter rallied too fast, launched up, and tackled Brett before he'd even realized his mind wandered. His back hit the ground and all the air was knocked out of his lungs. He then pulled a fist back and punched Brett in the face.

Pain erupted in Brett's cheekbone. He took a breath and tried to kick the guy off him, then cried out as frustration burned hot in his gut. He tried to fight, but it was no good. He was no good. The guy was heavier than him, and determined to do damage. He could barely breathe while the man punched his face over and over.

Brett tried to rally. It didn't work. He tried to find strength from the rush of emotion he'd felt when he realized this guy—

he assumed it was the same man—was trying to kidnap Kamryn. Trying to drag her away from behind the diner.

That didn't work either.

Brett reached for the guy. He had to do something or he was going to lose this fight, and everyone would know he wasn't good enough. He'd let his mom die, and he wouldn't be able to save himself.

Kamryn probably should just leave town again.

After all, it wasn't like he was worth sticking around for.

Before he could figure out what to do about the man on top of him, the guy grabbed his head and slammed it into the ground.

Everything went black.

23

Kamryn heard a rumbling truck pull up right as they loaded Maggie onto the ambulance. She spun around, her nerves still taut from the last half hour.

Jeff hopped out of the driver's seat. He moved quickly to her while Toni climbed out more slowly to make her way over on crutches. He strode all the way to her. "How is she?"

"She woke up after Brett left." There had been another shot, and Kamryn figured her scream was what woke Maggie. "She was in a lot of pain, so the EMTs gave her a shot. They're taking her to the hospital."

Toni got close enough to hear the last part. "I'll go with her." She glanced up at Jeff. "Do you want to find Brett and meet me there?"

He nodded, though it seemed distracted.

Toni got in the back of the ambulance with some help from an EMT, and they closed the back doors. A second later the siren commenced, and they headed off down the street.

Jeff turned to her. "Are the cops looking for him?"

"I don't think they're looking for Brett." She wasn't sure what was going on. "I think they're just looking for the shooter. But maybe they'll find him at the same time."

Jeff touched her shoulder. "Are you okay?"

No one had asked her that. Not when the cops showed up, or the EMTs began working on Maggie. She'd been glad for it, considering any hint of concern and she was liable to fall apart. As it was, now she had to steel herself against it. "Let's just find Brett. Then we can go to the hospital."

Only she didn't belong there, did she? Even though she was here when Maggie was shot, Kamryn was also the reason why it'd happened. She'd caused this. All because someone was trying to kill her to prevent her from learning the truth about her mom—and the accident.

"This wasn't your fault," he said.

"That's not true, is it?" She turned away and tried to figure out where Brett had gone. Where was he? He could be hurt, or dead. That would be her fault, too.

Jeff followed. Maybe he knew she didn't know where she was going, and maybe he didn't. Could be he was only going with her because it was the right direction.

She had no idea.

The only thing she knew was that she was having second thoughts about all of this. Especially if the worst happened to Maggie. Kamryn didn't know if she could continue after something like that.

Perhaps it was best to just leave it all alone and not risk anyone else's life. If she simply walked away then there would be no reason for anyone to try and kill her. And yet, this was bigger than just her. Someone had set up those campers, and somehow caused a bear to go rogue just to keep them from telling her anything.

She nearly gasped.

They'd known she was coming here to ask questions before she even arrived. They had to, or the camping setup didn't track.

Who knew I'd be coming here?

Kamryn bit her lip as she looked down a side street trying to find Brett.

Where is he?

"I'm sure he's fine, wherever he is." Jeff almost sounded mad. Like he was angry with his brother for being absent, keeping Jeff from being at the hospital.

She could understand that well enough, even if there had never been anyone in her life like what they had. She could count on her left hand the number of people she cared about the way he cared about his mom. Still, even though her life was a sad existence with no family, she understood what he was going through. Mostly because she cared about Maggie as well.

"Your mom just welcomed me back. No questions, only complete acceptance." She could hardly believe it was possible for someone to simply forgive everything and act as though it didn't even exist. The idea was so foreign to Kamryn.

"It's what she does," Jeff said. "She did the same with me a few weeks ago when she found out I wasn't dead. That I had been in town for two years, lying to her by not telling her I was here."

"I don't understand what that's like. To be able to just wipe everything away."

"She said it's grace. We get a clean slate when we don't deserve it, and we definitely didn't earn it."

"Grace." Even the word was foreign to Kamryn. "It's amazing she can do that."

"Honestly, it's been happening to me a lot lately. It's starting to not feel so bizarre." A smile appeared on his face despite the fear for his mom. "Let's find Brett so we can get to the hospital."

"I don't think I should go." She shook her head, still looking around for Brett.

Two cops stood together over in the construction area. One crouched. It seemed like the workers had marked out where new houses would go, but hadn't started building anything yet. And they'd left all their equipment there at the end of the last workday.

"Why do you say that?" Jeff asked as they headed toward them. "Mom cares about you."

"I'm the reason she got shot. I don't think I should be there, just in case something happens again."

First Savannah had been with her. At least with the kidnapping no one else had been injured or targeted along with her. But this time, Maggie was left fighting for her life.

All because her mom had an affair?

No, that couldn't be it. There had to be more to it than that, given the deadly retaliation.

"Over here!" One of the cops waved to them.

Jeff picked up his pace to a sprint, and she did the same, hugging her arm in the sling against her body so it didn't bang her side while she ran.

Brett lay on the ground between the two men. One of the cops patted his cheek. "Wake up, sleepyhead."

Jeff hissed a breath between clenched teeth. "Looks like someone did a number on him."

Kamryn looked around. She had to constantly watch for the next attack, just in case whoever was behind this tried again.

"Maybe the shooter attacked him." Jeff crouched and shook his brother's shoulder. "Time to wake up, bro."

As Brett moaned, Kamryn imagined Jeff had awoken him like that many times when they were kids. Probably when they'd been late for school, which she remembered happening often. There were a few years of difference between them, and that added to the hero worship Brett had for his brother.

After Jeff left for the Army, Brett had been almost desolate with the loss. She couldn't imagine what it felt like to hear his brother had been killed and then later learn he was alive. She could almost understand his anger. Still, the love they had for each other as brothers was an undercurrent between them, even while they were at odds.

Brett started to sit up.

Jeff helped him to his feet. "You good? We need to get to the hospital."

"I need a statement from everyone." The cop didn't look like he was going to take no for an answer, and Kamryn figured he wasn't accustomed to having to do so considering the sergeant stripes on his sleeves.

Jeff said, "You can do that at the hospital, right?"

The sergeant nodded. "That should work. I'll secure the house first. Are you good, Brett?"

"Yeah, Donaldson. I'm good. Thanks."

The two cops headed off, and Jeff watched Brett take the first few steps. When it was clear he was good, they all picked up their pace. "I don't think you should drive."

Brett said, "Kamryn can drive my car."

Jeff nodded. "Good enough for me."

"How did she look?" Brett asked.

Jeff motioned to Kamryn. "I don't know. Pale?"

She said. "The EMTs were in a hurry to get her to the hospital."

Jeff nodded. "Toni is with her, so if there's any change before we get there, she'll let me know." Kamryn got in the driver's seat, had passed the first corner, and was headed toward the hospital when he said, "Are you good?"

She didn't want to answer the question. Not that she wasn't prepared to be honest. She just didn't think he wanted to hear what she had to say when his mom was fighting for her life and it was all her fault. If she went down this road, opening up to him, she would only wind up losing it. He felt bad for her when he should be worrying about his mom.

"I'm guessing that's a no."

"Jeff already tried to tell me it wasn't my fault. We both know that's untrue."

What she needed to do now was decide whether to figure out what was going on, or to just leave it alone.

She needed evidence of what happened. The identity of the person who'd caused the accident, maybe the same person her mom had been having an affair with.

There was no time to worry about Brett or her feelings for him. Not now that his mom was in the hospital. He didn't need her to be confusing him, tearing him in two different directions. Not when she had other things to do, and she didn't want him to be in danger because of her.

Brett had been unconscious. His mom shot. Savannah and Tate could barely look at her they were so mad she hadn't told them she was Lenny's sister. Mia seemed to be fine, even if Rich was a target. Still, Kamryn didn't think she could face anything terrible happening to anybody else.

Not when that would be her fault as well.

Her dad and brother weren't here anymore, which meant it was all on her shoulders.

"This isn't about fault," he said. "But if we're going to be throwing around blame, some of it has to land on me. The shooter got away."

"You went up against him?"

"I'm not sure you could call it that. He wailed on me, I passed out and he probably just took off in his truck." Brett sighed. "I'm surprised he didn't run over me."

That meant the shooter was still out there.

She shivered. "Are you okay?" He could've been killed because of her and the fact she was being targeted. "You should be more careful than that."

He hadn't had a weapon.

He just waded in. Because of her.

Yet more guilt welled up. Brett shifted in his seat on the passenger side, silent probably because he knew she was right. The situation was dangerous, and he shouldn't be part of it. He'd probably decided to let her deal with it herself now that he'd been hurt. *Because of her.*

He probably realized she wasn't worth it. He should cut her loose.

She pulled into a hospital parking space.

A muscle in his jaw flexed. "My mom could be dead in there. And that guy got away."

She was right. He blamed her. "I know that. You think I don't? You think I'm not well aware of the fact that if I hadn't come back to Last Chance, none of this would've happened?"

He started to speak, but she didn't want to hear it.

Kamryn shoved open the car door. She got out before she realized she had no business being here.

He shut his door and started to walk toward the hospital front entrance. "Are you coming? We need to get inside because it isn't safe out here for you."

"I think you mean it isn't safe out here for *you*." She would be targeted, and someone else would be hit. She could see the bruises on his face. It made her chest feel heavy, squeezing as if steel bands wrapped around her lungs.

"Come on."

She took a step back. "I need to figure out who is trying to kill me before anyone else gets hurt."

"Kamryn—"

She shook her head. "You shouldn't be near me right now."

He took half a step. She heard a truck engine rev. The vehicle picked up speed as it bumped the curb of a planter and headed straight for them.

Brett ran toward her. She saw his life flash in front of her eyes, knowing full well he was about to lose it.

She screamed, and he tackled her.

They hit the ground and rolled. She felt the heat of the truck and heard the noise of the engine as it headed straight for them.

We're going to die.

24

Brett's entire body ached. He held onto Kamryn and kept rolling, praying the tire didn't drive over them. His legs clipped another car, and he scrambled up, taking her with him to hide between two cars. When he stood, he saw the truck speed away from them.

"Same truck."

Kamryn grasped onto his elbow. "What was that?"

"It's the same truck from earlier. That's the shooter who caught my mom." He moved toward the car, Kamryn still holding onto him. "Come on. We can catch up." Before she could object, he grabbed the keys from her hand and slid into the driver's seat. It was *his* car. He had the engine already running by the time she got in the passenger side and he pulled out before she got her door shut.

"Shouldn't we call the police?"

"Good idea," he said. "Or Jeff." Because now that he thought about it, Brett should be inside the hospital. Not chasing after an armed man who tried to kill them.

But this was the guy who had shot his mom. What else was he going to do?

She held the phone out between them. It started to ring.

"Hello?" Jeff answered. He apparently didn't recognize Kamryn's number.

Relief washed over Brett at the sound of his brother's voice. "It's me. Kamryn and I are following the guy who shot mom. He tried to run us over in the parking lot."

Or, at least they would be following if he found the truck so that he *could* follow it.

Brett glanced around.

Kamryn pointed with her free hand at the street. "Over there. See it?"

There was a rustling on the phone.

Brett hit the gas and headed for the street. He bumped up and out of the parking lot. The underside of the front bumper scraped the asphalt, and he winced. "Sorry."

"It's your car. Don't worry about me. He's getting away."

On the phone still, Jeff said, "Are you seriously telling me you guys are in a high-speed pursuit chasing the man who shot mom?"

"How is she?" Brett didn't want to ask, but he had to.

"They said she'll be in surgery for a few hours, but he's optimistic. Toni is on the phone with the police dispatcher. She'll get someone to take over from you."

"No." He didn't need any help. After all, he'd let this guy get away once.

"These people know what they're doing. When the cops get there, you need to back off and let them do their jobs. They're trained for this."

"Yeah, and I'm just a vet."

Out the corner of his eye, he saw Kamryn glance at him.

Whatever that was about, he didn't have time to ask. So what if they thought he wasn't good enough or skilled enough to run down this guy and bring him to justice? So what if he was only a vet? Just because the rest of them could do it didn't mean he couldn't make sure this guy never got away again.

"Brett—"

He tapped the screen and ended the call.

"At least the police will be on their way."

He winced. "Yeah, but we could lose him before then. That's why we have to do this." He weaved in and out of traffic, honked his horn, and pushed the gas down farther to try and catch up with the truck speeding faster than he was.

"Are you sure this is a good idea?"

"What other choice do we have?" Brett overtook a van. "He'll get away again."

Brett reached over and tapped the red button to hang up.

At least he didn't figure they had much choice, anyway. He knew this was, at least for the most part, about proving to everyone that he was capable of doing exactly what they did. He wasn't just a vet with no skills.

Maybe if he'd gone and hunted down that rogue bear with the state park rangers they wouldn't feel this way, but he would never know now.

"I know I don't want anyone else to be hurt because of me," she said. "So just be careful, okay?"

It was hard to believe she still cared about him after everything. But maybe she really did. He wanted to prove to them all that he could do this.

Brett took a sharp corner and spotted the truck up ahead. Beyond it was a red light.

"What is he going to do?" she asked.

He frowned. She had a good point. So far, the truck had been changing lanes and overtaking people. Now the traffic was stopped at the light and oncoming traffic filled the lanes headed toward them on the other side.

Where am I going to go?

The question persisted in his mind until he saw the truck swerve sharply to the right and bump up on the curb. After a second's jolt, the truck headed around traffic and straddling the sidewalk to do it. A man at the crosswalk had to jump out of the way, into the street in front of the first row of cars waiting for the light to change.

Kamryn sucked in a sharp breath. "He's going to kill someone."

Considering he already may have issued a death sentence for Brett's mom with that bullet, the guy driving the truck didn't much care.

Up ahead on the other side, a police car with flashing lights headed their way. The truck bounced back onto the street and kept going. A car trying to turn braked sharply and honked.

The truck kept going still.

The police car made a U-turn in the street.

Brett slammed his palm on the steering wheel. He couldn't get around traffic without doing the same thing.

"At least the police can run him down now." Kamryn sounded relieved.

Because she thought he'd been acting recklessly? "I wasn't going to let him get away again. That's twice he's tried to kill you tonight."

"That's why I didn't want you to get hurt."

"Not just because you'll never find out what you want to know if we're killed in a car accident. You'd never discover what happened to your mom."

She twisted in the seat. The brake lights from the car in front lit her face with a red glow. "So basically, you think I'm completely selfish. That I want to stay alive long enough to find out what happened to my mom, and other than that, I don't care about anyone?"

"That's not what I'm saying."

She started to fire back a retort but stopped herself from speaking. He wondered what she'd been about to say. Only maybe it was for the best that she was better able to control her tongue than he was.

As soon as it was clear, Brett pulled out of traffic and did a U-turn. "Text Jeff and tell him we lost the guy, but the police are on it. He'll want to know what's happening with the man who shot mom."

"But you're driving to the hospital?"

"Where else would I be going?"

She looked up from her phone. "I'll drop you off, but then I have things to do. I'll ask Toni to text me later and let me know how your mom is doing."

"You're not coming in?"

She shook her head no.

Of course, she wasn't. The moment the question left his mouth, he realized how absurd it sounded. She probably didn't want anything to do with him or his family. After all, they only got in the way.

"Someone is trying to kill me, Brett. People keep getting caught in the crossfire, and I don't want that to happen again. I don't want you to feel like you have to put your life in danger just to help me."

"I'm trying to protect you."

"You should be at the hospital, not helping me just because you don't think I can do this alone."

Brett pulled into the parking lot of a chain pharmacy. He put the car in park and turned to her. "Where are you planning on going?"

She stared out through the windshield.

"Please tell me." He needed her to trust him. That was what it came down to. Knowing whether or not she was willing to lean on him for once.

"So you can say I'm being ridiculous, or I'm putting my life in danger?"

"Are you going to be either of those things?" He didn't like the idea of her going alone. She was entitled to do it, but given the situation he figured it was better to have someone with her.

"Does it matter? No one else is going to get hurt." She folded her arms. "That's all there is to it."

"And if this guy trying to kill you succeeds? How are the rest of us supposed to figure out what happened? Someone needs to know where you're going."

She glanced at him. "Sorry if I don't know how it works when people care about you. I didn't know I'm supposed to check in, or take a buddy with me for safety. No one's ever had my back."

"They would have, if you'd told anyone you were leaving town."

"Because you'd have gone with me?"

He shrugged. "I guess we'll never know."

She huffed.

"Like I'll never know what you'd have said when I asked you to go to the same college as me," he added.

Sure, it would've been more complicated than that. He probably would've ended up proposing after what he assumed would've been an awesome senior year together. But all of that had only ever happened in his dreams.

Reality had turned out a whole lot different.

She twisted in her seat to face him. "You were going to ask me to go with you?"

He shrugged. "I couldn't go to vet school here, and I knew I didn't want to be without you."

"You say that like it's no big deal."

"You took the choice away from me." And he'd had to live with it all this time. Without her.

"What I did was give myself a choice about my own life. It was the only way to survive."

"Where did you go?"

She sighed. "I went to the airport. I was just going to fly away in a plane, any plane. I didn't even care if it went down and I perished with it."

Everything in him tensed. The idea she might have killed herself made him want to wrestle the steering wheel and scream as loud as he could. Yet another way he failed the people he cared about.

"My boss now, who was my flying instructor then? He found me and talked some sense into me. Maybe he knew what I was thinking about doing." She shrugged. "He helped me get a tiny apartment and I finished school. Then I went to community college. I worked for him at the airport, and after I graduated, I started flying for the nonprofit he runs."

"You could've called and told me where you were." Didn't she know she could always call him from wherever she was?

"I needed a clean break. You would have convinced me to come back, and I couldn't take the risk you would try and go with me. It would've ruined everything for you."

Brett shifted in his seat. "I don't think my life was as great as you think it was." He also didn't think they were ever going to agree on her leaving. But still, he needed to say something else. "I might not know how bad it was at home. But if you say you wouldn't have survived here, then you were right to get yourself out of that situation. And you're also right. I would've gone with you."

"Will you go with me to the airport?"

"You want to leave again?"

She shook her head. "The airport here. I want to find out what happened. So this stops. If I bring the truth to light, there won't be any more reasons to hurt me or anyone else."

"You're sure?" Even as he asked her, he put the car in drive and pulled out.

"I want to know what was buried."

25

———————

Kamryn shut her car door and stared over at the runway. It was hard to believe she'd been here not too long ago, and she'd faced down so many things since the day she drove back into town, determined to sort out the mess that was her past.

Brett asked, "Where do you want to start?"

"Let's go look at the wreckage." She figured that was as good a place as any to begin. "I didn't get to see everything last time."

"What about the photo album?" He popped the trunk and retrieved something. "Do you want to try and find it?"

"Why would I do that when it's been ruined by Lenny, just like everything else in my life?"

"I just wondered if you wanted any of the pictures of you and your mom." Brett walked beside her between the buildings, holding a flashlight in front of him to light their way.

The idea of having something like that for herself made her chest ache, the way it did when she thought about Maggie dying.

"My mom isn't here," she said. "I can barely remember

what she looked like. Why dredge up what I could no longer have?"

He glanced over at her, but said nothing.

"I'd rather figure out why the plane crashed."

As they neared it, he asked, "Have you seen any crashes before?"

"I've read a lot of investigation reports. I even thought at one point about becoming an investigator for the NTSB. Other than that, it's more of a hobby. Like people who think they can solve crime from their couch."

"I can actually do that, though." He grinned.

His smile was infectious. Then again, it always had been. Brett just had a way with his, lighting everything up. It was probably because he was so intellectual, and had so many serious pursuits, that if he was laughing then it meant whatever it was had to be genuinely funny. Kind of like the way he didn't do anything without a good reason.

She smiled back. "Thank you for coming with me."

He should be at the hospital, not somewhere with zero cell signal, where he wouldn't hear about it if something happened to his mom. "Of course, I came with you. Where do you think my mom would tell me to be right now?"

She didn't answer, because she knew. Maggie would be with someone she cared about if it was doing something that helped them. Especially if that person would be hurting otherwise.

They stopped, and she stared at the wreckage. "Can I borrow that?"

He set the flashlight in her open hand.

She didn't think she could solve a decades-old mystery and figure out what no one else had. But she did figure if there was anything to find, then she was someone who might understand its significance.

At the least, she was looking for the black box. But why wouldn't the investigators have found it? Even in all the chaos and trauma victims, someone should have located the one thing that could tell them what had happened.

Parts of the wreckage didn't even look like anything she'd seen before. The nose of the plane was completely disintegrated. She spotted part of the wing, and a piece of the interior wall with a significant amount of blood on it.

She closed her eyes, looking up at the night sky now the way she'd done that day. Even at four years old, she'd spent enough time at the airport to understand that a plane descending at such a high speed was nothing good.

"There wasn't any smoke coming out of it. It was just falling from the sky." She figured that was why so many people had been screaming. "They were just standing here watching. No one even ran until it got close to the ground. That's why spectators were killed, too."

"I can't even imagine seeing something like that."

She glanced over her shoulder at him. "I was only four. I couldn't testify as to what I saw, but it's still ingrained in my memory. Along with a few other things."

Because it wasn't just the plane crash that had been significant that day. Nor was it the way she'd been knocked around when people started running for their lives.

She walked around the wreckage, not even wanting to think about what happened after. How her brother had found her bleeding from a head wound where she'd hit the corner of the wall when someone bumped into her.

After that, things were a little more blurry. But in the confusion, she remembered one thing for certain.

She had seen her mother.

"She was looking for me earlier. Before the crash."

Did she see her mom then? After? She'd always thought she had.

Now, Kamryn wasn't so sure.

Brett came up behind her, walking a little back from her. Kind of like a bodyguard might. He was definitely here in a protection role, something she was infinitely grateful for. He hadn't left her the way she'd left him. Brett was a far better person than her.

Not that she'd ever been confused about that. Even now when she disagreed with her dad and brother's assessment, concluding she was obviously a bad person just so they'd feel like she was one of them. She still felt like Brett was better than her. It was just that she was no longer convinced there was an evil part of her—at least not more than might be inside everyone.

Who didn't need to give up a bad habit, or be better at something? Everyone did the wrong thing sometimes. But that wrong didn't define them.

"Everything okay?" he asked.

She stared at the wreckage. "I think we should look at Ellie's list of passengers and all the staff on board. Maybe we'll see something. Or if we look into their backgrounds, we'll discover a link."

"It's possible," Brett said. "But I think Tate is already doing that. After whoever that was who tried to kidnap you, Tate switched into high gear. He took everything Ellie had and he's been looking into this ever since we met with them at the diner."

"Are you serious?"

Brett nodded.

"Wow. I thought he'd written me off."

Now it turned out Tate was helping her? It might be at least in part to satisfy his own curiosity, but at the same time he had to know he was giving her what she wanted. If he didn't like her, or want to help her, then he wouldn't be doing so.

"Did either of them say anything about the black box?"

He shook his head. "Is it even really black?"

"No, it isn't." She figured he knew that, but was simply reassuring her by getting her to talk about things she was comfortable with. "It's actually orange. It's a cockpit voice recorder, and a flight data recorder. So whoever is investigating can hear everything from the cockpit. Two microphones for the pilot and copilot. And any alarms if they were going off. The data recorder is literally just graphs and stuff like that. They can see what the pilots were doing, like if they were over steering or anything."

"You do know a lot about this stuff."

She shrugged. "Anything that can make you safer isn't something you should overlook."

"Mmm."

She put her hand on her hip. "Just because I'm willing to risk my own life—"

"And mine."

"—doesn't mean I'd be okay risking anyone else's." She lifted her chin. "You chose to be here. I didn't force you to come."

"Do you think I would be anywhere else?"

She said nothing, too exhausted and wrung out to think of what to say. They'd had far too much deep and personal conversation in the last hour or two. Not to mention all the adrenaline, and fear for his mom.

"Are you praying for your mom?"

"It's what she would want me to do. I might not know exactly how to do more than I always have with faith. Or where it fits between my intellect and my ability to do my job and how I'm supposed to be unable to do anything without Him. But praying is the right thing."

She nodded, glancing over at the buildings.

Why couldn't that white structure have been destroyed? She would feel so much better if the whole thing had simply blown up. Or somehow been obliterated when the plane slammed into the ground at full speed.

Metal everywhere. Heat from the fire. The smell of oil, smoke, and burned flesh. So much destruction, and it was almost as if someone determined it remain untouched forever.

"I have to wonder if Lenny didn't purposely leave that building alone," she mused.

Brett glanced at the white structure, then at her. "What is it about that place?"

She knew he was going to come back at some point and get the album. Or maybe not, considering what she'd said about it. He probably thought he could change her mind the way he had determined already that she should think differently about so many things.

"Quit stalling, or thinking about how to change the subject. Just tell me what the deal is with that building."

Kamryn huffed. "I don't have to tell you anything."

"True." His lips twitched. "But humor me. Because there's some serious avoidance going on here, and it might jog your memory as to something that happened."

Kamryn strode to the front corner. She found a knot in the wall, low by her hip, and wondered if she'd hit her head in that exact spot. "I was bleeding. Probably it was instinct that sent me here when everything went crazy. Everyone was screaming and running, and I knew I had to get out of the way."

She sighed. "This is the office. I used to play in here while my mom was working at her desk. Dad was always out in those days, working on the planes probably. I don't remember because things changed after that, and we never came here." She thought she remembered tiny plastic animals on the floor. Lined up in rows, all going to the circus.

"Lenny found me over here." She stared over at the front door of the building, just a few steps and a tiny porch roof. "He grabbed my arm really hard and dragged me inside." She retraced those steps and opened the front door. It was unlocked.

I saw her.

"Right before he grabbed me, I saw her, searching for me. She called my name, but he pulled me inside instead. He said she was dead and I only saw her ghost."

Brett touched her arm. "Let me go first. Your brother left a lot of booby-traps around here."

Pulled under by the swell of her memories, Kamryn

couldn't do anything but comply. She didn't even want to go inside this place. She wanted to stare instead at the spot she'd last seen her mother—at four years old. She wanted to live there, with her mother searching so frantically for her. Calling her name and looking all over for her. Desperate to find her in the chaos.

"What did he do after he shoved you in here?"

She moved past Brett, hesitant to touch him because she knew if she did that, she would rely on him. She wouldn't be able to stand on her own two feet and face this. She would never know if she had the strength to do it.

In the corner was the cabinet. A wardrobe, really.

"He locked me in there. He'd done it before, and dad was usually the one who got me out. Maybe they never told her. Or maybe she didn't care. Dad was hurt." Kamryn went to the wardrobe, clicked the latch, and opened the doors. It was completely empty except for one thing.

On the floor was a small electronic device, blinking lights on the front. Tiny antenna like a modem.

She'd seen one of these before.

Kamryn pulled the wires from the back and disconnected it.

"What is that?"

She turned, holding in her hands. "It's a signal jammer. It has to be the reason this airport has no cell service."

26

Brett pulled out his phone looked at the screen. It now showed signal, where before there had been nothing. His phone came to life, registering messages and emails. A couple of missed calls, probably spam.

The messages scrolled down his screen. He unlocked the phone and pulled up his texts. The string from Tate continued beeping until it showed six new messages.

What does he want now?

"Tate is messaging me." Brett scrolled down the thread. "I already told you how he's looking through everything Ellie found about the disaster. He said the passenger list includes one missing guy. Investigators assumed the body burned up, or was somehow lost, and that's why they never found it."

"What does that mean?" Kamryn asked.

"Someone was unaccounted for." He lifted his face to hers. "They assumed he died, but no one ever found him. Tate thinks it's suspicious, as it means the guy could still be alive."

"What was his name?"

"William Herald." He waited to see if she recognized the name, but Kamryn only shook her head. "He was a copilot. Or, he was supposed to be. Maybe he never even got on the plane."

"He could've survived the crash and decided he wanted a clean slate with everyone thinking he was dead."

"Like he faked his death?" he said.

"Maybe he planned the whole thing to do exactly that. Or it was a spur of the moment thing when he realized what'd happened meant chaos and yet he was still alive. If we could find the black box, we might be able to answer that question."

He looked down at the phone again. "Tate also found out that the NTSB agent closed the case, and weeks later retired off the grid in Cabo. He's going to video call later with the guy so he can ask him all about the disaster and what happened."

He figured it meant Tate thought the guy had taken a bribe, and that would be his intention for this conversation—finding out what the guy was willing to share. After all this time, he might even tell the truth. If he no longer had a reason to keep the secret.

Brett texted back a thumbs-up, just so Tate would know he'd read everything. Then he added a note about the signal jammer and where they were before he put his phone back in his pocket.

He glanced around the interior of the office in the white building. Sparsely decorated, the whole place was dated. And not just because almost no one had been in here twenty years. Dust covered the eighties décor in a thick layer, only disturbed in a few spots.

"Do you think Lenny was the one who left the signal jammer?" he asked.

"I guess it's possible, but the implications are terrifying. Did he really want anyone who came across the airport to be stranded, unable to call for help?" She shivered. "I think I might have to get someone in here to look for buried bodies."

Not wanting her to have to talk more about her evil brother, he said, "Whoever caused the crash probably paid off the NTSB agent."

"And now they're trying to stop anyone from looking too deeply and finding out the truth?"

He shrugged. "That at least fits. Though, how it relates to your mom's disappearance, I don't know."

"So the copilot fakes his death, and the NTSB agent is paid off. Everyone is so overwhelmed with all the death that they don't look below the surface to find the cause. Other than whatever they're told by the investigators."

He figured if it was him at the time, he'd have stopped at nothing to find out what happened. Maybe someone had—and now they were dead. With people like Lenny in the mix, it was entirely probable no one knew what happened to them. He'd been a child when the plane crash happened, but he could've kept the secret for years.

Someone else was behind even that, though.

A mastermind with a drone who could orchestrate a kidnapping.

Meanwhile her brother had been a skilled killer as an adult. She was probably right to get someone out here to look for bodies. Even just on the off chance they could put someone's memory to rest and give the family closure.

His phone chimed, and he looked at the message.

You're at the airport with her?

Brett ignored that question from Tate and sent a text to Jeff asking how their mom was doing. He hit send just as another message came through.

I hope you know what you're doing.

Brett moved to the desk and sat on the edge, his muscles like heavy weights. Maybe he didn't know what he was doing. He was just sure he wanted to help Kamryn right now. The alternative was sitting at the hospital waiting to hear about his mom. Feeling powerless as he did now, just in a whole different way.

That was when Jeff replied. He told Kamryn, "Mom is in surgery still. Jeff said there's nothing new, and he's not expecting anything for a few hours. He had Toni go home and get some sleep."

Kamryn nodded. He watched her wander the room, probably lost in her memories. She'd hung out in here as a child. She was shoved in the closet he couldn't even look at, knowing she'd been trapped in there. He wanted to ask what she was remembering, but didn't risk her losing a memory before she fully recalled it. The last thing she needed was to be interrupted.

She could need considerable time in here to fully rediscover everything she might've forgotten. Or she might want to leave immediately. He wasn't sure staying would help them figure out what'd happened to her mother, but he wouldn't ask her to go.

It was more like this could help her put the past behind her and move on, something he was anxious to help her with. Not in the sense that he would rush her. He wanted to be there to help work through it, and fully planned on participating in the aftermath. When she realized she could live free of this. That she wasn't trapped here anymore.

Kamryn might be working through it for years to come. If it took that long, he would still be here. Or, if she left town, he would be there, too. Sure, he would miss his mom, and getting to know his brother again. But he could be a vet anywhere, and Brett just wanted to be where Kamryn was.

She crouched to run her fingers along the floor. She tapped what looked like nail heads in the wood planks.

Someone had at one point removed the flooring, exposing the wood underneath. Or maybe it had never been covered with anything.

"One. Two. Three. Four." Kamryn ran her finger along the nail heads. "This is where I lined them up. I can't believe I remember that." She sank to the floor and glanced up at the door. "I can remember someone coming in, and she talked to him." She shook her head. "I remember this room being a whole lot bigger than it is."

"You were a lot smaller then. Stands to reason it would seem bigger." Brett pushed out a long breath. The lingering aches and pains from being wailed on didn't feel super good. Probably he needed a glass of water and some over-the-counter pain meds.

Maybe a couple of ice packs. Things were getting stiff, and if he didn't stretch or something, it would probably feel like he'd been hit by a car by tomorrow.

He got up and started to circle the room. Mostly just for the sake of stretching his legs, but also to look around.

Kamryn was still on the floor, lost in her memories. It was heartbreaking to know she'd suffered so much, especially when he'd barely registered what she might be going through at home. He figured all teenagers were self-absorbed. He'd known things weren't great, but not that it had been so bad she felt like she had to leave to survive.

That didn't stop him from kicking himself over the fact he'd done nothing to help her—except what benefited his own burgeoning feelings.

Brett wandered some more, and found a spot that caught his attention. An anomaly on the wall. Just a slight difference in the drywall that didn't seem to quite fit. Beside a bookcase packed with binders and airplane manuals there was a tiny edge in the plaster. He poked at it with his index finger, but not much happened.

Was Kamryn going to be okay with him pulling the bookcase out and taking a look? He hardly thought it would amount to much of anything, but nothing about this airport seemed right. Or made any sense. Who knew what Lenny had messed with in the twenty years this place had been abandoned and he was left to do whatever his sick mind dreamed up?

She was probably right about there maybe being dead bodies. He wondered if the police department's new canine officer had a dog that could sniff out cadavers along with all the other things he could do. Maybe they only did one thing. Brett didn't know.

He'd started to look into military working dogs when the news came through that his brother Jeff had been killed.

After that, he didn't want much to do with any of that stuff.

"Kamryn." He turned. She was prying at the floorboards

with her fingers. He closed the distance between them and crouched. "Tell me what it is."

"Secrets."

"You need to get down there?"

Her face flushed. She nodded, the expression there so much like the shock from after his mom was shot.

Brett moved to the desk and pulled open drawers, rummaging through stationery until he found a metal ruler with a thin edge. He'd been hoping for a letter opener, but this would do.

"Here." He could've handed it to her, but instead wedged it in the floor between the planks and pried open the one she was trying to see under.

The one with four nails in it, hammered in the middle of the plank so that they were no help at all keeping the plank down. Someone had purposely set them here in a row for some reason.

She thought something was hidden beneath this?

Kamryn put her hand down under the planks and pulled free a drop cloth. It got stuck, and she yanked until the whole thing came out. "We need to get more of these up." She tapped on the next plank with her index finger. "There's something under there."

He pried up the next plank, and the one beside that. When they had a decent-sized hole, he saw what she had. Someone had hidden a storage crate down here.

"Help me get this out."

"After I do that, you should come and see behind the bookcase. There's something there as well."

Things could be tucked away all over this room. He had no idea what she was getting from this hidden spot. But it seemed she might know.

He helped her lift it out. "This is heavier than I thought." Still, it wasn't too heavy to lift. He put it on the table. "What is it?"

She popped the latch on an army green hard-sided case.

When she flipped the lid, he felt his eyebrows rise at the smaller case inside.

"Never mind." Because this was bright orange, disguised in a nondescript box and tucked away under the floorboards in the office. "It's the black box that's actually orange."

She never smiled at his attempt to bring levity.

"Maybe the signal jammer was to hide the black box?"

Kamryn frowned. "Maybe we'll never work out how any of this got here."

"I'm guessing Lenny never discovered this. Though, maybe he looked for it. Or he just didn't care and didn't know." Brett looked around again, half expecting something else crazy to happen. That was par for the course right now. "Can we listen to the cockpit recording?"

She shook her head. "Not without taking it somewhere we can plug it in and play it. I don't even think they'll have what we need at the police department."

"It's possible there's somewhere in town we can get to the bottom of this. There are people who live here with skills like that."

Currently Zander and his team of private security guys were out of town. They had been for weeks now, and no one knew when they were coming back. Not even Dean's brother Ted, who lived at the house and had lots of secret jobs he worked at all hours of the day or night.

"We can get this to the car," he said. "But I want to look behind the bookcase as well. See if there isn't more to discover here."

"Okay, sounds good. I'd like to listen to this as soon as possible." Despite that, she still came with him to the bookcase.

Brett wiggled it away from the wall. "There's obviously some kind of opening back here." He felt around his fingers and managed to pull at the seam.

A square of drywall big enough for a person to get through

opened. He looked inside. "There's a ladder on the wall going down." Other than that, it was dark.

The ladder meant there was some kind of space down there. What had Lenny hidden?

Brett leaned the square of drywall against the back of the bookcase. A wire was taped to it, leading down into the opening.

A click echoed up from below.

Instinct had him move immediately. "Run—"

Before he even got to his feet, everything exploded.

27

Kamryn's mind barely comprehended what was happening. She turned back to the black box even as the white building exploded around them and she started falling.

Brett reached for her. Their arms only collided, he never managed to grasp her and she came up with a handful of air.

Then there was only tumbling.

She hit the ground and landed awkwardly on something. Her body sprawled across the floor. Furniture. She didn't know what it was, just that she had fallen on it.

Pain erupted in her chest. She tried to breathe and fire stabbed through her middle. She could get air just fine, except the fact doing so hurt badly enough she wanted to pass out. But she didn't.

Darkness descended. She wasn't losing consciousness.

Above her, she could see the ceiling. Far too close now.

She blinked. What on earth had happened? There had been an explosion. But she hadn't been blown up, and there was no fire. The floor had fallen, and so had the roof. As though the building crumpled in on itself. Or sank into the foundation with the force of the blast? She had no idea.

"Trapped." She could just about get the word out, her voice

gravelly from the dust in the air. Then she had to take another breath and fire burst again in her chest.

Something was wrong. Her mind managed to catch up enough to have a reasonable thought, and she figured she had a broken rib maybe.

"Brett!" Her voice was quiet, all the noise she could make. She coughed again and moaned at how much it hurt. Where was he?

The wire in the panel. One of those booby-traps they said her brother set all over the place. The two of them hadn't even contemplated that in the moment. And she certainly hadn't when she was pulling up floorboards to find the black box. A black box that was now somewhere in the wreckage of the building.

"Brett!"

He didn't answer. Fear washed over her, as though she'd been doused with ice water. A tear rolled from the corner of her eye. Kamryn tried to shift her legs. Maybe she could roll over and try to get up.

Yet more pain stabbed, this time in her ankle. She hissed out a breath. This wasn't going to go down well with her boss. He'd texted most recently that she had a flight in just a few days. Someone needed to get supplies to a couple of missionaries in Guatemala.

It didn't seem like she'd be able to do that now. Yet another way she was letting him down. He knew that, and that was why his texts were getting more and more stoic. He didn't get mad, he only got so quiet it made her want to run away. She didn't often mess up. But when she did, his silence communicated just how greatly she'd let him down.

Alone in the dark, full of pain. Knowing somehow she was going to have to climb herself out of here, Kamryn let herself give in to the truth.

Tears rolled from her eyes as she finally realized she would never measure up. No matter what she did, it wasn't going to be good enough for God to help her. After all, she hadn't succeeded here. He must have abandoned her, because all her trying wasn't enough for Him.

If she had been sufficient on her own then she would've managed to find out the truth already. Not only had she been holding the black box, but she'd dropped it when she fell. Now it was lost in the debris. She wasn't going to be able to find out the truth. They'd triggered a trap, and Brett was probably lying dead where she couldn't see him.

He could bleed out. She wouldn't even know, let alone be able to help him. Or try to, at least. Knowing her track record if she did find him, she would either do more harm than good, or he would simply bleed out and she'd know it was her fault.

It was all her fault.

That was what the man had said.

"You're the one I did this for."

Katherine huddled in the closet. Lenny had told her not to move. If she came out, he would slap her again.

She didn't like it when he slapped her.

"You killed all those people!"

Mama. Her mama was out there. Katherine needed to go to her. She started to uncurl from her tight ball and push on the doors Lenny had locked.

"I did it for you! So we could be together!"

"You want to raise my daughter with me knowing you're a murderer." *Mama gasped. "They're all dead. Because of—"*

She heard a choking sound. One Katherine had heard before. She knew he was hurting her mama. And there was nothing she could do about it, locked in the closet.

Was it Daddy? Who was hurting her?

Katherine wanted to stop him, but she couldn't get out of the closet. She couldn't help Mama. Not until Lenny let her out.

There was only silence, and then a thud. Katherine bit her lip. The whimper escaped anyway. She didn't know how to hold it back.

All she knew was that something terrible had happened.

"Kamryn."

"Brett?" She could barely speak. "Brett, where are you?"

Maybe he was dead, and her mind just didn't want to let go of him. After all, her legacy was nothing but failure. And it always ended in death. Maybe it was for the better that her boss was displeased with her. Otherwise, he would only end up dying, too.

How could You leave me to be not good enough?

Maybe it wasn't fair to ask God that question. But if He couldn't handle her unfair question, then maybe He wasn't big enough she should put her trust in Him. Which meant He absolutely could handle it, especially when she had nothing left.

Because He was big enough. He simply chose not to help her.

And Kamryn had no idea why.

Now she'd failed everything and everyone. Her mom was dead. The plane crash had been buried. She hadn't been able to figure out who it was that did either. Now she knew it was the same person, she knew how thoroughly she had failed.

"I can hear you crying. My leg is stuck under a girder. You need to come to me." She saw a flash of light and realized it was the beam of a cell phone flashlight.

His phone.

"Brett."

"Yes, Kamryn. You need to help me."

How could she do that when she never managed to succeed? It didn't matter that she might be able to get to him. If his leg was pinned, she would never be able to get the beam off.

"You need to come here."

The second she attempted to sit up so much pain sliced through her that she cried out.

"I'm sorry, I'm sorry. I didn't know you were hurt." He gasped. "I'll use my phone to call for help."

She heard him dialing. The light flickered across the ceiling of the white building, the roof far too close now. As though it had simply dropped on top of them, sending them down into the basement. Kamryn didn't want to look around too much. Not when she had no interest in whatever Lenny had left here.

As Brett told whoever he called what'd happened, and that they needed help, she figured out how to roll over. Kamryn bit her lip the whole time to keep from crying audibly. He didn't need to know how much pain she was in when he was in pain himself. And she could maybe get them out of here if she could make it to him without passing out. He wouldn't get free unless someone helped him with the beam.

"Yes." He took a breath, audible more like a gasp. "Okay."

She focused on the sound of his voice. Moving over debris, she slithered and tried not to touch her front to anything. Even while she had to fight the fact bracing herself on her hands hurt probably just as much as doing that would.

Eventually she made her way to him, like a homing beacon, then collapsed on his arm and shoulder. "Sorry. You're probably hurt."

"It's okay. We both need help." His breath brushed lightly on her face.

She heard the other end of the phone call. A woman.

"Help is on the way. They'll be there as soon as possible."

"But it might be twenty minutes," Brett said between breaths. "We're pretty far out, and there's no one to fly the helicopter, right?"

"I wasn't going to tell you that. You need to hang on, regardless. They'll be there as soon as they can to help you." The woman barely waited a breath before she said, "Are either of you bleeding?"

Brett looked at her. "Kam?"

"Broken ribs, I'm pretty sure."

"That's bad," he said. "You could puncture a lung, so you need to stay still and we need to pray this doesn't get worse."

"I'm praying too," the dispatcher said. "That's why I took

this job. Because the chief said it was fine for me to pray all I wanted."

"Good. We need it." She managed to smile, but only a tiny bit. Her eyes were puffy from crying. Her whole body felt like she'd been hit by a semi and tossed in the air only to land on construction debris.

Brett said, "I'm pinned, but I don't think I have any injuries that can't wait until help gets here."

"Is that supposed to be a good thing?" Kamryn couldn't see anything good about the situation. They were both injured. Help wasn't here yet, so they had to wait for it. How could anyone be looking on the bright side right now?

The dispatcher said, "I, for one, will take grace wherever I can find it. You're both conscious and you were able to call for help when no one ever has cell signal over there. Now help is on its way, and you know they're running full speed to get to you. You don't think that's grace?"

Kamryn didn't have the energy to get into a theological debate. "I think if I try to get this beam off Brett's leg, I'm liable to do what he said. Puncture a lung."

He thought her injury could get worse. If that was true and she tried to help, then it absolutely would. Because that was what happened in her life.

Case in point, trying to solve her mom's murder. Now she knew the reason why her mom was dead. Because Kamryn hadn't been able to stop it.

If she'd been able to get out of the closet, he wouldn't have killed her mom.

"What is it?" Brett asked.

She shook her head in answer to his question. He didn't need to know exactly how bad things were. He liked her, and maybe even thought she was a good person. How was she supposed to admit to him that she was terrible? That she'd been quiet in the closet instead of doing something to save her mom.

Brett shone the flashlight around.

She looked at their surroundings as he illuminated it, trying to pretend she was anywhere but here. Although, having her head on Brett's shoulder felt pretty nice.

"I feel like we just fell through the floor," he said.

"Lenny's booby-traps?" She might've asked it as a question, but it really wasn't one. They both knew her brother was responsible for this. That core of evil had to be in her, too. There was no other explanation for the fact everything in her life always went wrong.

No matter how much she tried to use the skills God had given her, it just wasn't enough to do the right thing. It wasn't enough to make Him proud of her.

She continued, "I think he wired up the supports. When we tripped it, instead of destroying the whole place he made it so we're trapped down here." She didn't even want to think about it.

He said, "What is that?"

She heard sirens in the distance. "I guess they're here."

"No." She heard more than saw him shift the phone in the dark. The flashlight on the back of his cell phone lit the corner of the room. "I think that's the original basement over there." A section of the wall had fallen out. Maybe a door. What had been behind it was now exposed. "I meant, what is *that?*"

The head of the skeleton leaned out of the break in the wall. A necklace. Strips of material, almost disintegrated with age. That same pink shirt that had been Katherine's favorite.

"Mama."

28

A skeleton behind a wall. Buried in the basement. He could hardly believe it, but this wasn't about him. Brett managed to hold himself together until help arrived and someone yelled above them, "Let's get floodlights in here!"

Kamryn flinched.

He tugged on her hand, then her forearm, until she looked at him. "Stay with me, okay?"

His leg didn't feel too good pinned under a beam. He was stuck, but it didn't seem as bad as it could be. His leg didn't feel crushed. He could move his toes. It was just having the life squeezed out of it. Not exactly a super positive trade-off, but he needed to focus on Kamryn right now.

After all, they'd found her mother.

He'd heard her exclaim as much when he'd shone his light on the skeleton. Since then, he'd moved the beam away. Opting for darkness seemed like a better idea rather than face the nightmares from her past. Still, she'd looked that direction nonstop since—and didn't seem inclined to quit. Or respond to him.

But now, they were going to have to face everyone else. "Okay?"

Thankfully, she nodded. The distant look in her eyes didn't sit well with him.

"Once we get up and out of here, we can let the police take care of her."

He wanted to tell her that her mother would be treated with respect. But after being concealed down here for years, that could be too little too late as far as she was concerned. He wouldn't know what she was feeling about this unless she told him—and part of him figured she had no idea. Yet. This seemed like more of that shock she'd been in after his mother was shot.

"Hello!" someone called to them. "Brett! Kamryn! Can you hear us?"

"We're down here," he yelled back.

She flinched again.

"We'll be down there in a minute." It was Tate. "All good?"

That's a dumb question. Brett shook his head to dismiss the swirl of pointless and ridiculous thoughts. They weren't going to be any help. He squeezed Kamryn's hand and yelled back, "I don't think we're bleeding."

"If you aren't, it's a miracle," Tate replied.

Brett yelled back, "Amen to that."

Someone else called out, "Maybe we could quit yelling at each other and just get on with this." That was Basuto.

"It won't be long now," Brett told Kamryn. "We'll get out of here, and they can transport your mom. Pretty soon you'll be able to lay her to rest." He touched Kamryn's shoulder, wondering if he would be able to help her through something like this.

Maybe all those soldiers and spec ops guys in town knew what to do with a dead body. The pain of losing someone. His brother, the person he'd lost, was never really dead. And then there was his sister, who had her own problems and had been gone years before she actually died.

Brett had suffered loss. So maybe he did know how to walk

her through this. Or at least help somehow. It seemed like maybe God had prepared him for this.

Thank You, Lord.

"Now that you've found her," he said, "all you have to do is put her to rest."

He'd done the same with Annabelle.

She turned to him. In the dim light with his flashlight extinguished, he couldn't make out the expression on her face. "I was there. In the closet. When he killed her."

Everything in him shifted, like standing on ground he thought was solid and suddenly feeling an earthquake. "Kam—"

"He said he killed all those people for her. So they could be together."

"Kam—"

She shook her head. "Don't do that. Not right now, when I just remembered that I only sat there and did nothing."

"You were a child. What could you have done?"

"I could have died with her. The same way I was supposed to live…with her."

He opened his mouth to say—he wasn't quite sure what—when a light came on. The entire structure was illuminated in a yellow glow from one floodlight on the side at ground level.

Kamryn looked away from him. He couldn't say anything, not right now when it wouldn't penetrate because she was too absorbed in her shock. Later, when she had time to process everything that'd happened, he could sit her down and walk her through it. Or his mom could.

When she was better.

A therapist could surely help Kamryn understand that a four-year-old had little power, even when everything in them was desperate to do something. She'd been through serious trauma, hearing her mother get killed. He couldn't even imagine what that was like.

Once again, he felt woefully unqualified for this.

Help me, Lord. I need You to guide what I should say.

It turned out God was there at the end of everything Brett could do. Everything he knew through learning and study and years of experience. At times he would find the end of his capabilities, and now he knew there was God. With him. Doing what Brett couldn't do on his own. Bringing peace and wisdom.

Bring her that peace, God. She needs You so badly.

"Coming down."

Another floodlight came on as Tate descended on a rope. "It'll be tricky getting to you, but I should be able to do it. You guys doing okay?"

Brett said, "Thanks for coming."

"It's good you found that signal jammer and managed to turn it off. Otherwise, we would never have known you were in trouble."

Brett figured when none of Tate's texts were responded to, he probably would have started wondering where Brett was. Especially when he didn't find him at the hospital in the waiting room.

Mom.

His heart wrenched.

Soon enough, he would be there. In time to check out how things were going for her. According to his phone there hadn't been any change. If there was, then Jeff would have told him.

Right now, he needed to take care of things here with Kamryn.

Brett watched as Tate made his way over debris. He had to pause a couple of times while things shifted under him.

Kamryn didn't take her eyes off her mother. The skeleton was now illuminated in the glow of light. It made everything in here far too bright after the darkness of moments ago. Probably it would've been better to leave the lights off, but he could see why they thought they needed them. The whole building was a mess.

"It was one of Lenny's booby-traps." Brett didn't like admitting his mistake. "I was an idiot and pulled on a wire."

Tate looked around. "Seems like he hooked the support beams and blew the floor from where it was connected to the frame. Small charges, not enough to take down the whole thing and kill anyone inside. The whole first floor and the roof just descended into the basement."

Exactly what Brett had figured. "But if it hadn't happened, we wouldn't have found her." He pointed to where Kamryn's mom had been concealed all this time. "So maybe my failure wasn't as big of a screwup as I thought it was while we were falling through the floor."

Tate glanced back at the opening where the roof came to a point. Basuto was crouched at the edge. "You see that?"

"Yes, I'll send in Savannah just as soon as we get these two out. Assuming she's good to climb down there."

Tate reached Brett's other side, across from Kamryn. "My wife is the best detective in this town. Don't tell the other detectives I said that, but they already know I'm biased." He gave a small smile, but it didn't last long. "Kamryn, would you like us to find out what happened to your mom and take care of her?"

She tore her gaze from her mother to glance at him as she nodded.

Tate returned her nod. "We will be as respectful as possible."

When she said nothing, Brett said, "Thank you."

Tate looked down at the beam. "Don't thank me until after I get you out of here in one piece."

"You should take Kamryn first. Get her to ground level." Mostly he just didn't like her being down here with her mom's remains for this long.

She shook her head. "We should get that beam off you."

"You aren't lifting anything heavy. You told me you have cracked ribs."

"I don't know if they're cracked. Maybe I just hit them really hard."

Tate grasped the beam with both hands. "Let's see if I can get this, and then we'll know if I need your help. Okay?"

Tate got the beam off his foot. Kamryn helped him wiggle out from under it so Tate could put it back down.

Brett gritted his teeth. "Thanks."

"Let's get out of here."

Brett was down with that, and even with Tate helping him walk, his ankle did not feel good.

"What about the black box?" Kamryn asked.

Tate whipped his head up to look at her, nearly dropping Brett. "You found the black box?"

Kamryn nodded.

"In the floorboards." Brett still hadn't figured out who must've put it there. Especially not now that she'd told him the killer murdered her mother *after* crashing the plane. Why hide the black box after that? It made more sense he'd have taken it with him so no one ever found it rather than hide it in the same building where the body was buried.

Tate said, "Good job, Kamryn."

She shifted under his approval. Brett held her hand, and they started to make their way to the rope.

Thankfully, Basuto was currently lowering a ladder. He didn't think either he or Kamryn could climb up a rope. Not when he hadn't been able to do in PE, either. And back then, he hadn't been nearly as bruised as he was right now.

Basuto frowned. "Is the leg okay?"

"It will be when I can sit down." Brett shifted to allow Kamryn to go first up the ladder. "Ready?"

She didn't move.

Tate said, "I promise we'll take care of your mom. And we'll look around for the black box." After a beat of quiet, he continued, "You realize that with this one thing, you discovered what no one has been able to for years? Things that were covered up. Tragedy that should never have happened. And now, because of you, people will know the truth."

Brett watched her, worried that she wouldn't be able to handle this on top of everything else. "Once we get to safety, we'll be able to work it all out."

He couldn't help thinking about what she'd said. How she should have died with her mom. Essentially, that was what she'd meant. Had it been a spur of the moment reaction, caused by the shock? A deep longing for the life with her mother that she should've had?

What he did know was that it was something he would never be able to give her. No matter how hard he tried, he just couldn't fill that void.

Yet more areas where he would be lacking. But God would supply his need.

They made their way up to the surface, out into the evening air. The stars were like a blanket overhead there were so many.

Yet more things to be thankful for, even in the midst of what was tragic.

He didn't know how to fix this for Kamryn. All he knew was how to stick with her. Probably until she was sick of his support and wishing he would leave her alone. Then he would have his mother step in. Assuming Kamryn even stuck around in town.

Maybe she'd want to be anywhere but here once she'd taken care of her mother.

Tate walked him to the open door of his car and helped him sit. "The ambulance will be here in a minute. It wasn't far behind us."

"I can wait." Brett felt like a bull had used him for a punching bag, but that was likely nowhere near as bad as how Kamryn felt right now after having seen that.

Basuto stood with her. He was grateful for his friends, and also selfish enough to wish she would lean on him.

Especially now they had a shot at figuring this out.

29

———————

"We'll get to the bottom of this. You don't need to worry."

Kamryn barely knew how to respond to Lieutenant Basuto.

He clearly believed what he was saying. "It doesn't matter how much time has passed. We'll figure out who killed your mother."

He sounded earnest. He said all the right things, and some was the same things Tate and Brett had tried to tell her. But none of it made her feel better.

The reality was that her mother had been murdered.

She'd heard it happen and still couldn't believe it.

"Do you need to sit down?" he asked.

She shook her head.

"The ambulance will be here soon. You can get checked out at the hospital, and I'll come and see you when I have anything. In the meantime, you don't need to worry."

Kamryn stared at him for a second. The town of Last Chance these days was so much different than she remembered.

Everyone here seemed to be so nice. Or maybe the fact she'd grown up with her father and brother for her family clouded her view of everything and everyone. Plenty of people had painted her with the same brush as them, assuming she was horrible for whatever reason. They'd taken out their pain, or their dissatisfaction with their lives, on her.

Regardless, those people seemed few and far between now. Or she'd been gone long enough there was a new crop of people who made up this town—ones who weren't going to judge her based on who her family was.

Although now, she had no family left. Kamryn turned and looked at Brett. He didn't appear to be doing very well. With the bruises and the way he favored his ankle, even sitting down, she didn't think he was going to be super mobile anytime soon. And his mom was in the hospital, undergoing surgery.

It seemed like everything had turned into a disaster so quickly, when all she'd wanted when she returned to town was a shot at finding out what happened to her mother. And to figure out why the airplane disaster had been blamed on her family.

Brett lifted a hand and waved gingerly. She raised her fingers, but it was a halfhearted attempt at reassuring him. Still, he didn't need to worry about her.

She turned to the lieutenant. "The ambulance should take Brett. I'd like to stay here and wait while my mother is taken from that basement."

"You're entitled to accompany her to the county morgue. It's actually in the basement of the hospital. Once you're assured that she is secure, maybe you could go upstairs from there and get checked out?"

"Okay."

That was as much she was prepared to agree to. She felt listless, like a boat with no rudder. How was she supposed to figure out what to do next?

All this time her dad and brother had been right. Her mom was dead, and only Kamryn had known the truth all along.

Her dad had been injured in the plane crash. He couldn't have buried her mother, or hidden the black box. At the least she figured Lenny had maybe hidden the black box himself.

Even at seven, he'd known how high the stakes were. He'd spent nearly all his time at the airport.

It was possible the murderer had concealed her mom in the basement wall. Maybe in some kind of closet.

She shuddered at the thought her mother had been trapped like that for so many years. Kamryn knew what it was like to be shut up in a small space. But of course, her mom had been absent from the body. She was long gone now. Kamryn was the only one left.

Just her, and whoever murdered her mother.

She'd never seen their face. How could she figure out who it was? That person was still around today. They had to be, because they'd come after her to prevent her from finding out the truth.

She needed a way to flush them out.

"I'm not sure I like the look on your face." Basuto stared. "When my girlfriend gets that look, I know I'm not gonna like what she's planning."

"I don't know what you're talking about."

"She's at the spa this weekend with her best friend, the sergeant's wife, and their daughter. Girls' weekend. At least I only had to spend money this time. The last idea she had, I wound up paragliding in the Caribbean with two teenage boys."

"That doesn't sound so bad."

"I'm afraid of heights."

Oh.

"If I hadn't loved her since I was in middle school, I would probably object."

Kamryn glanced over at Brett. It seemed like she might know what that felt like. After all, there was a reason she'd never loved anyone since him.

Still, she couldn't allow the cops and their investigation to stop her from looking into who'd killed her mother. All along they'd been saying she knew things they didn't, and she'd proven that by finding the black box.

Her history had turned out to be the solution to everything.

This might not be over, at least not until they identified who the murderer was, but she believed now that she could see it through. Maybe she was the only one who could end this.

"Wanna talk about it?" Basuto studied her in that way cops had that made you want to tell them everything.

She glanced around for a way to change the subject.

Just then, an ambulance crested the hill and headed down the road toward the airport. "Looks like the EMTs are here." From the look on his face, he wasn't convinced about her tactic of stating the obvious.

As she watched it make its way to them, she could almost imagine lines of cars in both directions. Coming into the airshow. People everywhere, and the noise of a crowd. In its heyday, this place must've been a sight to behold.

Now it was nothing but a graveyard. And it was possible they didn't even know the extent of how much that was true.

Kamryn owned this whole place now. She had no idea what to do with it, and no money for that anyway. Unless she sold the entire property to a developer, there wasn't much else for her to use it for.

She walked with Basuto back over to where Brett sat in the front seat of Tate's car, his feet on the ground.

"Are you doing okay?" he asked.

She shrugged. "I'll be better when my mom is out of there."

They'd mentioned treating her with respect, and getting to lay her to rest. Kamryn appreciated both of those things. She wanted to see this through to its finish personally and not leave that to people who'd never known her mom.

"I'm sure the cops will let you know when that happens."

"They won't need to," she said. "Because I'll be right here. I'm not leaving her."

Brett frowned. "You'll need the doctor to wrap those ribs. You probably need an X-ray first to assess the damage."

"All of that can happen later. When I'm done here." Sure, it hurt to breathe, but she could sit and watch.

"Or you could do that first," Tate said. "Police investigations take time. You could be back here before they escort your mom out."

As though it was all about seeing a body bag get pushed into the back of a van. She lifted her chin. "I'm not going to the hospital right now. The ambulance can take Brett, and I'll go there later. He needs to check on his mom."

Brett shook his head. "Jeff will text me if there are any changes, or if she gets out of surgery. I'll stay with you here."

"No, you won't." Lieutenant Basuto decided to wade into the argument as well. "I'd rather both of you went and saw the doctor first. You were in the house that blew up. Taking chances with any potential injury you don't know about could be dangerous." He turned to Kamryn then. "We really will treat your mom with the utmost respect. You don't have anything to worry about with that."

"We'll also find the black box." Tate glanced between them. "So there's no reason either of you needs to stay."

Kamryn said, "I'm not going anywhere right now."

"Then I'm not either," Brett countered.

The EMTs strode over before she could argue with Brett and his ridiculous assertion.

He glared at her from his seat. "She has broken ribs, a previous throat injury you can see for yourself, and stitches in her arm."

"He can't put weight on his ankle without assistance, and is currently suffering from stubbornness." Kamryn folded her arms. "It's probably contagious."

The movement put pressure on her ribs, sucking the breath from her lungs on a gasp. She bit her lip to keep from allowing any noise to escape. They weren't going to make her go anywhere.

"Neither of you looks good." The EMT crouched to assess

Brett's ankle. "I vote you both go in and get that stubbornness looked at. It seems to be an epidemic in this town."

Basuto grinned. Tate outright chuckled.

"I don't think any of this is funny," Brett said.

From where Kamryn was standing, she actually agreed with him. "Me, either."

They immediately sobered, muttering apologies to her. In a way, she felt lighter than she had in years. The search was over. Her mother had been found, and she would get to bury her finally. Perhaps spread her ashes somewhere her mom had always wanted to go, but dad never took her.

The EMT shifted his hold on Brett's ankle. He gritted his teeth. "I'm not going to the hospital unless Kamryn goes as well. If she's staying here to wait for her mom, then I'm going to do the same."

"You're picking now to suddenly decide you can't leave my side?"

"It's my insurance policy. You can't leave without me knowing it if I'm standing next to you the whole time."

"Will you really be standing?" she said. "With that ankle?"

The EMT moved in front of her. They had a moment of silence where she wondered what exactly he expected of her.

"I'm not lifting my shirt in front of a bunch of people, so you can forget about that."

"Did I ask?"

She sighed. "I'm having a really bad week."

"I'm sorry to hear about that." His eyes scanned her face. "Does it have something to do with that destroyed building?"

"It kind of fell on top of us."

The EMT glanced at Brett, then back to her. "And neither of you wants to immediately rush to the hospital to make sure you don't have any internal injuries?"

Brett said, "I'm sure I don't."

"Me, either." Instead of being at odds, they were now united. The back-and-forth was starting to feel like whiplash. "I could use an ice pack, but I need to see a doctor later instead of now. Brett should go, though."

He started to argue but stopped when an engine rumbled in the distance.

They all turned, and Basuto took a step. "Is that a plane coming in?"

"Where is it? I can't see anything." Tate twisted one way, and then the other. "Do any of you see it?"

Kamryn tried to figure out why the sound was so distinctive. And why it sent a shiver of fear up her spine. "It can't land anywhere. There's no working runway."

"It's probably not trying to land." The EMT shrugged. "This used to be an airport. I bet people fly over all the time to look at it."

"At night?" Brett voiced the question she was thinking. "And I don't think it has its lights on."

She could hear it closer now, but couldn't see it. "That would be illegal." Still, it made the most sense.

"Up there." The EMT pointed. "Great, now we all saw the airplane. Let's go to the hospital and get everyone checked out. Sightseeing is over."

She didn't agree. And not just because something was off about this. She tried to make out what kind of plane it was. "Maybe a light bomber. The kind they used in the early twentieth century."

Those were equipped with both machine guns and missiles. She doubted it had any of either left, considering how many years it had been since World War II or any other conflict where these types of aircraft were used.

The nose of the plane dipped, and it headed straight for them, down the runway.

"It's making a run over our heads." Tate sounded almost excited. "But nothing about this seems right."

After the drone, Kamryn was inclined to agree. "There's a plane like that at the airport where I fly."

Basuto said, "Are there any ordinances—"

The plane dropped a missile. A whistle rang through the air, hit the ground, and the far end of the runway exploded in a ball of fire.

The plane picked up speed, still headed toward them.

As it approached their position, the pilot began to fire the machine gun.

30

"Get in!" Brett glanced at the plane, then back at her. She seemed to be frozen. "Kamryn! Let's go!"

She flinched and ran the few steps back to him.

Machine gun fire cut twin lines down the runway, headed right for them.

Tate got in the driver's side. She pulled open the back door just as he turned on the engine. The EMTs ran back for their ambulance. Basuto took cover. Brett spotted his head pop up, and the police lieutenant yelled, "Go, Tate!"

Kamryn whimpered from the back seat. Tate threw the car in drive and hit the gas. It jolted Brett back in his seat and his door clicked shut.

He shifted his legs and sharp pain rolled through his ankle. He hissed out a breath.

"You good?" Tate asked.

He glanced over. "My ankle won't matter if that plane shoots up this car."

Tate asked, "Kamryn?"

"I would say, 'Just go,' but you already are."

Tate's SUV bumped over something on the road. He gripped the wheel hard and turned away from the exit. The runway was covered in debris. There were so many destroyed buildings and alleys too tight for them to go down.

How would they get out of here?

Tate headed for the closest building, driving flat out at full speed.

Brett reached for the door handle to hold on if Tate slammed them into the side of the building. Instead at the last second Tate yanked hard on the wheel and the car turned.

The backend fishtailed. Brett was pretty sure at least two wheels left the ground. He was surprised they didn't roll into the front of the building rather than hit it. Not that doing that would be better.

Tate hit the gas again and headed for the exit road.

Brett shifted to look out the side mirror and found the airplane still firing at the ground. He prayed they wouldn't drop another bomb. How many did they have? With the number of bullets they seemed content to shoot at the ground, he wasn't sure they would run out anytime soon.

Whoever this was, they were determined to do maximum damage. Because they knew about the black box, and the body? Or was it simply another attempt to silence the truth? Brett didn't know which, and it was the unknown that always caused the most anxiety.

Like not having heard yet that his mom was out of surgery.

A car crested the hill, headed toward them. Then another after it. Three and four had flashing blue and red lights. The cavalry had arrived, and they were rolling right into the line of fire.

Tate gestured. "We can't go that way."

Brett peered out the window. "The second those bullets hit us, they'll be in the line of fire too."

The bomber accelerated rapidly, spraying machine gun bullets in two lines down the debris from the disaster still on the runway. Within seconds it was going to catch up to them. There would be nothing they could do about it.

"We need to draw the plane away from here." Kamryn's voice was shaky, but she sounded resolute in her decision. "Make sure we're the targets and not everyone else."

"Agreed." Tate pulled hard on the steering wheel and navigated between two buildings. "I'm going to head for the foothills. There's some cover in the trees."

Brett glanced at him. "Do you think he'll lose interest and pull off?"

"He didn't with the drone," Kamryn said. "He kept looking for us until we turned the tables on him and Savannah shot that thing down."

Tate shook his head. "There's no way to do that here. We're outgunned. All we can do is minimize the damage."

"Do what you need to do." Brett knew Tate had been an FBI agent at one point in his life. After that and up until now he'd been working locally as a private investigator. Aside from Jeff, there was no one in town he would rather have with him.

The plane banked right and followed them between the buildings. Tate found a road that ran parallel to the runway. He drove a quarter-mile and then cut left quickly, the way he had before. The rapid turns seemed to keep the pilot guessing, which made Brett wonder how much visibility he had up there.

That could work in their favor.

Rapid-fire bullets tore up the roof of the building. Something exploded, but he didn't think anything fell from the underside of the plane. Not the way the missile had that was dropped on the far end of the runway.

That had been this guy's idea of an introduction to what was going to happen now. Whoever flew that plane was bringing full force against them, determined to do harm.

Tate busted through the fence at top speed, sending the wrought iron flying. The car bumped and jostled. He heard Kamryn grunt but couldn't ask if she was okay while the pain from his injured ankle made him want to throw up. If he opened his mouth, he was going to make a mess all over the floor between his shoes.

As they reached the foothills, the trees washed above them, and Tate cut the lights.

Brett winced. How was he going to navigate without hitting the trunk?

His friend braked sharply, shut off the engine, and killed the lights. The engine clicked as it cooled.

Brett rolled down his window to hear the sound of the plane. Still coming for them. "I almost want to keep my voice to a whisper, as if he would hear me."

Tate said, "I almost want to tell you to do it."

The sound of the airplane engine grew louder.

Kamryn said, "He's nearly above us." They stayed where they were, hidden as the airplane flew overhead. The noise changed. "It turned around."

Brett figured Kamryn knew what she was talking about. "Do you think he'll come back and check again? Look around for us?"

The pilot could shoot up the trees. Or even drop another missile right where they sat, perfectly stationary. Like sitting ducks.

He'd never imagined he might die in a fireball after a World War II plane dropped a bomb on top of his head. Brett honestly couldn't ever say he'd thought of that.

Take care of mom. And Jeff and Toni.

He glanced at Tate.

Watch over Savannah and the kids. And all the other people in Last Chance County.

He'd spent his whole life in this town. Tears filled his eyes as he thought about this being his final few breaths. He glanced out the window and blinked to try and get the moisture to dissipate. If this was the end, then he would be strong.

Brett twisted and held out his hand. "Kamryn?"

She didn't turn from looking out the back window. "I'm okay, I think he turned."

She was quiet for a beat, and he dropped his hand.

"He's making another pass over us," she said. "I think we managed to hide where he can't see us."

The plane circled again, and then the noise of the engine retreated.

"He's headed back to the runway." Kamryn gave him a small relieved smile.

He tried to return it, but wasn't sure he succeeded. Or if she could even see him.

Kamryn shifted, clearly in discomfort. "What are we supposed to do now?"

"I'm not sure." Jeff would know what to tell her. Maybe he should call his brother. But admitting he was out of his depth and needed help wasn't good at the best of times, when his pride was thoroughly intact. Right now, when his mother was in surgery and Jeff was the diligent son in the waiting room, it would be far worse than that.

Tate twisted in his seat to look at Kamryn. "Any idea who is flying that plane?"

She said nothing, and he imagined she bit her lip. He couldn't see it in the dark of the car's interior.

Brett said, "Kamryn, any ideas?"

"Tate, do you have a picture of the man from the plane's manifest, the one whose body they never found?" When she spoke, her voice was soft. So quiet he barely heard it.

Tate grabbed his phone from the floor where it had fallen during their mad dash. "William Herald?"

"Was that his name?"

Tate nodded. "It's a pretty old photo." He turned his phone screen toward her.

Brett didn't like where this was heading. She wanted to see a picture of a man who should be dead. So she could identify him? That meant she thought she knew the guy. The person trying to kill her.

"Kamryn?" Tate didn't say anything except that.

"His name is Fitzwilliam Collins. He's my boss at the airport."

"Are you sure?"

Tate glanced at him, but Brett continued because they all needed to know, "Could it be a relative, or someone who just looks like him? It has been twenty years."

"It's him." She didn't sound perturbed that he'd asked clarifying questions. "He's in his mid-fifties. I know he has a drone because he talks about it all the time, but I've never seen it. And he has access to a plane exactly like the one shooting at us."

"If it was decommissioned," Tate said, "why does it still have ordinance on board?"

No one had an answer.

The machine gun fire started up again. They all flinched, but it was farther away than the last time. Had the plane returned to the airport to take more potshots at the people on the ground?

Tate pushed his door open. "I'm going to call Basuto, and then Conroy. Check in, and let Conroy know what's happening." He shut the door and walked away a few steps, his face visible in the light of his phone screen.

"I'm sure it won't be long." Brett tried to sound reassuring. "We'll be safe, and out of here."

"How did he know we found everything?" Kamryn asked.

He didn't want to say it, but thought it was possible that turning off the signal jammer at the airport had set this all in motion. Perhaps that was how the pilot—her boss, or someone else—had found out they discovered his secret. Then again, it could simply be that he knew they were here and wanted to stop them whether they knew the truth or not.

She continued, "If it really is Fitz, that means he's been lying to me for years. Since I went to him and he offered me a job. He probably knew all that time exactly who I was. He kept me close to him so he would know if I was looking into the past, trying to find out what happened."

"You can trust the cops here in town to find and arrest him if he is the one behind this," Brett said. "You can trust me." Whatever was between them seemed tenuous. As though at any time it could evaporate and they would be left with nothing.

"I've been lied to my whole life. I don't think I can trust anyone."

"I meant what I said. You can trust me." He felt the need to repeat it.

"I barely know you."

His chest squeezed. "You've always been able to trust me, and I hope that deep down a part of you knows it. Because I think at least part of the reason you left was to save me from them."

She fell silent. Then he heard, "Half of the awful things in your life that have happened to you were because of me."

Brett twisted to look at her. It was so dark, but he needed to at least try and see. "Make it up to me. Stay here in Last Chance."

She probably felt like this was her last chance. As though she may only get one more opportunity, and then there was no hope left.

Staying might make her think she needed to spend the rest of her life proving she was good enough for him. But if she agreed? If she chose him? Brett would spend his life showing her that he already knew it was true—they were made for each other.

Not only that, but she was the best he could ever have in his life. Better than anyone else he'd ever met.

"Stay with me, Kamryn."

She pushed the door open and got out.

Brett watched her take a few unsteady footsteps. He saw in the moonlight that she was breathing hard as she lifted her hands and ran them through her hair, elbows out. Clearly in pain. Distraught even.

The drone of that plane engine threatened to drive him crazy.

He'd pushed her too hard, too soon. Now she was freaking out, and because of his ankle, he couldn't even get out of the car and go to her.

There was nothing he could do. She needed to make the choice and come to him.

Choose him.

He opened the door and set his good foot on the ground. Just in case.

What he'd thought was the airplane overhead came into view—but it was on the ground. An ATV emerged from between two trees.

Brett yelled, "Hey!"

Tate yelled as well.

The driver swerved and grabbed Kamryn. She screamed, but it was already too late. The ATV driver raced off between the trees with her in his grasp.

She was gone.

31

———————

Kamryn couldn't breathe. The ATV rumbled under her hip, the man's arm around her waist. High enough his tight grip pressed against her ribs so that she cried out. If she screamed loud enough, maybe Tate would be able to run and catch up. Right? Or at least he might be able to tell where they were going.

"Shut up." The driver jostled her in his grasp, and she cried out again. "I don't care what he says," he yelled over the noise of the engine. "I'll just kill you and drop you right here."

She tried to get a breath past the excruciating pain. The air in her lungs emerged on a whimper. She didn't want to die. Not without even the slightest chance of rescue. She shut those thoughts down before her mind spiraled into how impossible that would be.

The man holding her turned the ATV and headed up the mountain. He skirted it and then climbed some more. Up, and up. The air grew colder and she saw patches of snow on the ground even though it was practically summer.

"Where are we going?" She could kick her legs and try to get him to let her go. She figured at worst she would pass out with just the attempt to get free. Let alone what he would do to her in retaliation—which was probably kill her.

The last thing she wanted was to be in some secret place, trapped with a guy who would do this.

It wasn't Fitz, her boss. That much she knew. She figured it was that guy who'd tried to kidnap her behind the diner—the one she hadn't been able to identify.

So many questions whirled in her mind. She could barely think through the confusion. She tried to think of Brett instead, just to try and calm down.

Stay with me.

Remembering those words calmed her, but the pain it birthed was like a bad taste in her mouth that left a sour feeling in her stomach—one that meant sickness was coming. She both loved and hated that he'd asked it of her right at that moment.

She couldn't stay. That would be impossible. Everyone in town would know who she was, and what had happened. People who cared about Brett would think he'd made the wrong choice, and he would stand by that choice—no matter what.

It would be his downfall.

She could cost him everything just because he thought he wanted to throw in with her. Be on her team. And even though she might like nothing more than that, it was the worst decision she could make if she cared about him like she claimed to.

It seemed like forever that he drove before he pulled the ATV up in front of a tiny one-room cabin. The toilet was probably little more than a hole in the ground—if not an outhouse altogether. She didn't want to know that part. Kamryn might be after a quiet life, but she didn't enjoy being off the grid so much she couldn't flush.

He shoved her away from him. Kamryn couldn't catch herself before she hit the ground and landed on her knees on the frozen solid grass, crunchy under her fingers. Rocks and pine needles poked her palms.

She gritted her teeth but didn't give him the satisfaction of crying out. Her head swam, and pain rolled through her. She hung her head and deposited her last meal on the ground.

"Gross," he said. "But at least you did it out here and not inside." Then he barked from behind her, "Now get up and get moving."

Kamryn shifted and rolled over in an attempt to sit on the cold ground.

"I said, get up." He pointed a shotgun at her.

She stared at the barrel and got to her feet. Somewhere in everything that had gone on today she'd lost the sling Maggie made for her. Not knowing where it was made her want to cry. But it also made everything hurt more, because there was nothing to take the weight from her stitches. She held the injured arm with her other arm, trying not to press against her ribs.

It took everything in her to move and not simply curl into a ball on the ground. Make herself a small as possible, and just hide from everything that was happening.

But then she would never find out why he'd done this.

"Who are you?" she asked. He seemed to be her age, but she didn't think she'd seen him before.

"It figures you wouldn't even recognize me. Always were too good to notice anyone else. Except Brett."

She glanced at him. His features seemed familiar now that she thought about it, and her mind called him back into her memory. "I'm having a rough day. You'll have to forgive me for being slow, Victor."

He'd been one of the camp guides with his brother when the bear had attacked. A man was shot that day. Craig and Victor had both been injured, and Rich had been forced to flee. Only the couple in the group had made it through, seemingly unscathed.

"She does remember." But he didn't smile. "Get inside."

As she crossed the threshold, he poked her in the back with

the barrel of the gun. She winced, stumbled a few steps, and headed for a chair.

"Shame you didn't choose the bed. We could've had some fun."

No way was she going over to the futon he was probably talking about as a bed in the corner. There was no couch, no refrigerator, and only a very dated looking kitchen with a gas stove that looked like it harkened back to the 1950s. The table was scratched and stained. The whole place smelled like gasoline and dirty socks.

"Why did you kidnap me, Victor?"

She figured he was the one who'd written the letter and tried to kidnap her behind the diner as well. Or, had the woman who gave her the letter written it so it looked like it was penned by a woman? Either way, she figured he was responsible.

She wasn't sure if she should bring up Fitz. Was it right to let him know she knew her boss was behind this? Maybe Victor didn't know about the disaster, or the black box. Or her mom. Maybe he didn't even know who was pulling his strings.

If that was even what was happening.

He eyed her. "I have my reasons."

That was good for him, but she didn't know if this was about the person trying to kill her or about him getting back at Brett. She looked around. "Where's your brother Craig?"

Violence flashed across his face. She was surprised he didn't cross the room and murder her with his bare hands. Or shoot her with that shotgun. "He didn't make it."

"He was in the hospital, wasn't he?"

"We don't like quack doctors."

"So after the bear attack, he took a turn?" She would've rushed her loved one back to the hospital, regardless of their preference.

"You think the bear attacked us?" The violence dissipated and angry laughter replaced his expression. "You have no clue what's going on, do you?"

"Why don't you tell me everything you know, and I'll tell you if I already knew that or not?"

He tipped his head back and burst out laughing. It didn't sound fun at all.

She didn't want that kind of humor in her life.

He pulled out a chair at the other end of the table and sat. "I should have you make the coffee. That's about the only thing that wouldn't be a waste of either of our time right now."

"I'll take a bottled water if you have any." She didn't want to ask for any medicine. He would probably give her something that made her pass out. After that, who knew what he would do. She didn't even want to think about it.

"What are we doing here?" she asked.

The more she could get him to talk, the better. He was liable to say more than he'd planned. And she needed him to spill as much as possible so she could get a handle on what was happening.

"Waiting for him." Victor held the gun across his lap.

"Fitz?"

"Clever girl."

And wasn't that just the most patronizing thing she'd ever heard in her life? But if she objected, she was liable to get shot.

"Might be a while before he lands the plane and drives up here," she pointed out.

"I guess we'll have to spend some time getting to know each other better, then."

"That's never going to happen."

He tipped his head to the side, his stare almost a sneer. "Because you already gave it to Brett, I'm guessing. Just like in high school."

Kamryn figured her relationship with Brett, and the intimacy level of it—which had been nonexistent, considering she'd been scared of everyone around her and God's judgment—was none of his business. But she couldn't tell him that, because it may very well encourage him to do something about it.

Fear was something she knew very well. She'd lived with it for years. Now that she had nothing left, what exactly was there for her to be afraid of losing except her own life?

Stay with me.

She almost wanted to hate him for saying that to her right before she'd gotten out of the car. But he hadn't known she was about to be abducted. He'd thought they were safe. To him that was the perfect opportunity to start talking about what was next, and what the future might hold for the two of them.

Brett didn't seem to understand that her life couldn't handle any of those things. She'd lived day to day since that closet where she'd heard her mom get killed. In high school, things hadn't been good. As much as she might've wanted to give him everything she had, eventually Kamryn realized there was nothing left to give him. She'd handed over everything, and it wasn't enough.

"I guess some things never change."

She didn't respond to that. What was the point?

It hurt to breathe. It hurt to sit, and to stand. If he tried anything there was going to be little she could do to fight him off.

And Brett wasn't coming. His ankle injury meant he wouldn't make it up here.

No one would save her.

If it came down to humiliation, pain and suffering, Kamryn just might choose to end her life in the quickest way possible. The alternative might not be something she was strong enough to live with.

"Maybe I'll make coffee," she said.

"You'll sit right there." He paused a beat. "In fact"—he walked to a drawer in the kitchen and pulled out a plastic tie— "put this around your wrists."

Arguing would expend precious energy she couldn't afford to lose. Kamryn had to bite the end of the tie, and tried to leave it a little loose.

All the while he pointed that shotgun at her.

She lowered her hands. "Done."

He held the gun with one, tugged on the ties and then tightened it so it bit into her wrists. "Nice try."

"What do you expect?" He couldn't think she would do nothing, or try nothing. Kamryn had been tossed around and battered her whole life. Fighting was second nature.

As he glanced at his cell phone on the table, his lips curled into a sneer. "Time's up."

Kamryn forced her body to tense to keep from reacting. Whatever was about to happen, she didn't have a good feeling.

An engine came close, and she heard it shut off. Seconds later, boots hit the front steps.

"Dad's here."

She twisted to look as the door opened.

32

The door to the hospital room opened, and Brett took notice as his brother stepped in, then rose from the bed and swung his legs over the side. His ankle had been bandaged but he doubted he'd be able to walk on it anytime soon. Still, he put his weight on his good foot and left the other one in the air as he stood.

"Sit back down," Jeff said.

Brett had been doing entirely too much sitting since Kamryn was grabbed from right in front of him. "We have to go find her. Who knows what Victor has done by now?"

Every second he wasn't looking for her was a second wasted.

It scared him that Victor hadn't even attempted to cover his face. The boldness didn't mean anything good. If he didn't care who knew he had her, that meant he didn't care about the consequences of whatever he was planning to do.

The fear was like a visceral thing. He didn't know what to do with all that hot anger and cold comprehension. He wanted to tear Victor apart, or worse. Thinking over what he might be doing to Kamryn was like being immersed in ice cold water.

"Tate already went after him," Jeff said. "That's what you told me, right?"

Brett frowned. "He hasn't called you?"

He didn't like feeling sidelined. The injury put him at a serious disadvantage, and everyone seemed content for him to stay here. To not do anything, when Kamryn needed him.

"Whatever." Brett looked around for his shoes. He would only need one since the other was bandaged and twice its size. "Let's just go."

"You expect to run after her?" His brother folded the one arm he had across his chest. The action only reminded Brett exactly how much Jeff had accomplished even after the injury that had taken one of his arms.

Brett had a few small broken bones, and all four limbs. Right now he could barely do anything. "I know I can't walk. I know I've had no training, so I'm no good. But I need to go after her."

"You really like this girl?"

"What does that have to do with anything? She's in danger. She could already be dead, and we're wasting time talking about feelings."

"Okay, so you love her." After that baffling statement, Jeff pulled out his phone. He dialed and put it to his ear. "He's ready." He hung up the phone and said, "Let's go." Then he reached outside the door and grabbed a pair of crutches, which he handed to Brett.

"You're letting me go with you?"

"Is anything I say going to stop you from going after her?"

"No." Brett stood up on the crutches. His ankle still didn't feel good, even suspended in the air. This was going to seriously suck. But Jeff was right that he had no intention of sitting on his behind and letting who knows what happen to Kamryn.

Jeff led the way out and down to the parking lot, where Stuart sat idling at the curb in a truck. Brett climbed in the back so he could lay his leg across the seat, and his brother got in the front passenger side.

"Where are we going?" Stuart glanced at Brett's ankle and winced before he headed out.

Brett kept his mouth shut so they didn't know exactly how much it hurt to move that much.

Jeff said, "Tate is going to meet us at the trailhead so we can head up in the mountains and start searching. He's also got Savannah on the line with the phone company, tracking her cell signal."

"Kamryn had her phone on her?" Brett hadn't even thought of that. He'd just assumed Victor would either disable it, or she hadn't had it after the building collapsed on them.

"I guess we'll find out if that leads to anything." Jeff buckled his seatbelt, then picked up his phone and scrolled with his thumb. "Tate is at Victor's house right now. He's going to call me if he finds anything."

"Thanks for doing this, guys." That was about as emotional as Brett planned on getting. Any more and the allowance would probably mean he'd lose it in the back of the car.

Be with her. Keep her safe, Lord.

He hadn't stopped praying since he'd seen Victor speed up and grab her, taking off just as fast as he'd shown.

And with Brett unable to go after her.

Tate had tried, but the ATV had been going so fast he hadn't been able to catch up. Brett had taken a couple of steps and wound up on his hands and knees in the dirt.

Right now he was beyond dirty, past exhausted and in serious pain. He'd taken something the doctor had given him, which only made him not want to think about how much worse it would be if he hadn't.

Jeff's phone rang. "You're on speaker." He held the phone over the center console. "What's up?"

"I cleared the house." Tate didn't sound like he found anything good. "Craig is dead in the bedroom. There aren't any visible mortal wounds, and he's not bleeding from anywhere more than the injuries he already had. Might've been a blood clot, or some other kind of complication no one caught because he wasn't at the hospital."

Stuart tipped his head toward the phone, still driving. "Or Victor killed him."

"He would never hurt his brother," Brett said. "They were partners in crime since they were little. I always thought it was because they lived with their mom, so they banded together."

Although, they had spent plenty of summers away at their dad's. Those had been some of Brett's favorite summers, when he didn't have to contend with them.

"Whatever the reason, Victor is alone now." Tate paused. "I still can't find the connection between him and Kamryn's boss, though."

Brett didn't much care what the connection was, as long as they found Kamryn. Conroy and the rest of these guys could figure out what to do with Victor and this Fitz guy who was her boss. The one who'd been lying to her for years.

As long as they found her, that was all that mattered to him.

His stomach churned. "How do we figure out where she is?"

Jeff glanced back with a look of concern on his face.

Brett mostly just ignored it, considering talking would only slow them down. He was at the point he needed action.

Tate said, "Savannah is still working on the GPS. She also got a warrant for Victor's phone, and is tracking him as well. I'll meet you guys at the trailhead. I'm hoping by then she'll have a general area for us to start searching."

"Copy that. See you soon." Jeff hung up the phone.

"What do we do when we find her?" Brett didn't exactly know how these things went. The fact Craig was dead might be an advantage, or disadvantage. Now they knew there was only one brother to contend with. The other could be twice as vicious, grieving the loss of his partner in crime. Literally.

Jeff shifted so the stub of his missing arm rested against the seat and he twisted around to nearly face Brett. "If I tell you that you need to stay with the vehicle, are you going to listen to me?"

Brett pressed his lips together.

"That's what I thought." His brother shifted on the chair. "Since we're the ones with guns, that means you'll be taking orders. You do what I tell you."

And if Jeff told him to stay in the car?

Brett didn't like any of this, but if it got Kamryn back, then it was a means to an end. He figured he could put up with a whole lot for the sake of having her back.

The last thing he'd done before she was taken was to ask her to stay. Even though she freaked out, he'd decided since then that her reaction was because it had been such an unexpected question. She did care. If she didn't want to stay, at least some part of her, then she'd have had no reaction. Least of all an emotional one. She would've simply turned him down instead of being overwhelmed just by the idea of it.

If he was honest with himself, he was overwhelmed with the idea as well.

Putting his heart on the line like that was a gamble. For a long time he'd been simply too scared to do it, or there just hadn't been anyone worth taking the risk for.

She was worth the risk.

They met up with Tate in the parking lot at the trailhead. He was driving an ATV, similar to the four seater Stuart had been using before. Maybe the same one. They all piled in and headed out, him in the back with his brother.

Brett was so relieved they all had the forethought to come prepared that he practically sagged against his brother. They knew what they were doing, and for once he didn't resent them for his lack of knowledge. His intelligence had always been his superpower, but with these guys he felt so lacking.

"You good?" Tate asked.

Brett nodded, straightening a little. Holding the crutches between his knees. "I'll be better when we find her."

Jeff squeezed his shoulder. "We will. Just have faith, and keep praying."

Brett immediately thought of the verse that goes, *Lord, I believe, help my unbelief.*

How appropriate that was right now, when he had so much and so little faith at the same time. He believed God could save and rescue her, but the faith to trust Him in how that would happen was hard to swallow.

"Head west on this trail." Tate pointed left where the path forked. It wound up higher into the mountains.

The farther they went, the more Brett's stomach clenched. The more he prayed. The more he leaned against his brother's arm, wondering if he should talk to alleviate the tension.

Maybe they were busy praying. He knew they were all believers, and Tate had often said that meant he was a work-in-progress as a Christian. Nowhere near complete. For so long Brett had assumed he either knew something, or he didn't. The idea he had to work out his faith in life wasn't always a comfortable thing. But he was trying.

Stuart slowed the ATV and stopped. "There's a cabin up ahead. I can see it through the trees."

Brett couldn't see anything in the dark, but he trusted his friend knew what he was doing.

They all climbed out and approached on foot so no one would hear them coming.

"Maybe you should hang back?" Jeff said.

Brett frowned at the cabin. What did his brother know that he didn't? Whatever it was, it made Jeff want to protect him. However, it made Brett feel like he was being abandoned all over again.

For a long time, he hadn't known how he actually felt about Jeff joining the Army. He'd figured it was some messy combination of sadness, or fear, and a whole load of pride in his brother's sacrifice. It was all of those, but he'd also felt like Jeff had left him and went off to live his own life.

Leaving him, kind of the way Kamryn had when she split town.

In the meantime, he had finished college and then stayed in Last Chance.

Forever. Alone.

Jeff touched Brett's shoulder, squeezing the tendon in his neck. "I'm sorry. I just need you to hang back so you're safe. If we need to retreat, you should be in front of us as we go."

Brett knew then that he was a liability being here. "Just get her back."

Did it really matter if Jeff was the one who rescued Kamryn? Brett just didn't want to hinder anything.

Tate trotted back to them. Stuart had since disappeared, but the private investigator hurried over. "Only one occupant. I didn't see Kamryn."

"Victor?"

Outside was the ATV Victor had used to take her, but there weren't any other cars.

Tate nodded. "Looks like he's drinking himself into oblivion."

"Great." Jeff led the way.

Brett hung back, entering the cabin half a dozen steps behind them.

As soon as Victor saw them, he threw the beer bottle he held straight at Brett, crying out in frustration.

Brett dodged to avoid it, and the bottle smashed on the wall behind him. "Tell us where she is."

33

———————

Kamryn took a couple of stumbling steps. Fitz prodded her in the back with his gun. "How much farther is it?"

She was losing the will to keep moving. They'd already walked at least a couple of miles. He had to know where he was going, rather than be walking aimlessly through the woods above Last Chance. Right?

From the moment he stepped through the front door of the cabin, Kamryn had known she was right. Fitzwilliam Collins, who had been William Herald before the airplane disaster, was the one behind it all.

After crashing the plane and murdering her mother, he'd set up a new life for himself. Moving on as though nothing happened.

As though he hadn't buried her mother in the basement of the white building.

It was even more a place of her nightmares tonight than it had ever been before. At least now she knew why she hated that building so much. And it wasn't because of Lenny having shut her in the closet. No, it was much worse.

From there, she had heard this man kill her mother.

Her boss.

Over the years she could even say she'd grown to see him as a father figure. Now all she wanted to do was vomit on the grass the way she had at the cabin.

He'd barely said much of anything since they left. It didn't surprise her that he hadn't answered her question now.

She glanced back over her shoulder. Her hands were bound in front of her. She had so many aches and pains and bruises she didn't even know which to concentrate on trying to ignore. Every breath she took was like being branded with a white-hot iron her ribs hurt so badly.

He walked behind her, only halfway looking at her. Sometimes barely even looking at her. As though eye contact meant he'd have to face what he was doing.

Did he think she was simply going to do whatever he said and accept the outcome? She turned to faced him and stopped altogether. He halted, blinking at her like she'd surprised him.

"I'm not going any farther until you tell me what's going on." If he had a plan, she wanted to know what it was. "Or you can just shoot me here and be done with it."

She was more than fed up right now. Exhausted and hurt. She wanted to see Brett, but that might not happen ever again.

He stared at her, finally willing to meet her gaze. He looked far older than he had the last time she saw him, barely days ago. Still the man she knew. And yet, now she barely recognized him. This was the truth of who he was—a murderer of not just her mother, but so many others as well.

"At least give me the respect of explaining." She figured that was a long shot, but it couldn't hurt to ask.

Fitz stared at her some more. Finally, he said, "You look like her."

Kamryn bit the inside of her bottom lip. Tears stung her eyes, but she wasn't going to give him any outward indication of how she was feeling. "What does it matter? She's dead because you killed her, just like you killed the people on that plane."

He exhaled, and his shoulders sank. "So you finally figured it out. Who I really am."

"I guess it's time to kill me, then."

He shook his head, sadness on his face. "It has to look like an accident. A tragedy."

"Are you going to crash another plane?"

"There's no time for that." As if there was even the question of harming a bunch of people all over again, just as a means to an end.

She wanted to slap him across his face. She wanted to shrug her shoulders. Or raise her hands, silently asking a question. If she did either of those things, she would be in even more pain than she was just from standing here.

A traitorous tear escaped and rolled down her cheek. "You killed her. You killed my mother, and now you're going to kill me too." All she'd had for years was a four-year-old's understanding of what'd happened. It was hardly comprehensive. She at least understood now that he was responsible.

"It wasn't as if I had a choice. She said she would go with me." He waved the gun around, gesturing. "We had it all figured out, and then suddenly she decides it wasn't the right thing?"

"She agreed beforehand that you should crash the plane to get away?"

There had to have been a solid relationship between them— or at least strong feelings, even if they were brief. No one in a casual relationship would consider murder just to escape a marriage…right? So had the affair lasted for weeks, or years?

Either way the outcome had been the same. He'd gone too far, and she'd realized she couldn't be with him.

Then he'd killed her for it.

His face reddened, strained by whatever turmoil was going on inside him. Maybe he wasn't convinced killing her was the right thing. Perhaps he just felt bad, but he still intended to go through with it. Or maybe she could persuade him to let her go.

The idea of running away made her want to curl up in a ball on the ground. She barely had the strength to even stand here.

How much farther was he going to make her walk?

He said nothing.

"And now you're going to keep killing people?" She had to play on his guilt if she was going to change his mind. "Trying to hide your secret even though it's inevitable that it will eventually come out. If it's not me, it'll be someone else. It's never going to stay quiet forever."

"I have to try. No one can know what happened."

She was glad she did. And he didn't know the police had found her mother's body, or that she'd found the black box. Otherwise, he wouldn't be still trying to hide it. He would take decisive action that meant he would kill more than just her. The airplane had simply been a distraction—another warning to back off. Meanwhile Victor was the one she figured had shot Maggie.

No matter how hard he tried to keep the secret, it was already out. But if she told him as much, he would begin killing people in town—Tate, Savannah, and the other cops. Maybe even Brett and his brother.

So much death, and she had the power to stop it right now.

"No one knows but me." She figured lying was okay when you were trying to save a bunch of people's lives.

Tate had shown her that photo, and she confirmed it was this man in front of her. It was only a matter of time before the cops caught up to him.

He was never going to get away with this.

Fitz studied her. "Is that even true?"

"You've been lying to me for years. You brought me up here to kill me." She managed a tiny shrug of one shoulder. Trying to appear strong, or as though she had bravado, wasn't going to get very far considering she didn't have the energy for it. But it wasn't as if she was going to lie down and just let him shoot her.

"It didn't have to be like this. You could have left it alone."

Let him walk free, after everything he'd done? Kamryn didn't have the strength to slap him, so she kept her mouth shut even though inside she seethed with the need to scream at him. He was determined to keep this all a secret for years? How he'd managed to get an entire town to let their questions lie, and leave it all alone, was crazy. She couldn't imagine how he managed to do it.

"Now you've ruined everything. I can't help people anymore, and it's all because you couldn't keep your nose out of it."

"Maybe you shouldn't have killed anyone in the first place."

"She was supposed to love me. She *betrayed* me."

"So you buried her in the basement wall and covered it all up so no one would ever know."

"I didn't need the hassle." He waved the gun and made a scoffing sound. "Everyone trying to find out what happened to the plane? It was sabotage, so that's what I made sure they figured out."

There was more to it. She'd known him long enough to see that plainly in his expression, and hear it in his tone. He wasn't disclosing everything.

Kamryn had to figure out what she was going to do. In the meantime, she decided she would keep him talking. "No one wanted more of an explanation than that? Seems strange they didn't care. And it wasn't like you could show your face in town and start a rumor mill if you were supposed to be dead. Right?"

"The boys' mom helped. I paid her enough, she did whatever I wanted."

"The boys." Her brain wasn't tracking. It refused to put the pieces together.

"Craig and Victor. My sons."

"The bear."

Fitz frowned. "The one that 'attacked'?" He laughed. "I needed a plan to kill those campers."

"Because they knew about you, or about the affair."

He huffed. "Victor and Craig."

Victor, who'd kidnapped her. Craig, his brother who'd been a camp guide with him. Two brothers who had mercilessly bullied Brett in school.

"They're your sons." Both had been injured by the bear, Craig badly, so things couldn't have gone completely according to plan.

"It wasn't easy to keep that hidden, but it worked well enough. They came in handy. Just like the NTSB agent."

"Because you paid them."

"Money talks." He shrugged. "But that's done now. And money won't solve this. It's time for action."

He was going to shoot her.

"Get moving."

She blinked. "What? Where?"

He motioned with the gun. "That way."

She looked. There was nothing there. "What are we doing up here?"

What she meant was, *I can't believe I ever trusted you.* Along with, *How could you do this to me?*

She didn't want to hope that Brett was coming for her. Not when he'd been more injured than she was. And how would they find her? When Fitz had pulled her phone from her back pocket at the cabin, the screen was shattered. It'd lit up when he put it on the table before forcing her outside. But they hadn't let her do anything with it.

Now she was cut off.

There was no way she could be rescued when no one knew where she was.

Fitz shoved her forward. He made her walk another mile, until they came to a cave. Then he pulled out his phone. She thought of rushing him while he wasn't looking at her. Between the gun and the phone, she didn't want to think what the repercussions would be if he hit her middle, or shot her.

The idea of bleeding out here, or dying some other way if a fractured rib managed to puncture her lung—it wasn't worse than knowing she would be alone as she took her last breath.

Brett.

Together. The idea of that forced her feet to remain where they were.

"Good. The bear isn't here." He looked up. "Inside."

"The *bear*?"

He couldn't—

He wouldn't—

"Get in there." He shoved her.

She tried to fight back.

Fitz jabbed the gun in her ribs, and the pain made her double over. He kicked her hip. She fell to the floor of the cave. He shoved her shoulder and dragged her bound wrists to an anchor in the wall with a carabiner hooked to it.

"Why are you doing this?"

"I wish I didn't have to. But I can't risk you telling everyone."

They already know.

If she told him, he'd go after them. It could mean the difference between her being rescued or them being delayed.

And then it would be too late.

Fitz turned and walked to the entrance of the cave. "I'm sorry it has to be this way." He was going to leave her alone to wait for the bear.

"Don't do this." She scrambled for a way to delay him. "I'll tell you what I know."

He frowned. "I'm listening."

34

———————

"You guys go. I'll stay with him." Tate put his hand on Victor's shoulder.

Stuart and Jeff were at the table where they'd talked with him. Brett had hung back, too angry to be of use. Stuart and Jeff had interrogated him like pros, but Brett still figured at least part of Victor wanted to tell them.

Maybe that was wishful thinking, even after all the pain Victor had dished out. But true or not, Victor was going to answer for what he'd done. For *all* that he'd done.

"Have fun with that." Brett readied his crutches.

Victor winced. He wasn't going to feel sorry for the guy, no matter that Tate wouldn't hurt him. That wasn't the point.

"Cops are on their way." Tate stowed his phone. He had a gun. They'd be fine.

It was time to go get Kamryn.

Jeff and Stuart headed for the door as though they'd been on countless missions together. Yet they hadn't. Brett had seen Zander's team working out in town, running sprints up and down the parking lot of an out-of-business big box store. They'd seemed in sync, like Jeff and Stuart now.

Not for the first time, Brett wondered what they knew—or

what experience they'd had—that he didn't. Except the entirety of their work lives involved guns and "operations." Not so much these days, since Stuart was a chef now.

"You good?" Jeff glanced aside as Brett made his way to the door.

He nodded, not wanting to get into that in front of Victor. They stepped outside. "Let's just get this done." He needed to focus. The alternative was risking failure.

"Stay here. I'll get the vehicle." Stuart sprinted off, far faster than Brett had ever seen anyone run.

"He's fast."

"We'll find her."

It figured Jeff knew exactly what he was doing. "But will it be fast enough? We're already miles behind. She could be—"

"Don't."

Stuart pulled up, and they climbed in. Brett kept his thoughts to himself the whole way there, eyes peeled for Fitz. He could be anywhere. After all, he was only tying Kamryn up in that bear's cave and leaving her to die there.

Only.

Lord, help her. Don't let it be too late.

His eyes stung. His nose tickled. Brett swiped a hand down his face and sniffed. They weren't going to be too late. It couldn't happen. He wouldn't let it. Not now that he had her back, after so long living without her. He hated that she was alone and in danger. He wasn't there.

As soon as Stuart halted the ATV, Brett was ready to jump out.

He could see the cave up ahead. Just a dark opening on the side of a hill. Inconspicuous, if he didn't know what he was looking for already.

He pointed. "There."

Stuart readied a gun and handed it to Jeff. "Are we sure that's the one?"

Brett just stared.

Jeff said, "If he says it's the one, it's the one."

He turned to his brother, surprise running through him even as he wondered how long it had been since Jeff stuck up for him over anything. Years, at least.

"What—" Jeff took half a step back. "Bear."

Brett hopped around to see the huge brown animal lumber out between two trees. He watched its gait. "Give me the rifle. Look at its hip. Victor was right, they did injure it."

Stuart handed it to him.

Brett lifted the scope to his eye and focused it. "I can't see well with it moving, but I think that's infected. He's probably not happy at all about how he's feeling." And when he encountered an intruder in his cave? "This isn't going to go well."

"What if we use tranquilizer?" Stuart's question was a good one.

"We could," Brett said. "If we have any." He lowered the gun. "Do we?"

"No." Stuart frowned.

Jeff said, "Are you going to kill it?"

"If I have to."

"Good, 'cause I don't do bears. I had a bad experience."

Whatever that meant, he'd ask his brother later. Right now all Brett wanted to do was run to the cave. Help Kamryn, get her out somehow. But he couldn't with his ankle like this. He asked Stuart, "Can you run up there fast enough to cut him off?"

"Yeah." He wasted no time sprinting up the hill.

Brett's stomach heaved. "The bear is going to see him." He lifted the rifle again, sighting the bear as it moved toward its cave. Lumbering along, favoring his back right leg. There were still at least two football fields between the bear and the cave. Could Stuart make it in time?

"She'll be okay," Jeff said.

No matter his intention, his words didn't reassure Brett. "She's in there. And the bear just saw Stuart."

It started to change course.

Brett fired a shot over the bear's back, like a warning shot fired across the bow of an old-time ship. Back in the days of maritime warfare. Some of his favorite movies were like that, and it worked for the bear now. Brett fired another round just to be sure.

The bear stumbled, going down with a roar.

"Good shot," Jeff said.

But it got back up far too quickly.

Stuart seemed to pick up speed. As though there was another gear in his engine, and he'd simply shifted up. His legs ate up the grass.

The bear headed after him, much slower now.

"He's going to make it," Jeff said.

"But what about when the bear gets inside?" Brett asked him. "What do we do?"

Stuart disappeared, and a second later a woman screamed.

"Kamryn!" As soon as Brett yelled, the bear turned.

"Good one. Get its attention." Jeff waved his arm. "Hey, bear! Over here!"

"This is a terrible idea," Brett said. "Hey, over here! I'm the one who shot you!"

"It's coming toward us."

"I see that." Brett hopped to redistribute his weight better, still trying to keep his injured ankle off the ground. He lifted the rifle.

"You're going to shoot it, right?"

"This thing will kill any of us—or all four. But only because we're in his territory." Brett aimed. Took a breath. *I'm sorry.*

This bear was a created being, just as he was. There were differences—the bear didn't have a soul. Still, every life was precious. Even in a fallen world.

Jeff said, "Brett, take the shot."

The bear closed in.

His shot rang out across the clearing. The bear dropped, a clean end to its pain.

Thank You for that. It wasn't suffering anymore, and it wouldn't hurt anyone else.

Brett intended on ensuring the party responsible for this faced the consequences, because it certainly hadn't been the bear's fault.

Jeff nudged him. "Let's go."

Brett grabbed one crutch and held the rifle in his other hand.

A weapon discharged.

Brett flinched. His brother walked faster on a reflex—the opposite of Brett's reaction that had him draw away from the sound. "Kamryn!"

Jeff glanced back. "Go!"

His brother didn't need to wait for him to find out what was happening in the cave with Stuart—and hopefully Kamryn, alive and well. But who knew? Until he got in there, he had no idea.

With his next step, Brett didn't quite lean all the way on the crutch. His injured ankle shifted, and his foot clipped a ragged bit of dirt. He cried out.

"Brett!" Her voice sounded so far away.

He fought through the pain, the nausea, and the urge to pass out. *Kamryn, I'm coming.* He needed her in his life. Wanted her with him every day, for as long as she would have him.

He stumbled to the entrance and stepped inside, nearly slamming into Jeff. He leaned his shoulder against his brother's back and looked around him. Jeff had his gun up.

Kamryn was across the far end of the cave, but it wasn't big. He could lay down, stretch out, and probably be touching her.

He wanted to drink her in. Still tied up, secured to the wall. On the other side, an older man had Stuart held in front of him. "Put your gun down."

"It's over, Fitz!" Kamryn yelled. "You don't need to kill anyone else!"

They'd gotten here in time to not only save Kamryn, but also to take down Fitz without a manhunt. Without the cops having to go after him. A possibly lengthy manhunt.

Brett nearly sagged to the ground in relief. He would have, if he hadn't had a gun pointed at him and his brother.

"Put it down, Fitz." Jeff sounded like he meant serious business.

But it still didn't reassure Brett. Not staring at the gun.

"Put yours down." Fitz tightened his grip on Stuart, whose face flushed. A knot had reddened his temple on one side and his eyes were glassy. He would pass out soon, but Fitz didn't even notice. "On the ground. You do that, and I'm gone. In five minutes, you can leave this cave. No sooner."

"Fine."

Brett was about to object. Jeff shifted. His shoulder hit Brett's chest. *Message received.* He kept quiet while Jeff said, "I'm putting it down."

Brett watched Fitz, ready to lift the rifle. He doubted he'd get it aimed before one of them was killed, but he would try. None of them in this cave would do anything while Fitz did whatever he wanted.

Jeff started to lower.

Fitz watched him with narrowed eyes, holding his gun on Stuart now.

Jeff reached out with the gun.

Stuart blinked. There was a heartbeat of silence and complete stillness before it seemed like everything erupted. Stuart kicked Fitz in the knee.

The gun went off.

Jeff brought his up almost at the same time. He squeezed the trigger on his pistol and caught Fitz in the arm.

Dirt kicked up beside Brett's foot as the bullet from Fitz's gun slammed into the ground.

Stuart twisted around. Fitz cried out, whirled, and ran for the cave entrance. Stuart grasped for him, overbalanced, and stumbled to one knee. He grunted.

"I'll go after him." Jeff raced for the cave entrance in pursuit.

Brett headed for Kamryn. Her eyes were closed, each breath sharp and fast. "Hey." He tried to crouch, but it hurt way too much so he just knelt and tried not to bend his foot. Or move it. Or put weight on it.

He cried out.

Her eyes flew open. "Brett."

He winced. "Let's get out of here."

She pressed quivering lips together and nodded. "You really came."

"Of course." He glanced around and saw Stuart had gone, probably to help Jeff catch Fitz. He said a quick prayer for them and got to work untying Kamryn. The multitool he kept in his pocket all the time—the tiny one he always forgot he had on him—made quick work of the plastic ties securing her hands.

"Thank you." She ran her fingers over the angry lines on her wrists, then the bruise on her neck.

"Can you walk?"

She nodded.

"Good, cause I'm not sure I can."

She didn't laugh at his joke, but he got a tiny smile out of her. As they stood, Kamryn wedged herself under his shoulder and helped him.

"Can you hold the rifle in your other hand?" Brett asked. He needed the crutch on his side to take some of the weight as they trudged out of the cave. "This will be slow going."

She shifted against his side.

Having her against him was more than a little distracting. But not enough not to notice. "The bear is gone."

"There really was a bear?"

He nodded. "I killed it. Now it's gone."

"So is Fitz, and your brother and his friend."

"Let's get to the ATV, and we can call them. See where they are."

"Good." She smiled up at him. "I'm ready to get out of here."

He smiled back, leaned down, and touched his lips to hers. Regardless of whether she stayed or went back to her life, he wanted that at least between them.

If not more.

His phone buzzed before they reached the ATV, keys in the ignition still. "Jeff said Fitz is keeping them running, and we should get to safety. They'll call the police to back them up."

Kamryn nodded. She held his crutches and the rifle as he drove with one foot, trying to ignore how much the other one hurt.

It took a second to decide which direction to take. While he deliberated and decided to head for the stream, then down to the highway since it was fastest, his phone buzzed again. "Toni." He exhaled, not even realizing he'd been holding his breath waiting—figuratively and literally. "Mom is out of surgery, and it looks good. She'll let me know when she's awake."

Kamryn lifted her face to the sun, and the warm glow brightened her features. "That's good."

He watched her for a moment. "I'm glad you're safe."

She nodded, opening her eyes to smile at him. "It feels different. Good, even if I can hardly believe it's done."

"As long as Fitz is caught, it will be."

"I still didn't see my mother escorted to the morgue."

He touched her shoulder. "We'll make it right."

Both were pretty quiet on the way back to the car. Kamryn shivered beside him. Brett wanted to wrap an arm around her, but needed both hands to drive.

"Are we by the river?"

He nodded. "Down there." To the right, the hill stretched up. Paths up and down delineated where some folks ran up and down it, or hikers made their way to look at the drop off that ended at the river—the bottom of the valley. It was pretty much a cliff.

Lately someone had died falling over it. Some guy, chasing Jess and Ted.

Brett was glad that with everything they'd been through, it hadn't involved that. Even if his skin was hot and gritty and cold would feel good on his injuries.

A few people from town had even jumped off the edge for fun. As though that would ever be a good idea.

Brett shook his head.

"What?"

"Nothing. Just rabbit-trailing thoughts. But it's keeping me alert."

"That's good." She sighed. "Did I say thank—"

A giant brown body lumbered in front of them, tumbling down the hill as it moved. Blood covered one side and with the bear came an almighty roar.

Kamryn gasped. Brett had a split second to realize what was happening before the bear slammed into their right bumper, going way too fast. Intent on them.

He tried to hold the steering, but the bear's weight shoved them to the side.

To the edge.

The wheel slipped.

Kamryn screamed, and they tipped over.

The ATV. The two of them.

And the roaring bear.

35

Strong hands dragged Kamryn from beneath the surface. Her entire body felt like it was frozen solid, her limbs too heavy to move. She couldn't object even if she wanted to.

She was deposited on the ground and rolled over. A heavy hand slapped her back until she coughed, and it seemed like half the river expelled from her mouth.

"There you go."

She was rolled to her back and blinked up at a wide face with deep set eyes and a big thick beard covering his cheeks and chin.

Through a flash of teeth, his gravel voice rolled over her. "Nice to have you back in the land of the living."

Her gaze dipped, and she began to descend back into the blackness. Kamryn fought the sensation with every bit of strength she had and found herself blinking again.

Black athletic shirt, long sleeves. Athletic shorts with a pair of those running tights that men wore covering the lower half of his legs. Beat-up running shoes that looked like they were about to fall apart.

From a way's away, someone yelled, "I got him. Give me a hand, kid."

She couldn't focus on it enough to figure out what was going on.

Kamryn thought through what she remembered. All she could remember was a huge bear, and the sense of falling.

"Do you know what happened to you?" His voice was the kind that made you want to fall asleep, though she imagined he could sound quite formidable if he wanted to. He also should have a side job as the host of a podcast that read children's stories parents could play to help their little ones fall asleep.

"Bear." That would make a terrible children's story. She was still shaking from how scared she'd been.

He set a hand on her shoulder. "Easy." Then he glanced aside. "We need to get them out of here before they get hypothermia."

Kamryn mustered up strength enough to say again, "Bear."

No, that wasn't what she wanted to know. She couldn't get her thoughts to work properly.

"The bear is long gone. We took care of him."

That didn't sound good. The look in his eyes said he'd seen far worse things than that, but it still didn't sit well with him.

"Brett."

"Is that your friend?" The bearded man frowned. "Isn't that the name of the town vet?" He looked over again at his friends.

"Oh hey, it is him," someone said. "It's that vet from town."

"Both of them are pretty beat up."

How many people were here? Kamryn tried to ask another question, not that she'd exactly managed a whole one so far. All she could do was whimper, too exhausted to tell them anything.

"I guess another one bites the dust." No one laughed, though the speaker seemed to think he was pretty hilarious.

The bearded man frowned. "There have been so many new couples in town lately I can hardly keep it all straight, even with all the wedding invitations. Baby shower invitations. Save the date cards. And now the vet? I guess we have another two right here with their last taste of freedom."

Kamryn had to figure out what that meant. Her mind couldn't wrap around it, except for the fact he seemed to think she and Brett were like any of those other couples in town.

She wanted nothing more.

But in her life she'd only received very few things she wanted. And now that she knew Fitz had been lying to her this entire time, she couldn't even appreciate what she had in her job and the work she'd done with the mission organization.

His actions had tainted everything good. And that was the least of what he'd done to her family. This town.

"Let's go." The bearded man picked her up in his huge arms as though she weighed barely more than a bag of flour. Considering she had no strength to move a single muscle, and could barely even blink, she was glad his team had come across her and Brett.

She tried to look around for him. Was he okay?

Her thoughts drifted in and out. He jostled her for a while, and then it felt like they were in a moving vehicle.

Lights flashed behind her eyelids. She heard people talking over her, then drifted out for a while.

When she blinked again, the lighting was soft, and a woman in pink scrubs stood beside her bed. "There you are." She smiled in a way that made Kamryn feel better, even though she couldn't feel much at all. "You've been through a pretty eventful week." She held onto Kamryn's wrist, then looked at her watch. "The doctor should be in shortly."

"Is Brett okay?" Thankfully she managed to get out those three words.

"The guy you came in with?"

She nodded, though it didn't amount to much movement. She just wanted Brett. Was he even alive? Was he here, somewhere? She wanted to see him. Hug him close again, the way she had when they'd walked to the ATV.

Fear still edged at her consciousness, threatening to tense all her muscles.

"I'll find out for you." The nurse patted her shoulder and then disappeared.

Leaving Kamryn alone. The way Fitz had been about to leave her for the bear, before Jeff's friend came in. She didn't even know where all of them were now. Maybe her boss had gotten away with it. He could have killed them, or anyone else, and escaped.

They'd been attacked by that bear again, trying to get back to town. Rescued from the river by those guys.

The door opened, and she spotted Conroy walk in with Mia.

Kamryn smiled as Mia came over, one hand over the bump of the baby growing inside of her. She could admit, to herself at least, that having a child of her own to love and care for was one of her greatest dreams. And even now, knowing how she felt about Brett, she wasn't sure if it would ever happen.

"How are you feeling?" Mia asked.

"I think I should be asking you that," Kamryn said. "I'm not even sure yet. I feel like I just woke up."

Mia squeezed her hand. "Just rest."

Conroy nodded, his arm around his wife. "You're safe now. I've been thanking God since they called me that Zander and his boys found you and Brett. If they hadn't been there so quickly, who knows what condition we would have found you in."

She could still remember plunging into the river and being enveloped by icy cold water. Even though it was summer, the runoff from the mountain peaks was freezing enough to numb her in only minutes.

He was probably right that they should be grateful to even be alive.

"How is Brett?"

Mia frowned. "He hasn't been here yet? I saw him walking around earlier."

Conroy shifted. "I'm sure he'll be in here soon enough."

They chatted for a few more minutes, but it was hard for her to keep her eyes open. When she woke next, she was alone again.

36

"Kamryn is perfect for you."

Brett shook his head, seated in a wheelchair beside his mom's hospital bed. She was pale and looked exhausted from the extensive surgery that came after being hit by that rifle round. Victor had almost killed her. And yet, here she was alive. Victor was in jail.

She wasn't out of the woods yet, but close to it. Things were looking hopeful according to her doctor.

"That's not what I came here to talk about. I just wanted to check on you."

She lifted one brow over her tired eyes. "Well, she's what I want to talk about."

Brett started to laugh. It hurt a lot, making him groan. He wanted to go and see Kamryn, but it was only right that he visit his mom first.

That was why he'd had Jeff wheel him over here.

"I want to talk about her, too."

He glanced at his brother. "Traitor."

They'd certainly reached a detente since Zander and his boys had pulled Kamryn and Brett out of the river. At least, that was what he'd been told had happened. He'd been unconscious the entire time.

Jeff had shown up almost straight away when Brett woke up in the hospital, with the news Fitz was in custody and Zander was reporting they'd killed the bear.

Conroy had offered to call the state park guys and tell them they could call off the search for the rogue animal.

All in all, there was nothing left for him to do after checking in with his mom. There was just him and Kamryn.

"Okay, so basically I'm scared to go talk to her." He wanted to roll his eyes, but managed to restrain himself. "I don't know what she'll say. I asked her to stay, and she freaked out. I think that means she's considering it."

Before he could say any more, his brother snorted.

Brett shot him a dirty look. "Anyway, it has to be a big deal or she wouldn't have reacted like that. But then she was kidnapped, and her boss—"

"And his son," Jeff added.

"They both tormented her. Who knows what happened before we caught up? Then that whole thing with the bear, and the river."

His mom's eyes were both wide. "That explains the dream I had."

He and Jeff both waited for her to explain.

Maggie waved a hand. "It wasn't much. But it was enough that I caught the gist of what happened, probably before you did. So when I woke up, I immediately started praying."

"Did you pray that a group of special forces guys would randomly come across us while they were exercising, just in time to pull us from a freezing river before we died of hypothermia?"

She grinned. "I'm sure it was something like that."

Brett grinned in return. His mom's spirituality wasn't a joke, but was a source of amusement between the two of them. It seemed as though she had a hard line straight to God and when it counted He came through. For her, for Brett and Kamryn.

At a time Brett had been completely unconscious, let alone unable to help himself, God had been drawing him out of that water by unseen hands.

Bringing him back to life.

Jeff tugged on the wheelchair, turning it with his one hand. "There's no time like the present. May as well go talk to her."

Brett twisted. His ankle didn't feel super good, but he had to say, "Right now?"

"Quit being a chicken." Jeff gave him a poke. "I'll wheel you in there, and you can tell her you love her. Job done."

His mom giggled.

Brett waved goodbye as Jeff wheeled him out of the room. "Did that work with Toni? Is that how you managed to convince her to fall for you?"

"You have no idea how charming I can be."

"And I don't want to. You can keep that stuff for yourself."

Jeff chuckled behind him, wheeled him to Kamryn's room, and opened the door. He pretty much shoved Brett inside and then shut the door behind him.

Brett called out, "Thank you!" to the closed door.

The muffled reply that came sounded a whole lot like, "Ask her if I can buy her airport!" But that was crazy.

Kamryn lay on the bed under the blankets, staring at him as though she didn't quite know what to make of his entrance.

"My brother is a crazy man."

She grinned. "It's really good to see you guys getting along."

"We're men. We performed a daring rescue together, and now we're good." No conversation required. Which was great, considering he needed to have one with Kamryn. And then all rational thought escaped his mind, and he couldn't think of one thing to say.

"How is your ankle?" she asked.

Of course, he should've asked her how she was doing. He said, "I can't walk on it for a couple of weeks. Then I see the doctor, and he's going to tell me if I need surgery. How about your ribs?"

She scrunched up her mouth in a shrug. "Three are broken, but thankfully it wasn't bad enough they couldn't just wrap them. Doesn't feel good though." She touched her waist with a hand. She still had marks from the bindings on her wrists, and a red line on her throat where her purse strap had dug in. Then there were the stitches on her arm, under the bandage.

"We've been through the wringer, haven't we?"

She nodded.

"I'm sorry about everything that happened. But I'm glad you know the truth now." He wanted to ask her what her plans were, but the words got stuck in his throat. "I seem to have a few days off work. Maybe I could hang with you?" She might leave soon. He didn't want to let her out of his sight—some of that residual fear from seeing her almost kidnapped once. And then kidnapped again for real.

"I'd like that. I've been thinking about adopting a dog." She said it without inflection. As though this was just a normal conversation between two people on the street. "Do you happen to know of one? Possibly one that was recently injured, and needs someone to take care of him. Any idea who I should speak to about that?"

Brett scratched his jaw. "You understand that adopting a dog means we have to be sure the animal is going to a good home. That requires plenty of visits."

"If I stayed here in town, that should take care of that, right?"

His eyes widened. "You'd stay?"

Kamryn nodded. "There are things to do. And then, after that, I'll probably find more things to do." She paused. "I might just wind up saying forever."

Brett pushed the wheelchair closer to the side of her bed and held out his hand. She put hers in it, smiling sweetly down at him. "Forever?"

"I want to be around people who genuinely care about me."

"I always have. Me…and the rest of my family."

"More than that, though, I want to be with people I love." She looked down at their hands. "Because I love you. Not just always, but right now. In a way that nothing else matters."

"When I woke up, I didn't have a single thought about my job. About the animals under my care. Not just because I know my staff has it under control, but because all I could think about was you." He squeezed her hand. Then he set his good foot down and braced his weight on the edge of the bed as he stood.

She gasped.

Brett leaned down so their faces were close. "I love you, too."

He pressed his lips to hers and sank into her kiss.

That's when he realized he was finally home.

EPILOGUE

Three days later

"Is that the strawberry?" Savannah was already reaching over with her fork, even before Mia pushed her bowl in her friend's direction. The diner was quiet, but it was eleven in the morning so the lunch rush hadn't hit yet.

Truthfully, Mia wasn't all that interested in her pie. Pregnancy was taking its toll. It was hot out, and she was eager to have this kid already.

Her dad was going to be out of the hospital soon.

The house was almost ready.

Conroy chuckled beside her as his detective ate from Mia's bowl. She smiled but didn't look over. He reached out and squeezed her knee, his fingers brushing the giant belly distending her shirt over her stomach that made her feel like a house.

Savannah grinned. "That one is *gooood*."

"Are you sure you're not pregnant as well?" Conroy glanced between Savannah and Mia.

Tate choked on his bite of pie. Savannah's mouth dropped open.

Mia pressed her lips closed and tried not to laugh. "They have four kids."

Conroy shrugged. "One more won't be that big of a deal." He motioned at Tate with his fork. "You already have a seven-seater SUV."

Savannah nearly spat out her pie. "How do you know it won't be that big of a deal? Yours hasn't been born yet." She eyed Mia.

"Don't drag me into this." Mia took another bite.

Conroy said, "You're supposed to be on my team."

"I am. If your team is 'Team Nap.'" She leaned back in the booth, but it was uncomfortable so she sat forward again. "I should go to the bathroom." *Again.*

Mia scooted to the edge of the bench seat, braced her palm on the table, and got her body up.

A rush of wet hit the floor between her feet.

Conroy jumped up behind her like he needed to catch her. "Babe." His arms cradled hers and he held on.

But she didn't fall. "We should let Hollis know I made a mess."

"Tate can do that." He shuffled her over it. "We're going to the hospital."

Their friends were on their feet. Tate said, "I'll go tell Hollis. You guys drive safe." He leaned down and kissed her on the cheek. "Everything will be fine, and we'll be there soon."

She nodded.

Savannah gave her a quick hug, and Mia was happy to see her steadier on her injured leg than she'd been recently.

Before she could ask, Mia said, "You can finish my pie."

Her friend grinned. "Thanks."

"Enough chit-chat. Let's go." Conroy started moving.

He looked more nervous than she felt. "Copy that, Chief."

"Not funny." He held the door for her. "Let's go have a baby, Lieutenant."

She stopped to touch his cheeks and press her lips to his. "Good idea."

He smiled.

She took a moment then, smiling back at him.

Until Tate yelled from the back of the diner. "Would you guys go already!"

One month later

"HOW MUCH LONGER DO WE——"

Dean tugged Ellie's elbow down. "Shhh."

"What is this, a library?"

Ellie slumped onto the grass beside him, tucked behind a fallen tree. They were half a mile from his new therapy center—the one that'd opened for select clients just a few days ago. The grand opening was in a month when they had everything up and running.

It was almost sunset. The orange glow across the sky caught his attention, but the sight of his fiance—who would be his wife in a few weeks—was more breathtaking.

Seeing Mia and Conroy's son had made him want children of their own. Something Ellie had been eager to talk about.

She smiled at him then, catching him staring at her in a way that made her cheeks flush pink. Dean leaned to her and kissed the hinge of her jaw, then the soft skin below her ear.

Behind him, Stuart cleared his throat. "Don't mind us."

Kaylee giggled.

Stuart had insisted his wife sit in his lap, and not on the dirt. Dean figured she'd have agreed even if she wasn't pregnant.

Dean looked at the trail, instead of letting his friends see his expression—whatever it was going to give away. He spotted Ted and Jess coming up the trail. "Here they come."

Ellie leaned close in a way he liked. She whispered, "She probably thinks they're going to the gazebo where you took me."

Dean needed to do that again. Have a date night with dinner, and look at the stars.

Kaylee said, "Jess told me he said he needed help with some new invention."

"He does." Dean grinned. The remote was beside him. "Ready?"

He waited for his cue…the two fingers his brother flicked out while Jess wasn't looking. Dean hit the button on the mechanism that dropped a rolled up banner vertically down a tree. They hadn't been able to use fireworks with the heat and all the trees, but the women had more than made up for that with ribbons and streamers.

Jess pulled up short on a gasp.

By the time she'd turned around, Ted was on one knee holding a tiny velvet box.

They were close enough to hear her gasp.

Kaylee whispered, "Love you," to her husband.

Dean glanced at Ellie. She looked over with a shy smile and he pulled her to his chest. When Ted jumped up and Jess launched herself into his arms, Dean pressed the second button.

Speakers they'd hung in the trees blasted a fanfare that made Jess tip her head back and laugh.

***

"I'M JUST SAYING."

Bridget glanced over. She lowered the paintbrush in her hand so it didn't drip on her. Despite being six months pregnant with her second child, she wasn't showing much. The doctor had reminded her that everyone was different. There was nothing to worry about. "What? I'm not following?"

Sasha rolled her eyes. "A drone, a rogue World War II plane, and no one thought to call us?"

"You're still mad about that?" Bridget went to put her hand on her hip and realized she still held the brush. "I'm pregnant. You think we should've gone looking for that bear?"

Sasha pressed her lips together. Bridget figured that meant yes, she did think they should've done that.

Bridget glanced at the guys to get some backup from the two cops in their lives—Bridget's husband, Aiden, and Sasha's boyfriend, Alex. Though, she was only still that because Sasha was seriously dragging her feet on the subject of getting married.

They were both looking across the warehouse that was being turned into a Community Center at Alex's mom, who was laughing and talking with Will's father. Right now Bridget was thinking of calling this place "Fresh Starts" but that was up in the air.

As soon as she decided she would order the sign.

Speaking of dragging her feet…

"You want an adventure?" Bridget asked. "Get married. There's no greater adventure than building a family."

Sasha lifted her hand and started counting off her fingers. "Hiking Mount Kilamanjaro. Visiting a volcano in Hawaii. Going hiking in Alaska. Riding rapids on the Colorado River. Going scuba diving in the Bahamas. Getting abducted and held for ransom in Mexico. Escaping and smuggling myself over the border. Meeting two kids that need rescuing, blowing up a car, and taking out a couple of cartel guys." —she'd long since run out of fingers to count— "Taking them to a shelter run by two people I've known for years—"

Alex swung his arm around her shoulder, looking a little pale. "We can do all that. Together, with my ring on your finger."

Bridget pointed out a pertinent fact. "That sounds like a threat."

"What sounds like a threat?" Will strode over with two heavy paper sacks.

Behind him, Hollis carried what looked like four pies in a stack.

Sasha said, "I was just talking about what I did last weekend."

Aiden burst out laughing.

Bridget looked at Alex, who met her gaze. He seemed as nervous as Bridget that Sasha might've been telling the truth.

"Relax." Sasha poked Alex in the side. "But if you want to get married…fine. I'll do it."

"Great. We'll plan something—"

"Right now."

Alex blinked. "Right—"

"Now. Tell your mom to call her friends. We'll go to the courthouse, and then hang out in her backyard. Everyone can come over for tacos or something."

No one said anything.

"Don't you have a ring already?"

Alex said, "This wasn't what I was thinking."

"I told you to hang onto it and I'd let you know when I was ready."

"And you're ready now?"

Sasha looked uncharacteristically nervous as she lifted her chin. "I'm ready for an adventure."

Alex swung her up into his arms and spun around. "Mama!"

Hollis leaned over to Will. "We're going to need more pies than this."

JEFF HELD the door for her because he'd insisted.

"It feels good to be off those crutches." Toni's leg still ached, but since she'd had her cast taken off life was moving on. The normal she had now was far better than anything she'd experienced before. Even her brother Judah seemed happy in his new position as part of Zander's team.

Jeff smiled but seemed nervous.

Toni eyed the yellow two-story house behind him. "I thought we were going to dinner."

"We are. I just wanted to show you something." He held out his hand, and she took it, aware it made him vulnerable. Holding his hand left him without one to defend himself with—an instinct, even if danger wasn't part of their lives anymore. She wasn't sure they would ever lose that heightened awareness.

They walked to the front door, past the FOR SALE sign in the yard.

"Nice house."

He nodded. "Sixty-four acres, and it backs onto the lake. Totally secluded, with a private lane."

"And we're close to the airport."

He glanced over. "You said you weren't mad."

Toni lifted her free hand. "I'm not. It's going to be a lot of work, but if you want to own an airport who am I to stop you?"

He paused on the front step. "I don't know where to start."

"Just say what you need to say." They'd never had a problem talking to each other. Their relationship had begun on the phone. In person was so much better. She loved looking at him.

"I want to buy the accountants' office business from Zander, so we can help people who need a safe place. A new identity."

"We?"

"I want to buy this house." He didn't move one single muscle, as though at the slightest inkling from her he would bolt. "I want to run the business together and use the airport to do it. As a team."

"Business partners?"

"And husband and wife."

"Both?"

He nodded in a jerky movement.

"What happens when you get sick of me?"

He blinked. "Sixty-four acres."

"I think I'll buy a horse."

"Good thing I know a guy."

She grinned. His head lowered toward hers and she knew she was in store for one of his ridiculously good kisses.

Right before their lips touched a car door slammed.

Brett called out, "Well?"

Jeff grunted, sounding frustrated.

Kamryn gasped. She leaned over to Brett and whispered something. He winced and they got close enough for Toni to see he held a brown puppy in his arms.

She frowned. "Whose dog is that?"

Kamryn glanced at Brett, then at Jeff. "Uh, well…"

Brett said, "He's an engagement present."

Jeff pulled down the collar of his shirt and lifted out a circle of twine with a diamond ring on the end of it. He lifted it over his head and held it up.

She touched the ring, watching it glint in the sunlight for a second. "This is beautiful."

"You like it?"

She nodded. "And the house. And the life you're giving me. All of it."

"I love you."

"I love you, too. So much I can't believe it sometimes." She buried her face in his neck and he held onto her.

Kamryn spoke quietly, "This feels like the best kind of happy ending."

"Happy, yes," Brett said in reply. "The end? Not even close."

Continue reading for the first 2 chapters of *Last Taste of Freedom*, the first book in my new series *Chevalier Protection Specialists! Find out more at* https://lastchancecounty.com/chevalier-series

I hope you enjoyed this series, would you please leave a review at your favorite retailer? It genuinely helps others find new books and is greatly appreciated!

LAST TASTE OF
FREEDOM
CHEVALIER PROTECTION SPECIALISTS BOOK 1 FROM
USA TODAY AND PUBLISHERS WEEKLY BESTSELLING AUTHOR
LISA PHILLIPS

1

To move among high society was to participate in a kind of Cold War all its own. Or so she'd always thought.

Nora Gladstone removed a glass of champagne from a silver tray but didn't sip. Nor did she thank the waitress. After all, no one else in this room did. And one didn't want to make a spectacle of oneself. Especially not on a night she wanted them to open their check books and be generous. Her foundation wasn't hurting for funds, but they could help so many more children with birth defects and health problems if she could convince these industry leaders and politicians to donate.

"I've so looked forward to this evening."

Nora smiled and gently squeezed the woman's hand, the skin so soft it was a little disturbing to touch. "Thank you so much for coming. I hope you enjoy dinner."

The woman moved on, not lingering long enough for Nora to get all those words out.

Nora sighed inwardly and moved to greet the next guest. Flute in her left hand, so as to look casual. An extended right hand. A polite smile.

"It's wonderful to see you."

"Thank you for coming."

"Oh, darling. It's been too long. We must catch up."

She was used to the quiet of her suite of rooms that extended from the east wing of her father's house.

Nora made it all the way to the floor-to-ceiling windows beside the stage, on which a jazz band played a soft number she couldn't remember the name of.

On the other side of the window the Seattle skyline stretched as far as she could see.

Nora tried to make out the mountains in the distance. That open space, where things seemed endless and animals could roam wherever they pleased. But she couldn't make it out. It was too far away.

"Nora."

She turned to the voice. "Yes, Father?"

He frowned down at her dress. "What were you thinking?"

"I was thinking this dress is beautiful, and this is an important event."

He pressed his lips together. "You can almost see your…"

He didn't say *scar.*

That would be uncouth.

Nora ignored the knot in her stomach and slid her arm through her father's elbow. "Thank you for coming." She took a sip of her drink. "You didn't need to come back early from D.C., but I'm grateful you did. It's nice to have a familiar face here."

He patted her hand on his arm. "I wouldn't have missed it."

That's when she noticed the man making his way through the crowd.

Taller than most. Alert ice-blue eyes that tracked every movement. Broad shoulders. Strength under the tailored suit. No tie. A thick beard covered the lower half of his face, the same light brown color as his short hair. Tanned cheekbones, as though he'd spent time in the sun recently.

Of course. Her father hadn't come here for her. No, he was utilizing this evening as a public place to meet with one of the men under his command as director of the Department of Clandestine Service, a branch of the government with close ties to the Defense Intelligence Agency, the CIA and military. The operations the DCS conducted were high level, often involving the politics of an entire nation.

At least, that was what she'd pieced together through research.

This had to be one of his men.

He walked like a soldier, and probably acted like one, too. She knew she would likely sound like a snob if she spoke. Better to keep her thoughts to herself than open her mouth and hand over the evidence to incriminate her.

She'd learned that with her father a long time ago.

The guy spotted them and shifted from his careful meandering into a stride that brought him to her father. "Sir."

She looked around again and saw her special guest at the bar enjoying a soda.

Nora's father motioned to her. "This is my daughter—"

"If you'll excuse me, I see someone I need to speak with." Nora didn't need to get into a lengthy introduction that would be meaningless.

Her father's lips pressed into a thin line.

She lifted to the balls of her feet and kissed his cheek. "I'm glad you like my dress."

"I never said that."

She turned away, almost smiling. Almost. She didn't look at the man her father had asked to meet him here. Whatever they were going to speak about wasn't her business, and she wouldn't get an answer if she asked. Her father didn't share about his work. His friend didn't seem like the kind of man who had anything soft about him.

He didn't seem entirely out of place here.

She shook her head internally. Being intrigued was one thing. Dwelling on it was another entirely. Relationships weren't something she entertained in her life. There was no time for the dance of attraction, followed by hope, culminating in rejection. She'd lost enough friendships over the years to know there was little point in reaching hope when the person would inevitably discover her health problems and walk away. Nora had the foundation, and all the children they assisted. That, and her father, was more than enough to keep her busy.

Besides, this wasn't a place to be genuine. No one here was interested in the real Nora Gladstone. They only saw what they wanted to see—an ice princess running her father's charity.

Beyond that, she had no interest in what they thought of her.

Nora headed for the bar, where she ordered sparkling water with lime and stood beside the young girl she'd invited to speak tonight, one of the children the foundation had sponsored since birth.

"How are you feeling, Charlotte?"

The girl looked queasy. She spoke with a strong accent that only added to her budding appeal. In a few years she would be a beautiful woman. "I'm nervous."

Nora studied her, looking for something beyond a basic fear of being in front of so many people. Asked to speak to a crowd. Was this more than stage fright? "I'm sure you have nothing to worry about. Did Miss Rachel help you figure out what to say?"

Charlotte nodded, her dark hair pulled back into a loose knot. She was almost seventeen now, and wore a lovely pink dress that didn't quite suit her features. She'd suffered a brain tumor early in her life. No doubt there was an ugly scar under her hairline. Nora had read her medical history, and it had felt so familiar she'd cried for a few minutes. Until her heart began to beat erratically and her breathing came in rushes she couldn't control and she'd had to take a pill and lie down for half an hour.

"Thank you so much for being willing to be here." She wanted to touch the girl's shoulder, or hand. Forge some kind of solidarity with their shared history of multiple surgeries and weeks on end spent in the hospital.

But she didn't.

Nora said, "The first time I got up in front of a crowd, I was walking up the steps to the stage. I tripped on my dress and went *splat* on my face. Can you believe that?" She smiled, feeling the heat of a blush on her cheeks. "I was so embarrassed."

The girl gasped, her smile unsure. "I hope I don't do that."

"I'm sure you won't. I know you'll do wonderfully."

"I am going to try." Charlotte took another sip of her drink as she glanced over at the bartender.

Nora spotted again the edge of that thing she'd noticed the first time she met the girl—a couple of days ago. They'd flown her over from the country where she lived, and she'd surprised Nora with her excellent English. It wasn't anything she could put her finger on. Just a lifetime mingling with people playing a part. But that made no sense. Charlotte had been one of the foundation's children nearly since birth.

Considering she'd already hired a private investigator to sift through everything to do with the foundation, she let it go for now.

"Thank you." Nora gave her a very slight squeeze of her hand. "You look beautiful, by the way."

Charlotte's expression faltered, deep in her eyes. For a split second everything seemed darker.

Most people might've missed the nuance. But Nora had studied people and how they acted her entire life so she could figure them out. Even after years of that education, she still couldn't figure out who would accept and who would reject her.

So she'd given up trying.

"Shall we?" She held out her arm, and Charlotte slid off the stool.

Nora led her to the stage. At the bottom of three steps, she turned to the girl. "We should have said no to these crazy heels and just worn flip-flops."

Charlotte grinned. "They are uncomfortable."

"Let's get this done. Then we can kick them off under the

dinner table and wiggle our toes free." Nora walked up to the podium. "Ladies and gentlemen, thank you so much for coming tonight."

ZANDER WAITED because Director Gladstone probably wouldn't want to talk while his daughter did her speech thing. Charity functions made him itch, but that was probably the suit. He hadn't busted this thing out for years—until the last ten months. Now it seemed like everyone in his hometown was hooking up and getting married. He'd received two invitations to coed baby showers in the last week.

"Let's step outside, Sergeant O'Connell."

He nodded, holding back his surprise that the director wanted to do this instead of listening to his daughter's carefully crafted speech.

It'd been a while since he was a sergeant. He didn't mind the director's use of his rank, though. Being in the US Army, and not just that but being part of Delta Force, had been some of the best years of his life.

Now he was freelance.

Gladstone wasn't his boss. But the assignments he threw in Zander's direction every once in a while kept the lights on at the house in Last Chance, where the team lived and trained—when they weren't on a job.

Truth was, they had three houses. Each was covered with a different story, usually that they were a team of ex-military guys who ran a training facility. People made up whatever they wanted to fill the gaps and try to explain what they didn't under-stand, or couldn't find an answer for. Then those stories became local lore.

They headed through the glass doors to the rooftop bar. The place was lit up and swarming with gala attendees who'd eaten but had no interest in the part of the evening where the foundation director attempted to pull on their heartstrings so they'd give generously.

It was exactly the kind of thing his mother would've loved—the chance to help a child have a better life the way she'd done every day as a cardiologist for a children's hospital. His father would have, too. Just for different reasons. He'd have seen it as a networking opportunity and made a business deal over a stiff drink.

Gladstone stopped at the railing that overlooked the street below. "A beard?"

Zander rubbed his jawline with the heel of his hand. "I lost a bet. Can't shave for three more weeks."

The director wasn't amused.

"What'd you want to talk to me about?"

"I'm hearing early rumblings that indicate a job could be headed your way in the next week or so. I can't be precise on the date, I'm afraid."

Zander shrugged, leaning against the rail. "Nature of the job."

"Indeed." Gladstone stood erect. His gold watch flashed in the light every time he took a sip of his drink. "I'm happy to hear you and the boys are available. This one is particularly… sensitive in nature."

In a lot of ways, Director Gladstone reminded Zander of his father.

Which was probably why he'd refused the offer to sign on officially with the Department of Clandestine Service and opted instead to stay a free agent. He could accept—or turn down—any job he wanted. Train the team as long as needed. Get it right. Every time.

Failure was never an option.

Not when he woke up from the nightmare where he recalled his parents the moment they fell to the ground. Dead. He could taste blood in the back of his throat every day. That wasn't going to happen to his men.

"Understood."

"You're able to stay in Seattle for the next week or so? I'd like to do the handoff in person."

Zander nodded. It wasn't uncommon for information to change hands face-to-face—leaving no electronic record. So much of what they did was top secret, eyes only. "The boys could use a few days of down time. Get some hiking in."

They were currently swimming in the indoor pool at the house he'd rented. He wanted to get back and join them for the last hour. Then it was bed, and an early kayaking trip tomorrow in the state park that would last all day. He could plan a coup that toppled a regime—and it had worked. They'd done a job in the middle of an earthquake once. A training itinerary for his boys in Washington State was nothing.

"Good. Get rested up so you can maintain peak performance."

Zander fought that equilibrium every day. Relaxing to recharge versus training to keep those gains. It was a tight balance.

"Probably why you and those four boys are the best." Gladstone glanced over.

"Five now." And they'd probably object to being referred to as boys—unless they were the ones using that term. "We were referred a guy from the CIA. Picked him up a couple of weeks ago."

"Oh?"

Zander nodded. "Seems like he could be a good fit."

That was all he could say about their most recent addition, the sixth member of his team. They'd lost and gained a few people over the years. Time would tell if Eas had staying power.

Under Zander was his best friend, explosives expert, Andre. His right-hand man. Then there was Ryder, who could hit his target every time from any distance. Those were the only two he'd served with in Delta, former teammates who'd followed him out of the army into the private sector.

Isaac was ex-CIA, and Judah ex-British Army.

None of them knew Eas's background. Kind of how they didn't know much of each other's. Their lives could end any second on a mission. One heartbeat living to the fullest, and the next…the heart stopped. Blood ceased. The brain shut down.

Nothing.

They lived fully in the present rather than expend energy on a past they couldn't change.

"Interesting," Gladstone said.

He wasn't wrong. Zander was aware they were a hodge-podge, that his team was a refuge for guys who didn't fit anywhere else. Men the world didn't understand, and probably couldn't handle. Intensity like theirs needed an outlet that could be found in only a few places—like wilderness firefighting, or competitive sports. They'd simply chosen to operate with a gun in one hand.

To make the world a better place in their own way.

So people like Gladstone's daughter could have their pristine lives doing their charity work, pretending they helped because they threw money at a problem. Someone else got their hands dirty. Not a woman like her.

Zander much preferred the sandbox to being here and pretending to be someone he'd never been. Would never be.

Through the window he saw her introduce the teenage girl. Her arm movements were stiff, as though she'd been strung so tight she was in danger of snapping.

She drew him, even if she appeared brittle. He wondered if she was always like that. Then he wondered why he was wondering about her.

Zander turned back to the skyline.

It didn't matter that she was…*captivating* was a good word. Long blonde hair, perfectly straight. Wide-set eyes. High cheekbones.

Meanwhile he had one purple fingernail, enough scars a

cutting board would be jealous, and a sunburn from waiting three days to take a shot that ended the life of a warlord.

He also had self-respect.

Zander didn't let himself wonder if she could say the same about her perfect life.

Great. He was still thinking about her. Even if it was judgy, she was in his head. That was the last thing he needed when the team had to have his full attention. When it slipped, people got hurt. No matter how beautiful she was, the woman had dismissed him as thoroughly as he needed to dismiss her from his thoughts.

He didn't need to start wondering why she seemed like she could snap at any moment. Or what she would look like in sweats, eating pizza. Hair a mess. Rumpled, and not uptight. Having fun instead of pretending she was enjoying herself.

He needed to get out of here before he was sucked back into high-society life.

The crowd inside applauded.

"I should head out."

Gladstone nodded. "I'll call and set up a meet."

That meant his assistant would, but Zander understood.

He headed for the ballroom and made his way past the bar, to the hall. The stage was clear now. The teen girl stood at the front, surrounded by the wealthy elite of the city. Chatting them up for maximum donations.

Wherever Gladstone's daughter had gone, Zander wasn't going to care. The princess was no doubt holding court somewhere, and he had a team to get back to.

He circumvented the crowded elevators and headed for the stairs.

Zander pushed open the heavy door and saw that dress. The metallic blue one that outlined her figure in a way that made his mouth water—but he wasn't going to look at it in front of her father. He did now.

She wore it well. Like she was born for this life.

His gaze lifted to her face, and the expression there. Something was wrong. "What?"

She flinched, and he realized he'd barked the word at her.

The ice princess lifted her chin and strode past him back through the door, leaving him alone in the stairwell.

Dismissed.

2

———

Nora strode into breakfast the next morning to find her father pacing between the breakfast nook and the conservatory patio area, phone in hand.

"Yes, sir," he told the caller. Then turned and spotted her, offering a warm smile. His body language completely neutral. No one looking at him would be able to tell how he felt about the person on the other end of the line.

He was a pro who never gave anything away.

"I understand, Mr. President." He hung up the phone.

She didn't sit before he came over, arms out, and hugged her. He kissed her forehead. "Good morning, darling."

And yet, his body language betrayed no more warmth than it had when he'd been on the phone. Whatever neutrality he displayed in talking to the president of the United States, he gave off precisely the same feel with her.

Absolutely nothing.

"Morning." She moved to the table. "Everything okay?"

She continued to attempt to read him, on the off chance he might give something away. But he never did.

She knew there were feelings under the surface. After all, she'd seen him lose his cool and get angry at a member of his staff. He had romantic relationships on occasion. She even thought that maybe she had observed him in a moment of grief over what had happened with Nora's mother. But that had been a long time ago.

Whatever he felt, he kept it tightly under wraps.

"Everything is fine now that you're here."

She offered him a small smile, took the cloth napkin from the plate, and laid it over the knees of her pajama pants. "Thank you for coming last night. It meant a lot to me that you were there."

The last thing Nora wanted to think about right now was that bearded man who'd stumbled on her in the stairwell. Everything in her flushed now at the way he'd looked at her, even if he had demanded to know why she was upset—not in so many words. And he'd essentially barked at her.

How crazy different was that from her father?

She'd evidently been upset. That had surged in him a response, almost as though he was angry on her behalf.

It made zero sense whatsoever.

"Donations were good?"

She nodded. "We exceeded all our goals."

And then some, considering there had been one particularly large check included. Someone named Zander O'Connell.

It was strange, considering she had no idea who that was.

She and her father passed dishes back and forth between them. Once she had a plate of eggs, whole wheat toast, and fresh fruit, he lifted the newspaper and opened it.

The front page caught her attention.

Local Private Investigator Killed In Fiery Crash.

She nearly choked on a piece of pineapple. He was dead?

Her father lowered the newspaper. "Everything okay?"

She nodded and took a sip of her tea. "Went down the wrong way."

He went back to his paper, and she studied the front page out the corner of her eye. That was the name of the private investigator she had hired. According to the tiny print she could just about make out, he'd had an empty bottle of whiskey on the floor of his front seat, and the police believed he'd killed himself.

After being sober for two years? He'd shown her the chip he earned at Alcoholics Anonymous. He'd been proud of it, and there was no indication she'd seen that he might want to kill himself.

Or perhaps, she was simply terrible at reading people.

Her father. The man from last night. The private investigator who was now dead.

Maybe she was wrong about everyone—or someone wanted her to believe that.

One of her father's enemies, maybe.

The private investigator had told her he thought someone didn't want him snooping around in the foundation's business. He had supplied her with a fake passport and enough cash to make her way to the center the foundation operated—one of four spread around the world—just in case she wanted to take a look for herself.

And yet, she couldn't help thinking when he'd handed the documents to her that something more was going on.

Now he was dead.

"Did you take your medicine this morning?"

She ignored her father's raised eyebrow and took the two pills from the tiny plastic cup beside her tea. She swallowed them down with a swig of English breakfast. "Yes, I did."

They shared a smile.

As soon as he was buried in his newspaper again, Nora dropped the heel of her hand over the scar on her sternum where they had cracked her chest open and replaced one of her heart valves.

She glanced back at the newspaper to keep from thinking about all that, and the doctor who had been the closest thing to her best friend for years.

So she would have to live with this the rest of her life, so what? So her father wasn't exactly the warmest person in the world. She hardly had a difficult life considering the things some people went through every day.

Illness, war. Persecution, and oppression.

She needed to find something to be thankful for. Except that a man was dead. Which meant, if she were the woman she wanted to be, she would find out what'd happened. Were her father's enemies targeting him through her?

It was highly unlikely she'd be able to fight them, but she couldn't prove her suspicions. Her father would dismiss the idea if she didn't have evidence.

Nora would have to accept the gift the private investigator had given her—the chance to find out for herself.

Just the idea filled her with fear, like so many things. But that had never stopped her.

If someone counted her as a vulnerability in an attack on her father, then she needed to know. No matter what it cost her.

Nora stood. "I should get dressed and get to work."

Her father flipped down the corner of the newspaper. "I thought you might work from home today. We could have lunch on the veranda."

"After last night there's simply too much to do, and everything is at the office." She kissed his cheek. "How about dinner?"

"Thai food?"

"Sounds lovely."

The words soured in her mouth as she wandered back to her room and got dressed. It would have to look as though she were going to work like normal. As though she hadn't been planning this in her mind since the private investigator mentioned it.

She wasn't prepared to kid herself that her father wouldn't find out exactly what she was doing. That would only lead to disappointment when he did. Even with the fake passport in the lining of her purse, she was taking a huge risk.

When the private investigator had handed it over, she'd been confused. Until he explained what it was for.

The chance to find out for yourself.

As though she was being deceived. Or as if he thought the truth would somehow set her free.

But it never did.

Why would Nora want to break free of a life she actually liked? After all, she made a difference in the world. Children who wouldn't have medical procedures got them because of the work she did.

Was it possible that someone had set the private investigator up to be killed? It was more likely he really had fallen off the wagon and gotten in a terrible car accident. Things like that happened every day. People let down those closest to them in favor of doing whatever they wanted to do in the moment, regardless of the consequences to anyone else. She'd seen it over and over again. It was the reason why she'd never moved out to live on her own.

Because after watching her mother do exactly that to her father, Nora couldn't stomach being the same way.

Her father would be devastated if she left the house. Why cause him such grief just for selfish reasons? She could be alone whenever she wanted. It wasn't like she needed her own house to do that.

Nora set her purse on the passenger seat of her BMW and pulled out of the garage. Then she drove her normal route to the office, trying to think through the variables of how she would make this work. A man like her father exercised full control over the people around him because he cared so much about their safety.

Now it might be his that was at stake.

She would have to ditch her car and her phone if she was going to pull this off. Otherwise, he would simply track her right to the center where the children lived.

She parked out front of the tiny office, located above a local organic honey shop. Nora employed four staff, including Rachel, who was her personal assistant. None would be in today, even though it was a Friday. She'd told them all to take the day off after the gala and have a long weekend.

A couple walked down the sidewalk, their young child between them, holding both of their hands. The child had a sparkly pink backpack on and looked to be about first grade. Two long blonde braids fell over her shoulders.

The mother smiled at her as they passed. Shared camaraderie, despite the fact Nora had no children. She never would.

She headed in the direction of the coffee shop where she usually bought a midmorning latte when she needed to stretch her legs.

Minutes later, she emerged with a white paper cup, and the couple headed through the disbursing crowd. Down the street, a school bus turned the corner.

She followed them around the corner to where a Subaru was parked, as though going toward the back entrance of her office, purse held tight against her side by her elbow.

They climbed in, both glancing at her. She didn't want to freak them out, but she was following them.

Nora opened the back door and slid in beside a child's booster seat. "I'll give you two thousand dollars if you drive me to the airport right now."

Zander opened the oven to check on his bacon and hash browns. If the boys didn't get up soon, he was going to have to wake them because breakfast was almost ready. Everyone except Eas, who was headed along the bank of the lake at a fast jog back toward the house Zander had rented for them all to stay in.

A little training, a little **R & R**. Sometimes they stayed in urban locations, but this time he had chosen a huge house on the coast to the west of Seattle with its indoor pool and huge game and media room. No sense in being uncomfortable.

He turned to the slight shuffle and saw Andre headed in, his dark hair ruffled from sleep, wearing basketball shorts and a rumpled T-shirt, his feet bare. "You didn't wake us? It's nearly nine." He made a beeline for the coffee pot and poured a cup for himself.

"Breakfast is almost ready."

Andre lifted his head, the mug close to his mouth. "Hash browns?"

"I found hot sauce in the cupboard."

Andre's eyes lit. "Is it my birthday?"

Zander nearly laughed. "You guys have been working hard for the last few weeks. I figured sleeping in and eating well would do everyone good." The early morning kayaking trip had been pushed back a few hours.

"Who are you, and what have you done with my hard-nosed team leader?" Before Zander could answer, Andre narrowed his eyes. "This kayak thing is overnight now, isn't it? You switched it up to some kind of three- or five-day survival thing with no food and only a pocket knife."

Zander said nothing.

"I knew it. You're buttering us up so you can torture us later." He groaned and took his coffee to the table. "Eas wasn't in his bed."

"He's out running." Zander had done his own workout this morning. Their newest team member seemed to have a different way of doing nearly everything, but Zander figured that didn't mean he needed to change to fit in with the team.

Things were evolving, as they tended to do. Seasons ended and new ones began. People came and went, and by the grace of God it wasn't because Zander had buried someone.

Isaac trailed in, wearing sweatpants and a tank. He was the only team member who didn't have more than four scars. As a former CIA agent, Isaac's tactics had a little more finesse than

Andre's tendency to build a bomb out of whatever was in his backpack and blow something up.

"How long has he been out there?" Isaac stared out the patio doors by the dining table.

Zander poured him a cup of coffee and took it over.

"Thanks," Isaac said.

"It's been an hour and a half, almost to the minute." Zander watched as Eas picked up his pace to a sprint and headed up the grass of the lawn between the lake and the house.

"Are you going to tell us what you know about him?"

"It's for Eas to decide what he wants to disclose." The truth was, Zander didn't know all that much about him other than what Homeland Security had opted to say. If anyone could find out more information on the man, it was Isaac. "The CIA has nothing?"

"I'm sure if they were speaking to me, they might have something to say. But I doubt it would be about Eas."

"Then I guess we'll just have to wait for Eas to tell us who he is on his own time."

Isaac headed for the dining table, where Andre attempted to drag him into an arm-wrestling match.

The patio door opened, and Eas stepped in, pulling up the hem of his T-shirt to wipe his face. On the side of his abdomen was a long nasty-looking scar beside a tattoo that looked like some kind of dragon. He'd pulled a beanie down over his ears, which he removed, along with his sunglasses. He only did that indoors, when he felt safe.

Eas lifted his chin and trailed away to the hall, probably to take a shower. As he turned, Zander got a full view of the jagged scar on his face.

Zander called out, "Shake Judah and Badger out of bed, will you?"

"On it." The words didn't sound precisely comfortable coming from Eas's lips. His accent probably made Isaac wonder which Asian country he was from. But he was putting a concerted effort into assimilating. Just not into letting anyone in on his personal business.

Zander tried not to look too closely at his eyes. What he saw reflected there spoke a little too loudly of all the things he had seen and done. He wasn't sure Eas had ever served in the military—but he was skilled nonetheless. Deadly like the rest of them. But with an edge that was all his own.

Considering none of them were all that interested in getting personal, it worked out pretty well.

"No need to wake me. I'm up." Ryder—everyone called him Badger—trailed down the hall wearing only shorts, with his California surfer hair sticking every which way. "Please tell me there's a reason I can smell bacon."

Andre lowered the mug from his lips. "It's because Isaac farted."

The former CIA agent slapped him on the back of the head. While Andre yelped, he said, "I also poop rainbows."

"And I make breakfast that's actually edible." Zander turned off the oven and took out the baking trays.

Ryder looked over his shoulder. "Bless you. I'm starving."

"You're always starving."

Isaac's dig at him didn't go unnoticed. Zander spotted how it affected Ryder. If he hadn't known the kid grew up dirt poor—literally—he might not have noticed.

"Get some coffee, Badger."

Judah strode in and hit the button on the electric kettle to boil water. The rest of them drank coffee, but the British man among them always needed tea first thing.

"Get the milk while you get your creamer, Badge."

Ryder nodded.

Zander watched them all move around the space he had rented, content to be among men he considered to be his family. Still, his thoughts gravitated toward the blonde woman from the night before.

His mother had been warmth and light. In comparison,

Gladstone's daughter was cold. If he hadn't seen her at an event for a children's charity, he would have thought her incapable of compassion. Just another high-society woman.

The kind who, when they found out who he really was, tried to stick around for the payday.

As if he didn't see through that play.

He was too old for games now. Whatever was going on with her, Zander wasn't interested.

Eas came back from the shower in time for them to dig in. He grabbed the open can of evaporated milk from the fridge and made tea of his own.

Conversation was pretty quiet while they all stuffed their faces. Andre said, "Fuel up, or kayaking is gonna suck."

Ryder lifted his face and grinned. "Maybe for you, old man."

Isaac groaned. "I hate water."

Judah and Eas both seemed content with Zander's brand of training. Or maybe they just hadn't been part of the team long enough to give him crap about his methods the way the others did. Joshing around like they had in the army when they'd served together in the same Delta

Force team.

Whatever it was, no one could argue with his success rate.

He pushed the team hard, but as a result they were highly skilled and had never lost a man.

The laptop Zander had left on the kitchen counter began to ring, an incoming video call. He opened it on the table so the caller could see each of them, except Eas, who backed his chair up from the table.

"Ted?"

The young man from Last Chance County, who they all shared a house with, grinned. He brushed back the dark hair that fell over his forehead almost constantly. He was in his midtwenties and had formally been the police department's technical expert. After his father ruined that career, Ted had received multiple offers from different companies. Zander figured he moonlighted in a couple of fields. "She said yes."

Cheers erupted around the table. Zander grinned. "Good for you."

He'd figured Ted's now fiancée Jess was going to say yes to his proposal. But it was good to hear the Last Chance County police detective had a brain in her head. And it was good to see Ted happy.

The kid's father had terrorized him. A sociopath with grand plans who took advantage of his genius son? Now Ted worked for Zander, and he made it worth the kid's time to be available all hours of the day and night sometimes.

Judah lifted his mug of tea in a salute. "Here, here."

Zander figured that was some kind of British version of good job.

Eas was the only one who remained quiet. Those watchful eyes assessing everything. The rest of them only turned on that same steady gaze when it was time for a mission.

"DCS called this morning. They have a job for you guys."

The Department of Clandestine Service only made him think of the woman again. He dismissed the memory of how she looked in that dress—probably a good thing considering it would be seriously distracting and all the guys would notice his mind was elsewhere.

"I guess kayaking is going to have to wait." Ted grinned.

No one was sad about that. And they didn't even know half of what he'd had planned.

Zander said, "Run it down for us."

<hr>

Don't let the fun stop… get *Last Taste of Freedom* NOW!
Find out more at https://lastchancecounty.com/chevalier-series

OTHER BOOKS BY LISA PHILLIPS

Find out about other stories in Last Chance County by visiting Lisa's Website:

https://lastchancecounty.com/

And all of Lisa's other books at her main website:

https://authorlisaphillips.com

All of the books in the Last Chance County series:

Book 1: Expired Refuge

Book 2: Expired Secrets

Book 3: Expired Cache

Book 4: Expired Hero

Book 5: Expired Game

Book 6: Expired Plot

Book 7: Expired Getaway

Book 8: Expired Betrayal

Book 9: Expired Flight

Book 10: Expired End

Also Available in 2 Omnibus collections!

ABOUT THE AUTHOR

Follow Lisa on social media to find out about new releases and other exciting events!

Visit Lisa's Website to sign up for her mailing list to get FREE books and be the first to learn about new releases and other exciting updates!

https://www.authorlisaphillips.com